ESCAPE FROM HELL

Historical Fiction by V. A. Stuart
Published by McBooks Press

THE ALEXANDER SHERIDAN ADVENTURES

Victors and Lords
The Sepoy Mutiny
Massacre at Cawnpore
The Cannons of Lucknow
The Heroic Garrison

THE PHILLIP HAZARD NOVELS

The Valiant Sailors ✓
The Brave Captains ✓
Hazard's Command ✓
Hazard of Huntress ✓
Hazard in Circassia ✓
Victory at Sebastopol ✓
Guns to the Far East ✓
Escape from Hell ✓

Not Read
~~ASW III~~
12 JUNE
2020

For a complete list of nautical and military fiction
published by McBooks Press, please see pages 251–254.

THE PHILLIP HAZARD NOVELS, NO. 8

ESCAPE FROM HELL

by

V. A. STUART

McBooks Press, Inc.

Ithaca, New York

Published by McBooks Press 2005
Copyright © 1976 and 1977 by Vivian Stuart
First Published in Great Britain by Robert Hale & Co. Ltd.,
Also published as *Sailors on Horseback* and *Action Front*

Cover: *1857, Delhi Stormed* lithograph by G. McCulloch after
Captain G. F. Atkinson. Courtesy of Mary Evans Picture Library

Library of Congress Cataloging-in-Publication Data

Stuart, V. A.
  Escape from hell / by V.A. Stuart.
    p. cm. — (The Phillip Hazard novels ; #8)
  ISBN 1-59013-064-2 (trade pbk. : alk. paper)
  1. Hazard, Phillip Horatio (Fictitious character)—Fiction. 2. Great
Britain—History, Naval—19th century—Fiction. 3. Lucknow
(India)—History—Siege, 1857—Fiction. 4. Great Britain. Royal
Navy—Officers—Fiction. 5. British—India—Fiction. I. Title.
  PR6063.A38E83 2005
  823'.92—dc22

                                        2004024252

Distributed to the trade by National Book Network, Inc.
15200 NBN Way, Blue Ridge Summit, PA 17214
800-462-6420

Additional copies of this book may be ordered from any
bookstore or directly from McBooks Press, Inc., ID Booth
Building, 520 North Meadow St., Ithaca, NY 14850. Please
include $4.00 postage and handling with mail orders. New York
State residents must add sales tax to total remittance (books &
shipping). All McBooks Press publications can also be ordered
by calling toll-free 1-888-BOOKS11 (1-888-266-5711).
Please call to request a free catalog.

Visit the McBooks Press website at www.mcbooks.com.

Printed in the United States of America

9 8 7 6 5 4 3 2 1

FOR DAVID AND LEE ZENTNER

in gratitude for an unforgettable visit to New York,
the house opposite Walter Winchell's,
and the American Booksellers' Fair, 1975.

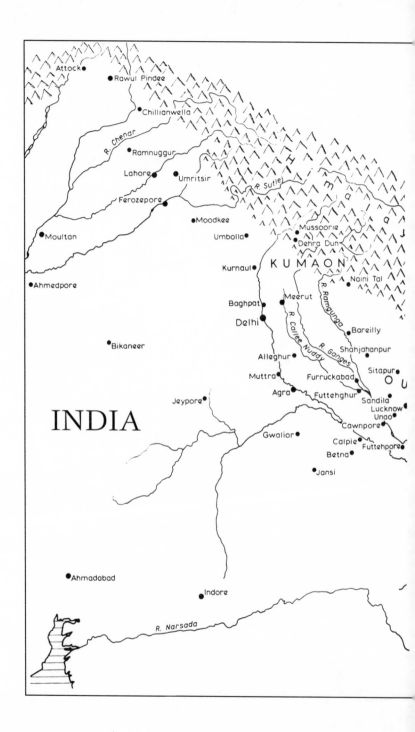

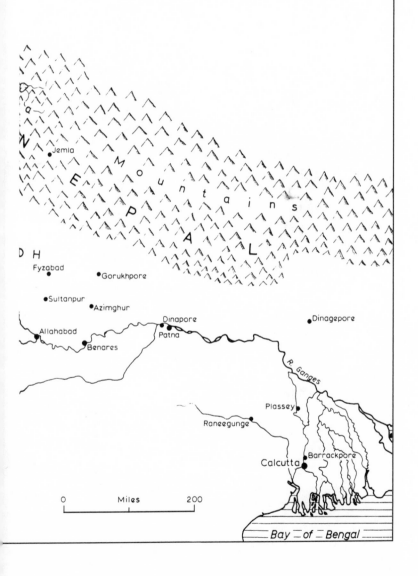

TIBET

Jemla

NEPAL

Mountains

D H

Fyzabad

Gorukhpore

Sultanpur

Azimghur

Dinapore

Dinagepore

Allahabad

Patna

Benares

R Ganges

Plassey

Raneegunge

Calcutta

Barrackpore

0   Miles   200

Bay of Bengal

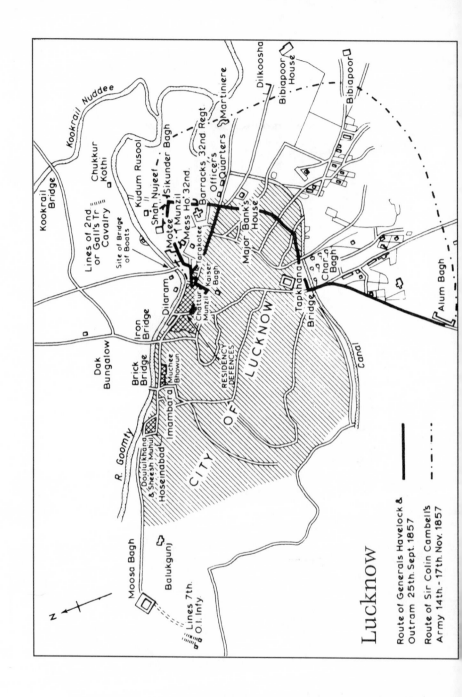

Lucknow

Route of Generals Havelock & Outram 25th. Sept. 1857 ——————

Route of Sir Colin Cambell's Army 14th. – 17th. Nov. 1857 — · — · —

Kookrail Nuddee

Kookrail Bridge

Chukkur Kothi

Lines of 2nd or Gall's Tr Cavalry

Site of Bridge of Boats

Kudum Rusool

Shah Nujeef

Sikunder Bagh

Motee Munzil

Mess Ho. 32nd.

Barracks 32nd Regt

Officer's Quarters

Martiniere

Dilkoosha

Bibiboosha House

Bibiapoor House

Bibiapoor

Farakotee

Chuttur Munzil

Kaiser Bagh

Major Banks's House

Char Bagh

Tapkhana

Dak Bungalow

Brick Bridge

Iron Bridge

Dilaram

Doulutkhana & Sheesh Muhul

Hoseinabad

Imambara

Muchee Bhowun

RESIDENCY DEFENCES

CITY OF LUCKNOW

R. Goomty

Canal

Tapkhana Bridge

Alum Bagh

Moosa Bagh

Balukgunj

Lines 7th. O I. Infy.

N

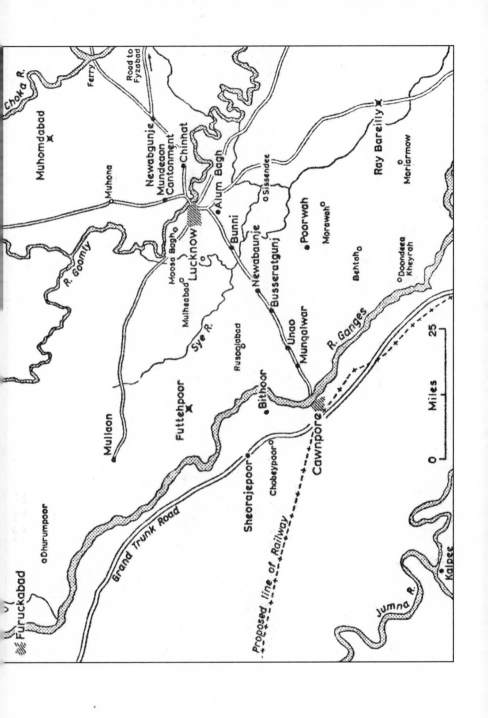

PROLOGUE

For *days past* warnings of an impending attack by the Nana Sahib's army and the ten thousand strong Gwalior Contingent had been reaching Cawnpore and, on 24th November, 1857, Major-General Charles Windham called a conference of his senior officers to decide how best to meet the threat.

A Guards officer who had won great distinction in the Crimean War, where his personal heroism had earned him the honoured nickname of "Redan" Windham, the General had been appointed to command of the Cawnpore garrison on the departure of the Commander-in-Chief, Sir Colin Campbell, two weeks earlier, with the Lucknow Relief Force.

It was an unenviable command, since every soldier and every gun that could be spared had gone with the Relief column on its desperate, do-or-die mission, and Windham had been left with a bare holding force of four companies of Her Majesty's 64th Regiment, some military and naval gunners and small detachments of other British regiments amounting, in all, to five hundred officers and men. When he had decided to advance to Lucknow's relief before dealing with the threat to his base at Cawnpore, Sir Colin Campbell had, General Windham was aware, taken a carefully calculated risk. Sir Colin had only forty-two hundred men of all arms under his command—even with the addition of the two hundred seamen of HMS *Shannon*'s Naval Brigade and of a Brigade from Delhi, which had fought every mile of the way south to join him.

The Gwalior mutineers had established themselves on the far side of the River Jumna and—since all the available boats were in their hands—any attempt to bring them to battle could be indefinitely delayed should their wily commander, Tantia Topi, so choose . . . and even a few weeks' delay might well lead to the fall of the hard pressed Lucknow garrison. Already the siege of the Residency, by an estimated fifty thousand fanatical rebels, had lasted over four months.

The first small relief force, under Generals Outram and Havelock, had fought valiantly to rescue the garrison but had suffered so many casualties—five hundred out of a total strength of twenty-five hundred—that, since the end of September, the survivors had been trapped in the Residency, aiding its defence, admittedly, but also adding to the number of mouths its slender stock of provisions had to feed. With women and children, wounded and sick, there were now close on two thousand non-combatants in the garrison, whose lives depended on swift evacuation and Sir Colin Campbell, determined to save them if he could, had openly conceded that he was taking the greatest gamble of his long career. In a letter to the Duke of Cambridge, he had written:

"I intend to trust to the valour of my small but devoted band, make a dash for Lucknow, withdraw the garrison and return— swiftly enough, I hope—to save Windham from any danger that may threaten him . . ."

General Windham's orders were to hold Cawnpore at all costs, pending the Commander-in-Chief's return. His first responsibility was to guard the Bridge of Boats, which crossed the River Ganges into Oudh, from enemy attempts to capture or destroy it. The bridge was a vital link in Sir Colin's line of communication; by it, the evacuated garrison of Lucknow would have to be brought into Cawnpore and, recognising its importance, Windham had done all in his power to strengthen the fortified entrenchment sited at the Baxi Ghat, on the Cawnpore side of the broad river, mounting guns to cover the approaches to the bridge.

The entrenchment had been originally constructed in July for the same purpose, when General Havelock had first been compelled to leave Cawnpore with a handful of men to hold both city and bridge and, by dint of employing several thousand native coolies, it had been considerably enlarged. Now a wall, seven feet in height and some eighteen feet in thickness, extended for half a mile to form an inner defensive circle surrounding a high mound overlooking the river. The parapet was turfed over to prevent its being washed away by the rains; the walls were fitted with sally-ports, and embrasures and platforms for the guns, constructed of brick, had been set in concrete by native masons. An outwork beyond enclosed four acres of ground and included a mile of loop-holed parapet and this was connected to the *enciente* by a covered way, closed at the canal end to the rear by a high stockade, with a *tête-de-pont* descending to the river bank and mounting two guns.

By comparison with the mud-walled entrenchment, nearly a mile away on the open plain, which General Wheeler's ill-fated garrison had defended so heroically in June, Windham's was a fortress but nevertheless it possessed a number of disadvantages. It was dangerously close to the native city, for one thing, and the ground about it—although flat—was encumbered by houses and walled gardens, with two narrow ravines leading up from the river, which had constantly to be patrolled. A resolute enemy would have little difficulty in bringing up guns with which to bombard his stronghold and the bridge it guarded, the General was unhappily aware—particularly if he were compelled to withdraw his troops from the city of which, for the moment, he was in control.

The opportune arrival of Brigadier Morden Carthew's Madras Brigade had to a certain extent assuaged his anxiety and during the last few days, drafts from the Rifle Brigade and the 34th, 82nd, and 88th Queen's Regiments had raised his total force to some seventeen hundred men. These he had been directed to retain, in a note from Sir Colin Campbell's Chief of Staff in Lucknow, which had reached him on the 15th. Since the 19th, however, communication with the Commander-in-Chief had been abruptly cut off and, as yet, he had received no reply to his request to make the best possible use of his reinforcements by going over to the attack. A fighting soldier, Charles Windham had always believed that attack was the best means of defence and now, as his commanders gathered about him, he again studied the written orders Sir Colin Campbell had issued for his guidance, heavy dark brows gathered in a frown as he did so.

"You are to make the best show you can of whatever troops you may have at Cawnpore, leaving always a sufficient guard in the entrenchment . . . by encamping them conspicuously and in somewhat extended order, looking, however, well to your line of retreat . . ."

Up to now, he had done precisely as ordered, Windham told himself, still frowning. His main body was encamped, as conspicuously as possible, just outside and to the west of the city, with strong pickets posted at the junction of the Delhi and Calpee roads, two more at the northern boundary of the city, whilst detachments of the 34th and the 82nd covered the road from Bithur, to the east. The entrenchment, with its well-positioned artillery, was defended as adequately as it could be; to his rear, at Fattehpore, he had detached the 17th Madras Native Infantry to patrol the road to Allahabad and, with the 27th supported by a European field battery, he had retaken the Bunni Bridge, on the Lucknow road, which had been overrun by the rebels. He had forwarded all the detachments required of him, in wings of regiments, to augment the Lucknow column, and the Commander-in-Chief had thanked him, in the warmest terms, for his support. Now that, at last, he had been permitted to bring his own force up to reasonable strength, it would surely be the height of folly not to seize the opportunity this afforded him to take the initiative.

He would have to make certain that he had the full support of his senior officers, of course. The final paragraph of Sir Colin Campbell's orders called for him to retire to the entrenchment, should he be seriously threatened and— General Windham glanced down at the paper in his hand— *"not to move out to the attack unless compelled to do so by the threat of bombardment."* A prudent order, when he had had a scant five hundred men with whom to hold his position but with treble that number—and the majority Europeans—it smacked of over-caution, even of cowardice and, as such, went sorely against the grain. In his own case and . . . He subjected the faces of the officers gathered about him to a searching scrutiny, glancing first at those most likely to offer him the support he wanted.

Brigadier Carthew, of the Company's Madras Army, had given him most admirable backing since his arrival and he was now peering down, with lively interest, at the maps which the Chief of Staff, Colonel Adye, was spreading out on the table in front of them. Equally dependable, Windham felt confident, was Colonel Wilson of the Queen's 64th, now acting Brigadier and his predecessor in the Cawnpore command. Wilson was in his late sixties, white haired and somewhat slow of movement but a fine soldier, very popular with the garrison and as eager as he was himself to bring the Gwalior rebels to heel. Colonel Walpole, the Rifles' CO, was an old and well tried friend—he need have no doubts on that score—and Major Stirling, acting commander of the 64th, had been with Havelock's Force since it left Allahabad in June. The 64th had done a lot of hard fighting and there had been some scandal or other, in which Stirling had been concerned, during the advance on Cawnpore. Something about an unmanageable horse that had compelled Stirling to go to the rear, whereupon Havelock had sent his son to lead the regiment into an attack in its commander's place—and had then recommended the boy for a Victoria Cross. Or so rumour had it . . . General Windham smiled to himself. Clearly Stirling would welcome the chance of action, if only as a means of repairing the damage to his reputation.

As to the others—Kelly of HM's 34th was a fighting Irishman, Maxwell of the Connaught Rangers an officer of the same calibre, and Watson of the 82nd and Harnass of the Engineers were both conversant with the details of the proposed plan of attack and had wholeheartedly approved of it. The only stumbling block therefore was Dupuis, commanding the Royal Artillery. As a Major-General, Dupuis outranked all the others so that his opposition—*if* he opposed the plan—was likely to be formidable. There was no questioning his courage, of course; Dupuis did not lack courage, but he was inclined to set great store by a rigid adherence to orders and would almost certainly advise waiting until a reply had been received to the urgent despatch he had sent to the Commander-in-Chief, setting out details of the proposed attack. That an affirmative reply would be received, Windham did not doubt, since the plan he had worked out was a sound one but . . . it was unfortunate that communication with Lucknow should have been interrupted at so vital a time. Any delay in putting his plan into action would rob him of the element of surprise, which was essential to its success. And it would give the enemy, at present divided, time to join forces . . .

"Gentlemen, if I may have your attention," General Windham said. He gestured to the map. "You know our own depositions, of course. What I want you, if you will, to consider are those of the Gwalior mutineers. Until the middle of this month, they made no attempt to cross the Jumna. Indeed, although well armed and disciplined and excellently supplied with artillery, up to now their movements have been hesitant, even timid, but since the Commander-in-Chief marched to Lucknow, they have been gradually advancing upon us. According to reports from the spies I have sent out, five days ago their main body of about three thousand men, with twenty guns, was still at Calpee. A force of about twelve hundred, with four guns, had advanced to Bognepore, here"—he jabbed at the map with his forefinger—"two others, slightly smaller, were at Akbarpore and Shewlie, and a body of about a thousand, with cavalry and guns, was at Shirajpore, here. The remainder are at Jaloun."

The General paused, allowing his assembled officers time to pick out the places he had named on the map, and then went on, "They thus form the segment of a circle about us gentlemen which, I venture to suggest, is an indication that they intend to launch an attack on this city while, as they suppose, we are depleted in numbers and hard put to it to defend ourselves."

"You do not think, then, that they will try to join the Nana's

army in Oudh?" General Dupuis asked. "Clearly their hesitation caused them to miss the opportunity of attacking the
Commander-in-Chief's column on the way to Lucknow but it
is possible, is it not, General Windham, that they may fall upon
Sir Colin when he returns here, impeded by the Lucknow
women and children and the wounded?"

"It is possible," Windham conceded. "But unlikely, in my
view. Our spies all tell us that the Nana is moving southward at
considerable speed . . . away from Lucknow. Captain Bruce will
give you chapter and verse, gentlemen." He nodded to the
Intelligence Officer and Bruce—another veteran of Havelock's
Force, now in overall command of Cawnpore's newly-raised
police—gave crisp details of the reports his men had brought in.

He added wryly, "The Nana isn't anxious to be observed,
gentlemen—three of my unfortunate fellows have been sent
back with their tongues cut out. But everything points to his
joining Tantia Topi and the Gwalior mutineers on this side of
the river, probably within the next two or three days. His prestige suffered when he lost Cawnpore to General Havelock—
he wants the place back and, once he joins forces with the
Gwalior troops, I'm quite certain he'll attack us."

"I feel," General Windham put in, "and I feel very strongly
that we should take the initiative—strike a swift and decisive
blow against them before they've had time to join forces. And
I propose to make use of the canal, gentlemen. You'll see from
the map that it runs from here northwards and passes between
Shewlie and Shirajpore, both of which are fifteen miles from
us. My plan, the details of which I have forwarded to the
Commander-in-Chief, is to transport about twelve hundred of
our available force by boat along the canal during the hours
of darkness. There are plenty of boats, and field guns can be

moved up with them, along the tow-path. The men, instead of being fatigued by a fifteen mile march, will arrive fit and fresh and can fall upon either of the two rebel forces—which of the two will depend on the intelligence reports we receive— taking them by surprise at first light. Having met and dealt effectively with whichever force seems the more vulnerable to attack, our troops will at once return to Cawnpore."

"You would, of course, leave the entrenchment adequately defended, General?" Brigadier Wilson suggested.

"Of course." General Windham's bearded lips parted in a smile. "And in your safe hands, my dear fellow. We now have a strength of some seventeen hundred bayonets, have we not, Adye?"

"We have, sir," his Chief of Staff confirmed.

"Then you'll have your four companies of the 64th and your artillerymen, my dear Wilson."

The old Brigadier nodded his satisfaction. "We could never count on more. But we know the defects of the entrenchment and, for the information of those commanding officers who have recently joined us perhaps, General, you would wish me to point them out?" Receiving his superior's permission, the Brigadier proceeded to list the deficiencies of the earthwork under his command, ending ruefully, "General Windham's orders call for him to retire to the entrenchment if attacked, and not to move out unless compelled to do so by the threat of bombardment. Which means, in effect gentlemen, that if the enemy succeed in penetrating the native city, such is the nature of the ground that they would be able to bring up heavy guns with which to bombard our defences, and the Bridge of Boats. We could not reply to their fire if they position guns on the north side of us."

"Then we should have to move out to take them with infantry?" Colonel Kelly offered, frowning. "Since the bridge must be preserved at all costs?"

"Precisely, sir," Wilson agreed. "The bridge is our sole link with the Commander-in-Chief's forces in Oudh." He hesitated, glancing at General Windham, who gestured to him to continue, sensing that his revelations concerning the entrenchment had had a profound effect on his listeners. Wilson sighed. "In my considered opinion, gentlemen," he said flatly, "we cannot abandon the city and simply wait, in our defensive works, for the enemy to attack us. With the bare five hundred men we were originally left with, such a course might have been forced upon us but with your reinforcements, we have room for manoeuvre and in my view, we should use it. Apart from being militarily unsound, to abandon the native city to pillage and arson by the Nana's troops would greatly damage our prestige . . . and prestige is important in our present situation. Every defeat we suffer gives birth to more rebels, but every victory brings the waverers and the fearful flocking back to their allegiance. They are simple people, gentlemen, to whom might is right and who see safety only in being on the winning side." He talked on, persuasively, and General Windham listened with controlled impatience, inwardly cursing the failure of his *cossids* to bring him the answer he needed from his Commander-in-Chief.

One victory, as old Wilson had said, might be all that was needed to send the Gwalior troops back across the Jumna . . . but the chance of such a victory was now, without further delay, when the rebels were in detached bodies and each vulnerable to attack by his twelve hundred British bayonets. Once they joined forces, the initiative would be theirs, even to the choice of battlefield and the time and manner of attack. But

Wilson was now going off at a tangent, losing the thread of his argument and laying too much stress on the defence of the native city . . .

"Apart from any question of morale," the old Brigadier said earnestly, "we are expecting a large influx of ladies and little children, as well as wounded, from Lucknow. Bungalows have been made ready to receive them in some degree of comfort, poor souls, which they will need after their long ordeal. To attempt to accommodate them in our entrenchment would result, I fear, in many deaths due to chaotic overcrowding. And then there are the stores and baggage, the reserves of ammunition Sir Colin's force left here. We—"

"General Wilson"—the Artillery commander, General Dupuis, interrupted him, his tone curt—"are you advocating the attack on Shewlie and Shirajpore or merely that we should defend the native city against the Nana's anticipated attack?"

"I . . ." The staunch old Brigadier reddened, turning to glance unhappily at Windham. "I'm endeavouring to make the situation clear to those who have just arrived here, sir. I have been here for a long time and . . ." Meeting Windham's gaze, he broke off, and added with more than a hint of resentment, "I'm advocating the defence of the native city, certainly, sir, and in my view, General Windham's plan to use the canal is a sound one, provided—"

"Provided the Commander-in-Chief agrees to it, I imagine," Dupuis put in. His eyes, blue and hard beneath their beetling white brows, met those of General Windham. "Which, I understand, so far he has not?"

Faced with a direct question, the General reluctantly shook his head. "I've requested his approval. As I told you, I sent details of my proposal to use the canal but communication with Lucknow has been cut off for the past five days, so I have no means of knowing whether or not my messenger got through."

"In that case, sir," Dupuis returned bluntly, "I fear you have no choice but to wait until you receive a reply from Sir Colin or his Chief of Staff. *We* do not know how they are faring, do we? And your orders allow you no latitude, save in the question of whether to defend or abandon the native city. In the light of what Brigadier Wilson has told us, it would seem desirable that it should be held, since to abandon it would place both the bridge and the entrenchment in a precarious position. And"—he shrugged—"with only ten guns and seventeen hundred bayonets all told, I think the task will tax us to the limit, without running the risk of a reverse at Shewlie or Shirajpore, fifteen miles away. That, sir, would be disastrous, to say the least."

It was what he had expected of Dupuis, General Windham reflected, conscious of disappointment nonetheless when he heard the murmurs of agreement with which the other commanding officers greeted the old artilleryman's words. None of them were prepared to back him up if he exceeded his orders. Even Wilson had struck a note of caution although yesterday evening, when they had discussed his plan to attack the mutineers' divided forces from the canal, the Brigadier had appeared enthusiastic. He could overrule them, of course—*he* was in command, the final decision his alone but . . . He gave vent to an audible sigh. Without the support of his senior commanders, the risk was too great and he dared not take it.

"General Windham." Dupuis laid a hand on his arm. His voice had lost its note of harshness as he said, "At any other time, I'd have agreed wholeheartedly with your proposal to attack an advancing enemy . . . boldness always pays. But at all costs this place—and the bridge—must be held and, if things have gone badly for Sir Colin Campbell at Lucknow, we may be called upon to send the major part of our force to his aid. That's a possibility of which we must not lose sight, sir . . . and you've had no news for five days, have you?"

Windham shook his head. "Then, General," the Royal Artillery commander suggested, "why not advance your main body to the bridge by which the Calpee and Delhi roads cross the canal?" He jabbed at the map. "Their main body was last reported at Calpee, so that it will advance from there and you would be showing a bold front, which might well deter them, if they're still hesitating. You would have sufficient troops available to patrol the roads should they attempt to get round your rear, and the canal to serve as a wide, wet ditch along your entire front. In addition, you would be in position to carry out your canal operation, should the Commander-in-Chief give his assent to it, would you not?"

"I should, yes," Windham assented. He was relieved that this suggestion should have come from Dupuis; it was the position he himself had earlier decided to take up, whether or not his canal plan met with their approval, since it left him the option of carrying it out if this seemed expedient. To the rear of the Calpee Bridge and his present camp lay an area of open ground, broken by high mounds which had been built up over some abandoned brick kilns and here, since the mounds offered a ready-made defensive position, he had resolved to meet an enemy attack. Field guns could be mounted in commanding positions on the mounds, there was adequate cover for infantry and supply waggons and, from the summit of the highest mound, a good view of the surrounding countryside could be obtained. He and Brigadier Carthew had reconnoitred the area soon after the arrival of the Madras Brigade . . . He met Carthew's gaze and saw that he was smiling. Evidently the Brigadier had been talking to Dupuis and . . . Gratefully he acknowledged the Madras officer's smile.

"An admirable compromise, General Dupuis," he acknowledged. "Unless anyone has an alternative suggestion to offer, I . . ." He was interrupted by his aide, Lieutenant Swires, who hurried to his side and excitedly thrust a tiny spill of paper into his hand.

"A *cossid* from Lucknow at last, sir!" he said. "I thought I had better bring it to you at once."

"Thank you, Roger." Slowly and carefully, General Windham unrolled the wafer-thin spill and the other officers watched him in silence as he sought, with some difficulty, to decipher the message it contained.

"Is it from the Commander-in-Chief, sir?" Carthew asked eagerly. "Are we to attack from the canal?"

Windham slowly shook his head. His voice was strained as he answered. "No, it's from the Commissariat Officer of the Lucknow column. He asks me to send ten days' provisions for the whole force. He gives no news of the garrison—simply says, devil take him, that he can express no opinion on military matters!"

"But for God's sake!" General Dupuis exclaimed, exasperated. "Ten days' provisions—that can only mean that Sir Colin has met with a setback!"

"Or that he has the rescued garrison to feed," Carthew argued.

"It also means," General Windham stated grimly, "that if I send him these provisions, I shall have to send a strong escort and all my available transport. Far from launching an attack on the enemy, gentlemen, we shall have our work cut out to defend ourselves if we're attacked!"

"But you will send them, sir?" old Brigadier Wilson questioned. "You will send the provisions? The rescued garrison and the women and children will be starving."

"What choice have I?" Windham spread his hands helplessly, hard put to it to conceal his dismay. "As General Dupuis has pointed out, my orders leave me with little latitude. I must support the Commander-in-Chief and, if he requires ten days' provisions, then I'm bound to send them."

"This request comes from the Commissariat, not from the Commander-in-Chief, sir," Colonel Adye reminded him. "And it will take at least 24 hours to assemble the supplies and the necessary carriage."

A gleam of heartfelt relief lit General Windham's dark eyes. "By heaven, you're right, John! We'll make the necessary preparations but delay despatching any supplies to Lucknow until tomorrow evening. By then, perhaps, the Commander-in-Chief or General Mansfield will confirm these instructions and give me some idea of their situation. In the meantime, let us make our show of strength while we've still sufficient troops available to make it. We will move camp to the Calpee Bridge this afternoon, gentlemen!"

Leaving four companies of the Queen's 64th and the usual complement of gunners to hold the fort, the rest of the British force crossed the Ganges Canal by the Calpee road bridge and made camp. Next morning a second *cossid* arrived, bearing a despatch from General Mansfield, in which he stated that the Commander-in-Chief would commence the journey to Cawnpore on the morning of November 27th bringing with him the evacuated survivors of the Residency garrison. No mention was made of commissariat stores or of his proposed plan of attack on the Gwalior mutineers, and General

Windham reluctantly rescinded his order for the collection of canal boats.

Just before dusk on the evening of the 25th, a police sowar galloped into camp with the information that *zamindari* levies were crossing the river from Oudh and that a division of the Gwalior rebels, numbering about three thousand, with cavalry and six field-guns, had taken up an offensive position on the Pandoo Nuddy River, less than three miles from the camp. Windham did not waste time conferring with his commanders.

"Have the camp struck and the troops under arms at first light," he instructed Colonel Adye. "We'll aim a swift, hard blow at them across the Pandoo Nuddy and then fall back on the brick kilns to cover our base. If we can hit them hard enough, it may deter their main body and the Nana's levies from coming any closer. God, how I wish we had a squadron of British cavalry to bring us reliable intelligence of the Nana's movements! It makes me deuced uneasy, not knowing for certain what he's up to or how many of the Delhi regiments have joined him—it's like going into battle blindfolded."

At dawn, escorted by nine men of the 9th Lancers and a handful of Native Irregulars—all the cavalry he had—the General rode forward to reconnoitre, still uneasy. But seeing, through his field glasses, that the red-coated Gwalior sepoys were preparing to continue their advance, he ordered his own troops to commence their attack.

They did so, in dashing style, led by four companies of the Rifle Brigade in skirmishing order under their Colonel, Walpole, to be met by a heavy fire of artillery from guns posted on the far side of the dried-up bed of the Pandoo Nuddy. From the enemy's right, a large body of cavalry made a spirited charge but this was repulsed by the 34th who formed square, smote them with a crashing volley from their Enfield rifles, and sent them flying back in confusion. The British column deployed and, led by the 88th—the Connaught Rangers— charged with the bayonet, cheering as they went. The river bed was crossed, the position carried with a rush, and a village, more than half a mile to the rear, taken at bayonet point. The mutineers retreated rapidly, leaving two 8-inch howitzers and a six-pounder gun behind them in their haste.

But Windham's jubilation at his easy victory was short lived. As his troops gathered, cheering, about the captured guns he saw, from a raised mound on the other side of the village, that the mutineers' main body—rank upon rank, numbering at least ten thousand—was advancing to meet him. Smartly uniformed and perfectly disciplined, the Gwalior infantry marched with parade-ground precision, with their Colours in their centre. Cavalry skirmishers were spread out ahead of them and their teams of horse-, bullock- and elephant-drawn guns were positioned at their centre and on either flank.

Some distance to their rear, an ominous cloud of dust rose skyward, heralding the arrival of still more troops—the Nana's levies, General Windham thought dully, seeing the sunlight glint on steel-tipped lances and catching the far-off sound of beating drums. The Nana's levies, which he had supposed to be forty miles away in Oudh! Fervently cursing his lack of cavalry, he lowered his field-glasses and turned to Dupuis.

"It would seem, General," he observed wryly, "that we delayed too long—the rebels will join their forces within the next two hours. Those we have just defeated formed only their leading division."

General Dupuis inclined his head gravely. "I take it, sir," he said, "that you will now fall back to protect the entrenched fort and the Bridge of Boats?"

"I can do little else." Windham shrugged despondently. His voice flat, he gave the required orders to his staff. "I intend to save the native city from pillage if I can. We'll fall back to the old brick kilns on this side of the canal. If they attack us, we'll meet them there."

"We shall be out-gunned, as well as outnumbered, General," Dupuis warned. "I think, sir, you would be wise to send a messenger to inform Sir Colin Campbell at once. Perhaps he may be able to hasten his return."

"Perhaps," General Windham spoke bitterly. "But I doubt it—I doubt it very much, sir."

CHAPTER ONE

As *the long line* of plodding gun-bullocks moved slowly past the walls of the Alam Bagh Palace, four miles to the south of Lucknow, Commander Phillip Horatio Hazard, of HMS *Shannon*'s Naval Brigade, inspected the great twenty-four-pounder siege-gun to which they were yoked with a critical eye. All appeared to be in order and he waved to the crew to proceed.

The sixty-five-hundredweight iron monster was one of six which, together with two 8-inch howitzers and a pair of rocket-launching tubes, were manned by the two hundred seamen and Royal Marines of the Naval Brigade attached to the Lucknow Relief Force. In addition to the gunners required to serve their formidable weapons, the Brigade had two seaman-rifle companies, trained to march and fight like soldiers, and six light field-guns, each commanded by a midshipman. All had proved their worth in the hard fought battle to save the beleagured British garrison in the Lucknow Residency and now, their task accomplished, the Brigade was bringing up the rear of a ten-mile-long column making its way back to Cawnpore.

Not all in the column were fighting men. A force of four thousand, with 25 guns, had been left in the Alam Bagh, under the command of Major-General Sir James Outram, to hold off pursuit and keep the rebel-held city in check. In consequence, only three thousand men of all arms remained to guard the women and children and the sick and wounded—numbering almost two thousand now—whose *doolies* and hackeries formed the bulk of the procession. Moving with equal slowness were the ammunition and baggage waggons, the native camp followers and servants and the host of camels, elephants, and bullocks which carried the column's tents, provisions, and camp equipment.

It had taken the better part of a week to bring them this far. Phillip Hazard's mouth tightened, as he remembered the gnawing anxiety he had endured when first the garrison's sick and wounded and then the surviving families had been smuggled out of the Residency under cover of darkness, with only a thin line of piquets between them and the thousands of mutineers who still held the city in a ring of steel. The *Shannon's* heavy siege-guns had bombarded the enemy-occupied Kaiser Bagh 24 hours a day, for three days, in order to delude the rebel leaders into believing that an attack on their fortress was imminent. Instead, leaving lamps and candles still burning in the shell-scarred Residency buildings, the garrison's rearguard had slipped silently from their posts—gaunt, half-starved men in ragged uniforms—to join the ranks of their rescuers in the Dilkusha Park . . . and the rebels had not known that they had gone until long after the last man had completed the perilous journey.

And . . . Phillip's expression relaxed. Miraculously his prayers had been answered—his sister Harriet, with her two small children, had been among those who had lived through the 140-day siege. All three of them were in a packed bullock cart, already several miles along the dusty road to Cawnpore where, tragically, his younger sister, Lavinia, had died . . . brutally murdered, with the other women and children of General Wheeler's garrison, in a small, yellow-painted house in the native city where the traitor, Nana, had held them captive. He had seen that house, seen with his own eyes the evidence of what had been done there and . . . for all his familiarity with the horrors or war, Phillip shivered, wishing that he could erase the memory of what he had seen from his mind.

There had been so many deaths on both sides, since the sepoy Army of Bengal had broken out in mutiny nearly seven months ago. Lucknow had already cost more than a thousand lives in the two Relief columns alone, and the siege had taken heavy toll of the original defenders of the Residency, British and Indian alike. Seven hundred of the sepoy garrison had remained true to their salt, fighting loyally beside the soldiers of Her Majesty's 32nd Light Infantry and their Sikh comrades from the Punjab . . . as indeed had many others in the Relief columns.

But now they were marching out, leaving their dead behind them in mass and unmarked graves. They were leaving the hero of the siege, Sir Henry Lawrence, Chief Commissioner of Oudh, thanks to whose foresight in fortifying and provisioning his Residency their brave defence had been made possible— although he had not lived long enough to witness it. They were leaving General Havelock also and . . . The last of the massive siege-guns came jolting past behind its twelve pairs of straining bullocks. Phillip watched it go and then turned in his saddle to look back at the towering, loopholed walls of the Alam Bagh, behind which Major-General Sir Henry Havelock had been laid to rest two days before.

Hailed throughout British India as the saviour of Lucknow,

the little General, who had battled so valiantly to bring the first relief to the besieged garrison, had sickened during the seven weeks that he, himself, had shared the ordeal of those he had endeavoured to rescue. Careless as always of his own safety, he had gone out with Sir James Outram and other officers of the Residency garrison to receive the Commander-in-Chief, Sir Colin Campbell, in the building known as the Mess House which was under enemy fire. He had been knocked down by the blast from an exploding shell but had gone on, insisting that he was uninjured, to be informed of his promotion and his knighthood by the man who had led Lucknow's final Relief Force. With the garrison's congratulations ringing in his ears, Henry Havelock's strength had failed him, and barely a week after his historic meeting with the Commander-in-Chief, he had succumbed to an attack of dysentery against which his frail, emaciated body had had no resistance.

Even so, the news of his death had come as a profound shock to the entire Force and Phillip—who had attended the brief funeral service with William Peel, the *Shannon's* Captain—recalled with a pang the tears which had glistened in the eyes of the mourners, as six stalwart Highlanders of his favourite regiment, the Queen's 78th, had borne Havelock's body to the hastily dug grave, preceded by a piper, playing "The Flowers of the Forest."

They had fired the traditional volley at the graveside, Sir Colin Campbell standing on the newly turned earth, his hand raised to his cocked hat in salute, with Sir James Outram and Brigadier Inglis on one side of him, his elder son, Harry Havelock, of HM's 10th Foot and his devoted, young aide-de-camp, William Hargood of the Madras Fusiliers, on the other. As the high-ranking mourners had started to move away, leaving the two young officers to their private and personal grief,

William Peel had said, a catch in his voice, "They may well weep for him—a brave soldier and a better Christian never drew breath. I confess, Phillip, that I shall be satisfied if I can say, as General Havelock did when he knew that he was dying, 'I have forty years so ruled my life that, when death came, I might face it without fear.'"

Amen to that, Phillip thought, and amen to . . .

"Sir!" Midshipman Clinton, his right arm, injured at the attack on the Shah Nujeef ten days before, still in its sling, drew rein beside him. His good-looking young face was thickly coated with dust and he was breathless with the effort it had taken him to reach the rear of the column. "The Captain's compliments, sir, and he'd like a word with you. He's up ahead— about a couple of miles—with the First Lieutenant. I'm to inform the gunnery officer of a change in his orders, too, sir— can you tell me where he is?"

"He's there"—Phillip pointed—"if you can see him for dust! Carry on—and thanks."

He found Captain Peel, as young Lord Arthur Clinton had predicted, some two miles further along the dust-clouded road with the *Shannon*'s First Lieutenant, James Vaughan, and a Royal Artillery officer, Captain Travers.

"Ah, Phillip, I'm glad you've got here." Peel's handsome, fine-boned face wore an expression of unusual gravity as Phillip edged his sweating horse to the road verge where they had halted. "It's quite a job, is it not, getting anywhere or finding anyone in this crush? And it's worse up there." He gestured to the road ahead, where glimpses of red-curtained *doolies* could be seen in an apparently endless procession, their native bearers jolting the occupants unmercifully as they jogged along the rutted road three, and sometimes four or five, abreast.

"Those poor devils of wounded," Phillip said wryly. "They're being pushed along at quite a rate, aren't they, sir? Is quite so much haste necessary?"

"The C-in-C thinks it is," Peel returned. "I've just been talking to him. He's worried about Cawnpore. No"—he answered Phillip's anticipated question—"there's been no word from General Windham as yet but that's not to say he hasn't sent word. Communication with Cawnpore has been, to say the least, uncertain—*cossids* haven't been getting through. But I gather it's the lack of news that is at the root of Sir Colin's concern. He says he feels it in his bones that all is not well and—that's why I wanted to see you, Phillip—he wants our guns and Tavers's heavy battery brought nearer to the head of the column. Brigadier Hope Grant's Delhi Brigade, with the Lancers and the horsed guns, form the advance guard, as you're aware. Well, he wants our Brigade to move up to their immediate rear. If Cawnpore *is* under attack, we're to be pushed forward, in advance of the column, to Windham's aid. The Chief is anxious about the Ganges Bridge."

Phillip nodded, frowning. The Commander-in-Chief's anxiety was understandable. "When are we to move up, sir?" he asked.

"This evening," Peel told him. "Camp is to be made at the Bunni Bridge—Hope Grant should be across it by now. We're to move up as soon as the road is reasonably clear, passing through the camp while the rest of the column is halted."

"In semi-darkness, Phillip," Jim Vaughan put in. "We shall have to put two crews on each gun—watch and watch, more or less. But at least there'll be a moon, for which thank heaven—because it will take us all night and well into the early morning to get those guns shifted. The men will have a dinner halt and another short one at Bunni. For the rest, they'll have to keep on the march, I'm afraid."

"The Jacks will cope with that," Phillip said. "But what about our gun-cattle? They won't."

"Hughie Hare is trying to get us some relief teams," Captain Peel answered. "Captain Travers"—he nodded in the direction of the Royal Artillery officer, who had ridden across the road to greet a party of wounded in a bullock cart—"says he'll use elephants for his battery, and we may have to, if we can't track down any spare bullocks. But I'm not keen on the brutes, I must confess, and I certainly don't want to go into action with them if I can help it. However, the Madras Regiment should have commandeered some spare transport animals at the Bunni campsite; they were warned." He sighed and then demanded sharply, "Phillip, our Jacks did break their fast before they marched, didn't they?"

Phillip smiled. William Peel's obstinate insistence that the men of his Brigade were to shave and eat breakfast before going on duty was in defiance of the Commander-in-Chief's standing orders, which called for the meal to be eaten at the second halt when the column was on the march.

"Yes, sir," he said. "They did—although the Column Marshall nearly had apoplexy when I informed him that I was acting on your instructions."

"Men fight better on a full stomach," Peel observed, the suspicion of a smile giving the boyish curve to his firm mouth. He took a small silver watch from his pocket, and his smile faded. "Jim and I will ride back to the guns, Phillip, and get things organised. I want you to resume your duties as liaison officer with the chief staff, if you please."

"Aye, aye, sir," Phillip acknowledged. He waited expectantly and the *Shannon*'s Captain went on, his tone faintly defensive, "Sir Colin likes to play his hand a mite close to his chest but I want to *know* what's going on—you understand, Phillip? If there is any news from General Windham—good or bad—send me word, will you? I'll let you have one of the mids, to act as galloper. He can catch up with you . . . and, Phillip—"

"Yes, sir?"

William Peel gave vent to an audible sigh. "If the news should be what Sir Colin fears, he'll almost certainly ride ahead of the column to make a personal reconnaissance. In that case, go with him, if you please, and make sure that young Hay and his party are all right. If necessary, take over command yourself and see to it that our Jacks and their two guns are put to the best possible use—you have my full authority to do whatever you consider expedient. But above all, send *me* a full report on the situation as soon as you can."

"I will, sir," Phillip assured him. He saluted and, kneeing his horse into a reluctant trot, started to make his way towards the head of the long, slow-moving column. It took him almost two hours to catch up with the Commander-in-Chief and his staff, such was the speed with which they were pressing forward. Sir Colin Campbell, small and dapper, rode in grim silence, hunched in his saddle, his eyes half-closed against the glare of the sun and a kerchief tied about the lower part of his face in an effort to keep out the dust. He made no acknowledgement of Phillip's presence and seemed unaware of it but his senior aide-de-camp, Sir David Baird of the 98th, told him, with a smile, "The Chief's seen you, my dear fellow, make no mistake about that. But it's as much as our lives are worth to interrupt his thoughts at the present moment—even General Mansfield's keeping out of his way!"

"I gather he is anxious about Cawnpore?" Phillip suggested.

"Indeed he is, Commander." Baird's smile faded. "There's been no news, of course, but he insists he can hear gunfire, although none of the rest of us can."

By the time the head of the column reached the camping ground, two miles beyond the Sai River Bridge at Bunni, however, the distant rumble of heavy and prolonged cannon fire was clearly audible to them all, coming unmistakably from the direction of Cawnpore. An urgent request to Captain Peel to expedite the movement of his siege-train to the front was followed by a general order, from the Commander-in-Chief, for the whole convoy to prepare for a forced march next day, and, well before first light, the camp was astir, with the naval guns now in position to the rear of the Delhi Brigade's cavalry and horsed guns, and the infantry dropping back to protect the convoy.

The first news from Cawnpore was brought by a native *cossid* who emerged, sweating and breathless, from his hiding place in a field of corn as the advance guard of the 9th Lancers trotted past. The note he carried was marked "Most Urgent" and addressed to "Sir Colin Campbell or any Officer commanding troops on the Lucknow road." Written partly in Greek characters, it stated that General Windham was under attack by an estimated twenty to twenty-five thousand rebels, with powerful artillery—the Gwalior troops, under Tantia Topi, having joined forces with those of the Nana.

At noon, a second message, evidently penned some ten or twelve hours after the first, urged the Commander-in-Chief to return to Cawnpore with the utmost speed. The native city and the Ganges Bridge were threatened, the defenders having been compelled, after a severe and daylong battle, to retire within the fortified entrenchment with their guns. The rebels had at least 70 guns, some of heavy calibre and he was being hard-pressed, Windham concluded. Nevertheless, a counter-attack had been ordered for the following day in the hope of carrying off some of the guns or driving them back, beyond the range of fort and bridge.

"They're not in possession of the city yet," Captain Baird said, passing this news on to Phillip. "According to the fellow who brought the second message—and General Windham has strong out-piquets posted to cover the Bridge of Boats. Pray God he can hold out until we get there but the Chief's worried—if that bridge is lost or destroyed, it will be disasterous for them and for us."

With all his earlier fears for the safety of his base at Cawnpore now confirmed, Sir Colin Campbell ordered the speed of the convoy increased, while he himself pressed on with the cavalry and horse artillery. The thunder of the guns could now be heard even by the rearguard and, with each mile the weary convoy travelled, the sound became louder and more menacing. Thirsty and footsore, the infantry marched doggedly on; the travel-worn *doolie* bearers and the heavily laden coolies could scarcely stagger under their burdens. Men, horses, and gun-cattle dropped from exhaustion; and the sick and wounded died, tired beyond endurance by the pain inflicted on them; and children sobbed in their mothers' arms, their pleas for water ignored, since no halt could be called and the contents of the water-carriers' goatskin bags had to be kept for the fighting men who might, at any time, be called upon to defend them.

Thirty-eight miles were covered before, at long last, a halt was made outside Mungalwar and the suffering of the wounded and of the poor fugitives from Lucknow in their hot, dusty conveyances, found some relief. Anxious for his sister, Harriet, and her two small children, Phillip dared not leave his post, but William Peel, anticipating his anxiety, sent Midshipman Lightfoot to search for them and the boy reported that he had found them an hour or so before the convoy reached the campsite, tired and suffering from the heat but otherwise unharmed. Greatly relieved by this news, Phillip was waiting, with other members of the Commander-in-Chief's staff at Mungalwar, where the cavalry had halted, when a third *cossid* from Cawnpore was ushered into Sir Colin's presence, to thrust a spill of native-made paper into his hand. The old General's thin, deeply lined cheeks drained of their last vestige of sallow colour as he unfolded and read it.

"Gentlemen, there can be no rest for us this night," he announced. His voice, with its grating, Lowland Scots accent, sounded strained. "This is the third message I have received from General Windham. He is in serious danger and his force has sustained nearly five hundred casualties. He informs me that he has been compelled to withdraw once more into the entrenchment which, with the Ganges Bridge, is now within range of the rebels' heavy artillery. The native city is in their hands and, when he wrote this report, he was expecting them to attack his position and the bridgehead in overwhelming numbers. He begs for immediate aid; As you can hear"—he gestured, with a bony hand, in the direction from which came the relentless roar of the guns—"the attack is still in progress and General Windham's small force appears still to be holding out. I intend to ascertain the situation by making a personal reconnaissance and, if the bridge is still intact, I shall cross to the entrenchment and confer with the General."

He issued his orders with his accustomed precision and Phillip listened, admiring his calm control. The cavalry and horse artillery were to remain at the campsite, to give both men and horses time to eat and snatch what rest they could but, he warned Brigadier Hope Grant, they must be ready to move at a moment's notice, should the need arise.

"Despatch your young gentleman to Captain Peel," he said to Phillip. "And say that I regret the circumstances which compell me to ask him to bring up his heavy guns with all the speed he can muster and without respite for his gallant seamen. But I must have those guns by dawn tomorrow, at the latest, Commander Hazard. Impress that upon him, if you please. And you yourself had better ride on with me, in case my orders to your commander require to be changed . . . although I fear they will not."

Within ten minutes, Sir Colin was again on his horse, a small, bowed but oddly indomitable figure, riding purposefully towards the sound of guns. His staff and an escort of a dozen Lancers rode with him and they covered the six miles which separated them from the Oudh bank of the river at a steady trot, which increased to a gallop when the bridge was sighted.

"The bridge is still there, sir!" an ADC reported breathlessly. "But the city is in flames."

He was right, Phillip saw, glimpsing the pall of smoke which rose from the huddled buildings on the opposite bank, obscuring the sunset. The Bridge of Boats stretched like a dark thread across the wide expanse of water before them and, as he studied it, he saw a roundshot strike one of the two small islands to which the centre of the bridge was attached and bound over it, to fall harmlessly into the reeds beyond. There were at least two batteries of heavy guns playing on the bridge but they were firing at extreme range and, as far as he could make out, not very accurately. Instinctively he watched the flashes, pinpointing the position of the enemy's guns. They were well positioned and cleverly masked; the guns of General Windham's entrenchment could not bear on them, whereas—

if the rebel gunners chose to turn their attention from the bridge—both batteries could bombard the fort and its surrounding buildings with virtual impunity. But as long as the bridge remained intact, there was a chance that they could be silenced . . . he was conscious of an upsurge of hope, as he recalled Captain Peel's parting words to him.

"See to it that our Jacks and their two guns are put to the best possible use," Peel had said. He had no means, as yet, of knowing whether the two 24-pounders left under Edward Hay's command were still in the Cawnpore entrenchment—it was possible that both guns might have been put out of action or that their crews might have suffered so many casualties that neither could be worked. General Windham's last message had stated that his casualties had been close on five hundred and that estimate had been made some hours ago . . . suddenly conscious of a sick sensation in the pit of his stomach, Phillip urged his flagging horse into a canter and followed Sir Colin Campbell down the river bank to the bridge.

A guard of about company strength was posted at the bridgehead. The officer in command, a youthful subaltern of the Rifle Brigade in a torn and filthy uniform, came to meet them in response to the sentry's excited shout. Recognising the Commander-in-Chief, an expression of heartfelt relief spread over his wan, unshaven face and he stumbled across the swaying, turf-covered surface of the bridge towards the little group of horsemen.

"Thank God you're here, sir!" he exclaimed. "We are at our last gasp. When the rebels seized the city, we feared that all was lost, sir, and—"

Sir Colin Campbell rounded on him furiously. "How dare you suggest that any of Her Majesty's troops are at their last gasp, sir?" he demanded. "Shame on you, sir!" Waving the abashed young officer contemptuously aside, he turned to one of his staff, a tall man in the uniform of Barrow's Volunteer Horse. "Find yourself a fresh horse and ride back to Mungalwar, if you please, Colonel," he requested, his tone crisp and decisive. "Tell General Grant that I want his heavy guns in position to cover this bridge before daylight—Captain Peel's twenty-four-pounders, too, if it's humanly possible. And warn Grant that I shall require his cavalry and horsed batteries to be ready to cross into Cawnpore at first light. I shall go across now to consult with General Windham and decide what's to be done, but tell the Brigadier-General that I'll rejoin him as soon as I can."

Dusk had fallen when Sir Colin led the way into the Cawnpore entrenchment but, despite the dim light, the men guarding the out-works recognised the small, bowed figure on the white horse and started to cheer. The welcome news of his arrival spread like wildfire and the cheering was taken up and echoed by those manning the batteries and the perimeter and even by the wounded as they lay, helpless, in the over-crowded hospital, on which the rebel battery in the churchyard had now ranged.

Phillip, followed on the heels of the Commander-in-Chief's aides, saw a white-haired officer in Irregular Cavalry uniform move forward to take his horse's rein. Sir Colin dismounted, thanking him courteously for his assistance, to be assailed by a loud-voiced complaint as the white-haired officer, relinquishing the rein, planted his stout and perspiring body in the General's path.

"I wish to protest, sir, at the manner in which this defence has been conducted! Quite reckless and unnecessary risks have been taken by General Windham and men's lives uselessly squandered. Indeed, sir, he—"

Sir Colin cut him short, his tone icy. "And who, sir, might you be?" he asked, with dangerous calm.

The white-haired officer held his ground. "My name is Cockayne, sir—Lieutenant-Colonel Cockayne, lately in command of the 21st Oudh Irregular Cavalry at Ghorabad. I—"

Again Sir Colin cut him short.

"Your regiment mutinied, did it not, Colonel?"

Colonel Cockayne inclined his white head. "It did, sir. That is why I am here—I came to seek aid for the British garrison at Ghorabad, when I made my escape. My wife and daughter are with the garrison and all of them are in mortal danger. But I have been unable to obtain aid—there are not sufficient British troops, I am told. Yet General Windham squanders five hundred of them in this . . . damme, sir, in this insane attempt to engage a vastly superior enemy in open country, outside the city and his fortified entrenchment! I have the right to protest to you, sir, as Commander-in-Chief, when British lives are being sacrificed to no avail. With even half the men Windham has lost in the past three days, I could have saved my people in Ghorabad. Indeed, I could have brought aid to others who sorely need it and—"

Sir Colin Campbell lost patience with him. "Be silent, sir!" he thundered. "I'll thank you to keep your insubordinate opinions to yourself. Were it not for the fact that due allowance must be made in the light of your anxiety for your wife and family, I'd have you placed under arrest."

"But, sir . . . Sir Colin, I beg you to listen to me—"

"Stand aside, Colonel Cockayne," the General bade him, his tone one that brooked no further argument. "I have no time to listen to you. *I* have two thousand British lives in peril—wounded men and women and children from Lucknow for whom I've risked everything to save. And they will be in peril unless the Ganges bridge is held for long enough to enable me to bring them and my force across the river tomorrow."

Colonel Cockayne looked as if he were prepared to carry his protest a step further but the DAAG, Captain Hamilton, slipping quietly from his saddle, gripped him firmly by the arm and drew him back. "General Windham's coming, sir," he warned Sir Colin, and the Commander-in-Chief gave him a nod of approval and then walked, a trifle stiffly, towards the tall figure hurrying through the gathering darkness to meet him.

Left to his own devices, Phillip went in search of the *Shannon* party, finding the young acting-mate, Henry Garvey, in charge of a battery of the fort's eighteen-pounders. Firing from the fort had ceased with the coming of darkness and the men lay or squatted about their guns in a state of complete exhaustion, only rousing themselves when a petty officer and two cooks made their appearance with the grog ration and buckets of steaming coffee.

"Mr Hay was wounded twice, sir," Garvey explained, when they had exchanged greetings and both had been supplied with pannikins of coffee. "He's in the hospital."

"How bad is he, Mr Garvey?" Phillip asked, sipping appreciatively at his coffee which the petty officer, unasked, had lashed liberally with rum.

"He's bad enough, sir, but out of danger, the surgeon told me this morning. He was hit a second time by a grapeshot which fortunately struck the buckle of his sword-belt—otherwise he'd have been killed." The young mate hesitated and then said feelingly, "I can't tell you how relieved we were to see Sir Colin ride in just now—it's been touch and go here, believe me, sir. But how did you fare? I take it your return means that Lucknow was relieved?"

Phillip nodded. He gave a brief account of the battle for

the Residency and the final evacuation of the garrison, aware
that the seamen were also listening eagerly. Then, moving out
of earshot of them, he invited Garvey to tell his own story.
"From what I've heard so far, Mr Garvey, things have been
going badly here. Have they for you?"

Henry Garvey's expression was wry. "Frankly, sir, yes." He
described the movement of the defenders to the Calpee road
camp and their first—and highly successful—brush with the
Gwalior rebels at the Pandoo Nuddy Bridge, followed by the
shock of learning that, instead of the three thousand they had
expected, some twenty-five thousand insurgents were preparing to attack and drive them from Cawnpore.

"We just weren't prepared for that, sir," he went on unhappily. "There had been no warning and it started a panic. It . . .
to tell you the truth, our guns were . . . well, mishandled from
then on. We were expected to move them about like nine-
pounder field-guns and, on the first occasion that Mr Hay was
hit, his gun was up with the skirmishers near the junction of
the Delhi and Calpee roads. It was some distance ahead of
mine and to my left, and we both came under fire from enemy
guns at very close range—four hundred yards in Hay's case,
sir, and there were about fourteen of theirs to our six. We had
Captain Greene's battery to our right, two howitzers and two
9-pounders. We kept up our fire until we started to run out of
ammunition, and then they launched an attack on our left
flank, with about a couple of thousand infantry and some
Irregular cavalry."

He paused, frowning, and Phillip prompted, "Well, what
happened, Mr Garvey?"

"The skirmishers were called in, sir," Garvey told him bitterly. "And the order came to retire. Hay yelled out 'Rear
limber up!' when a shrapnel shell burst right overhead which

stampeded our bullocks and the drivers all deserted. Our supporting infantry and Captain Greene's battery obeyed the order to retire, so we were left unsupported, without ammunition or limbers. The CRA, General Dupuis, ordered us to spike the guns and retire, because the enemy cavalry seemed to be preparing to charge us. With only 25 men, there wasn't much else we could do. Mr Hay was hit spiking his gun—in the arm, sir, not severely—and he told me to get the men to fall back to the infantry's new position, which we did and—"

"Are you telling me that the guns are lost?" Phillip questioned sharply.

"Oh, no, sir—we got them back!" Henry Garvey's tone was indignant. "We knew what Captain Peel would say if we let them fall into the enemy's hands! The cavalry thought better about charging us and Captain Greene had got his nine-pounders in action again, so Mr Hay called for volunteers to bring them in. We managed to catch the bullocks and yoke them and then, with volunteers from the 88th, we gave 'em a bayonet charge and secured both guns. Young Harry Lascelles borrowed a rifle and bayonet from a wounded fellow and led the Connaught Rangers' charge—he fairly put the fear of God into the darkies, sir, hacking away with his bayonet and yelling his head off!" Garvey's haggard young face was lit by a reminiscent grin. "You should have seen him, all four-foot-nothing of him, surrounded by cheering Irishmen!" His grin faded. "That was when poor Hay was hit a second time and I had to have him carried in."

Lascelles was a naval cadet, Phillip reminded himself, whom Captain Peel had deliberately left behind in the hope that he would be safer in Cawnpore than in the Lucknow column . . . He sighed, as Garvey continued his story.

"Mr Hay's gun, which was well and truly spiked, was

ordered back to the fort," he said. "And I was instructed to place mine at the entrance to the city, to cover our infantry's withdrawal. I took all our Jacks with me, because we still hadn't seen hide nor hair of our native bullock drivers, and I sent Lascelles and two of our slightly wounded men with the spiked gun. Harry Lascelles's Irishmen had volunteered to escort him and I thought they'd be all right but—" he broke off, reddening.

"But what, Mr Garvey?" Phillip asked

"Well, sir, they capsized it in one of the narrow streets of the city," Henry Garvey confessed. "The first I heard of it was when I'd seen Hay into hospital and was snatching a bite to eat. General Windham sent for me and told me I must recover the gun. He said that firing in the city had ceased and that the rebels had withdrawn. He promised me a strong escort but warned me that it might be an ugly job."

"And was it?" Phillip asked. The youngster had done well, he thought; he was only eighteen, promoted from senior midshipman, but he had taken command when Edward Hay had been incapacitated and had exercised that command with courage and good sense. And, it was clear, he had not lost his guns . . .

Garvey grinned. "Not as ugly as I expected, sir. The worst part was getting the gun back on an even keel because we daren't make a noise, for fear of bringing them down on us. We had to clear away a lot of stones and rubble before we could tackle the gun but our fellows were first-rate. They'd been in action since five in the morning and they were all pretty done up but when I said 'Heave!' they made an almighty effort and righted her, and we got back here without a shot being fired. Since then, we've been manning the batteries here, apart from one sortie, when we were ordered to support General Carthew's piquet at the bridge."

He went into graphic detail and Phillip listened, a thoughtful frown creasing his brow. The boy was right, he decided—the military commanders *had* attempted to employ the naval twenty-four-pounders as light field-guns, with little regard for the sheer weight of each piece and the difficulty of manoeuvring twelve pairs of bullocks, even with their native drivers. Without them, the guns' speed over rough ground would inevitably be greatly reduced since—according to Garvey—only the bare number of men required to work and fight each gun had been permitted to go out, the remainder of the seamen being ordered to assist in manning the fort's batteries. But with a double crew, perhaps . . . His frown deepened.

"It was the hottest fire I've ever been under," Henry Garvey added, referring to his sortie in Brigadier-General Carthew's support. "But there was the Brigadier, sitting his horse as cool as you please and refusing to take cover—he has more guts than any man I've ever seen, sir, honestly." His voice was warm with admiration. "But I heard a little while ago that he's being forced to withdraw because his position has become untenable—it was untenable when we were there and that was about three hours ago. He sent us back; from where we were, we couldn't bear on any of the rebel batteries and the Brigadier was afraid they'd make a rush and cut us off. They . . . look, sir, below you—that's Carthew's advance guard, coming in now, with some of the wounded. Poor fellows, it's not before time."

"What about the bridge, if Carthew withdraws?" Phillip questioned. He peered down anxiously from the embrasure at the shadowy, running figures below him. It was an orderly withdrawal, with no sign of panic but . . . A burst of rifle fire from somewhere near the bridgehead was echoed by a volley from the fort's perimeter.

"The guns behind the out-works can cover the approach to it," Garvey said. "And we have riflemen posted along the perimeter; the rebel infantry won't get on to the bridge, sir." He barked an order to his own guns' crew, as one of the hitherto silent nine-pounders posted in the out-works opened up. His seamen, moving like sleepwalkers, took up their position round their guns, silent, too exhausted even to grumble. After a while, the firing petered out and, when a procession of curtained *doolies* was followed into the entrenchment by a company of the 34th and six or seven mounted officers, Garvey permitted his men to stand down.

"They're in, sir," he told Phillip, relief in his voice. In the wan glow of the newly risen moon, he pointed out a bareheaded officer in shirtsleeves, who was dismounting from his horse with the slow, stiff deliberation of one nearing the limit of physical endurance. "That's General Carthew and it doesn't look as if he's been hit—which is nothing short of a miracle, sir, truly it is."

It probably was but what, Phillip wondered uneasily, was likely to be Sir Colin Campbell's reaction to the bridge piquet's withdrawal—now, of all times, when that slender line of anchored boats stretching across the Ganges was the only link between his Lucknow column and Cawnpore? It was to be hoped that young Henry Garvey was right concerning the rebel infantry's chances of seizing the bridge before Hope Grant could bring his cavalry and horse artillery across. The Pandies were not noted for their courage, it was true but . . . He smothered a sigh. There were still those two batteries of heavy calibre guns, mounted beyond the fort's range, whose now desultory thunder warned that some of them were continuing their endeavours, even in darkness, to sever the link. When the moon rose to its full height, the danger of their hitting their target would increase and, with the coming of daylight—if Peel's guns had not arrived to silence them—the risk would be doubled.

Garvey, as if reading his thoughts, offered confidently, "Those twenty-four-pounders are firing at extreme range, sir, and they were making pretty poor practise when I was watching them from the bridgehead this afternoon. I fancy they'll give up soon—they don't usually waste shot after dark."

But they could move in closer with the darkness to aid them, Phillip reflected and, once they realised that Brigadier Carthew's piquet had been withdrawn, it would be surprising if they failed to take advantage of its absence. A plan of action was beginning to form in his mind and he glanced, with narrowed eyes, into the night sky. They would need Sir Colin's approval, of course, but . . . He turned again to Garvey.

"I endeavoured to spot their position when we crossed the bridge," he said. "But it was dusk and Sir Colin wasn't wasting any time. You'll have had a better opportunity to observe them this afternoon, I imagine; can you pinpoint them accurately, Mr Garvey?"

The young acting-mate did not disappoint him. "Oh, yes, sir," he answered readily. "We hadn't much else to do, since our gun couldn't bear on any of their batteries, so I set the cadets to making sketch maps and working out ranges. I thought it would keep them up to the mark and it did—Teddy Watson produced a beauty. I've got it somewhere." He fumbled in his pockets and brought out a crumpled sheet of paper, which he offered apologetically. "I'm afraid it's only in pencil, sir, and it's got a bit smudged."

"This will do admirably," Phillip assured him. "You are certainly keeping the cadets up to the mark. Mr Watson shows talent."

By the spluttering light of the battery lantern, he studied the neatly drawn sketch. As he had earlier surmised, to bring a gun to bear on either of the enemy batteries would require it to be positioned on the bridge itself or, better still, on the nearer of the two small islands in midstream. Once there, a certain amount of cover for the gun's crew could be provided by riflemen, strategically posted in the fort's out-works and—he checked Cadet Watson's sketch map—by a nine-pounder already mounted on the perimeter, which could be swung round. It would be a fairly lengthy task to haul one of the *Shannon's* twenty-four-pounders into position on the island if bullocks were employed and it would have to be done silently but . . . Phillip's brain was racing now, as he examined the possibilities. Garvey had already proved—when he and his gunners had retrieved their damaged weapon from the native city the previous night—that a well-trained crew could work swiftly and efficiently in darkness, without attracting unwelcome attention from the enemy. And with a double crew . . .

"Mr Garvey, how many fit men have you?" he asked.

"Counting the Marines' party, sir, I have 42." Garvey's round, powder-grimed face betrayed his inner excitement but he was too well disciplined to ask questions. "They've eaten, sir," he added. "I sent them for dinner when we withdrew from the bridgehead. Mr Lascelles and Mr Watson are sleeping—I told them to go off duty; I thought they'd earned a rest, poor little devils. But," he added eagerly, "I can have them called if you need them, sir."

"Not yet," Phillip answered. "I have to speak to the Commander-in-Chief first." It was a pity, he thought regretfully, that only one of the *Shannon's* heavy guns was serviceable. Sir Colin Campbell might have reservations on that account, but unfortunately there was no time now to rebore the gun poor Hay had been ordered to spike. He asked about gun-cattle and ammunition supplies and then mentioned the spiked gun. Once again Acting-Mate Garvey surprised him.

"Mr Hay's gun is ready for action, sir. It wasn't well and truly spiked, you see, and I got Brown on to it this morning."

"Good man!" Phillip exclaimed, with sincerity. "You've done damned well in your first command, Mr Garvey, and I shall see to it that Captain Peel is informed of your conduct." He rose, tucking the sketch map into the breast pocket of his coat. "I'm going to report to Sir Colin Campbell that—thanks very largely to your forethought and efficiency—the Naval Brigade detachment is at his disposal if he wishes to engage the enemy's long-range batteries."

Henry Garvey beamed his delight. "Shall I have my men relieved at these guns, sir? We could be yoking up the bullock teams and limbers while we're waiting."

Phillip nodded. He went in search of Sir Colin, to find his staff gathered round a tent on the *glacis* normally occupied by General Windham. From its lamp-lit interior, his voice sounded wrathfully, the strong Scottish accent contrasting with Windham's quieter, more cultured English voice.

"Unless you've something exceptionally good to tell him, I shouldn't go in, if I were you, Commander," Captain Baird warned wryly. He drew Phillip aside and added confidentially, "The Chief is greatly put out by General Carthew's decision to withdraw his piquets, which he fears may jeopardise the bridge before General Grant's Brigade can cross. And if your Captain Peel's siege-train isn't able to reach the Oudh bank before sunrise then . . ." He shrugged resignedly. "Poor Carthew has been given a very severe dressing down which, according to the people here, he hardly deserves. They say he's displayed the most magnificent personal courage and that he and the 34th fought like tigers for 24 hours before being compelled to retire. But Sir Colin will have it that he should have hung on and General Windham's had to admit that he retired without orders. The Chief is upset, of course, over General Wilson's death—he was killed leading a counterattack this morning, poor, brave old man. Stirling, too, and Morphey, and young Richard McCrae."

"I hadn't heard that," Phillip said, conscious of sadness. Brigadier Wilson had been much loved by all who knew him. He hesitated and then offered quietly, "I believe I do have something useful to suggest, Captain Baird."

"Precisely what, Commander?" Baird asked cautiously. Phillip outlined his plan and saw the ADC's expression relax. "By George, sir, I believe you do!" he agreed with relief. "Hold on for a few minutes, will you please? I'll have a word with General Mansfield."

Within ten minutes, a summons came from Sir Colin himself. Standing hatless, his sparse white hair blowing in the slight evening breeze, he was waiting at the opened tent flap as Phillip approached. As always, when crisis loomed, the Commander-in-Chief was brusque, and he came to the point bluntly and without wasting words.

"You think you can engage those two batteries and keep their fire down until Captain Peel gets here with the rest of your guns?"

"I think so, sir. Thanks to Mr Garvey, the young officer who has been commanding the naval detachment since his senior was wounded, both our twenty-four-pounders are serviceable." Phillip went into brief details and saw the old General's tired face light with a smile.

"Then go to it, Commander Hazard," Sir Colin bade him gruffly. "You'll earn my gratitude and so will your Mr Garvey.

I'm returning to Mungalwar now but you have my authority to call on this garrison for any assistance you need. Just get those guns into position without delay."

"Aye, aye, sir," Phillip acknowledged. He crossed the *glacis* at a run and, as he did so, one of the rebel batteries opened on the fort and, with greater accuracy than they had hitherto shown, sent half a dozen roundshot into the hospital on its north side.

CHAPTER TWO

Both *naval guns* were in the positions Phillip had selected for them two hours before dawn. The attack he had feared at the bridgehead did not materialise but Hay's bullock team had proved their unreliability once again, and when random shells from a howitzer—aimed at the fort—had burst overhead, the whole team had been thrown into panic-stricken confusion, and he had been compelled to have the heavy gun manhandled on to the bridge.

It had taken the combined efforts of the *Shannon*'s 42 seamen and Marines to drag it there but it was a measure of their willingness and discipline that they had performed their difficult task without breaking silence, requiring only a few whispered orders to direct them. Finally, in response to Phillip's request, two elephants had been brought down and these had been a godsend, under the expert supervision of an unexpected volunteer in the shape of the Irregular Cavalry Colonel, whose bitter tirade had earlier provoked Sir Colin Campbell's wrath. Colonel Cockayne was fluent in the native dialect and, under his urging, the *mahouts* had handled their huge beasts with great skill, hauling the sixty-five-hundredweight of unwieldy metal along the turf-covered surface of the bridge as if harnessed to a child's toy. The movement of the guns had, apparently, been unnoticed by the rebel gunners in the opposing batteries; they continued to throw shot at the bridge at fairly lengthy intervals but without success and, long before the *Shannon's* guns were unlimbered, both batteries had ceased fire.

"They are probably closing in for the kill," Colonel Cockayne suggested grimly. "Damme, the swine must know that the Commander-in-Chief's column will attempt to make the crossing soon after first light! They don't lack artillery. They'll be bringing up all the heavy cannon they've got and trying to shorten the range, no doubt, in the hope of giving themselves an easier target. Do you really suppose you can stop them, with these two guns of yours, Commander Hazard?"

Before Phillip could reply, a rebel twenty-four-pounder opened on the fort, the dark mound at its summit starkly outlined against the blazing buildings immediately to its front. By the same glow, the gun itself was revealed, only partially masked by a fold in the ground, and two others also commenced firing on the fort, all three situated on the far bank of the canal. They had, as Colonel Cockayne had predicted, moved in considerably closer and Phillip turned, with a grin, to his gun's crew, which was under the nominal command of Cadet Lascelles.

"Right, my lads—action front and let's see if we can't teach the Pandy gunners how it's done! Stand aside, Mr Lascelles, if you please—I'll lay her myself."

The naval guns had been borrowed from the Bengal Artillery, since the *Shannon's* own sixty-eights—too heavy to be moved on existing wooden carriages—had been left in the fort at Allahabad, pending the construction of suitable carriages for them. On Captain Peel's instructions, the borrowed guns had been fitted with sights to enable them to be ranged accurately—a refinement their previous owners had considered unnecessary. The additions were simple but effective:

a dispart, with a notch cut along it, on the gun muzzle, and a tangent sight in the form of a long screw fitted into a hole bored through the cascabel, pointed at the top and with a cross-arm to turn it round, by means of which the elevation of the gun could be adjusted. After days and nights of practise in Lucknow, all the *Shannon* gunners attached to the Commander-in-Chief's column had become very expert and Phillip's grin widened, as he recalled William Peel's claim for his twenty-fours. *"It should not be said of these guns that one can shoot with them as well as with a rifle, but rather that one can shoot with a rifle as well as with them . . ."*

Still smiling, he laid the gun, loading with spherical case. The first shot went over the target, the shell bursting too high. As the great gun ran back six feet from its firing position, it was sponged, re-loaded, and run up; Phillip adjusted the elevation, and the gun-captain stood ready, his smouldering linstock in his hand. The third shot was on target and one of the canal bank battery was silenced, its crew sythed down by the exploding shrapnel. The other two ceased their bombardment of the fort and brought their gun muzzles round in the direction of the bridge but their first ragged salvoes fell into the river well short and after a brief duel, in which Garvey's gun joined, the Gwalior gunners abandoned their canal bank positions and withdrew out of range.

"Very impressive, Commander," Colonel Cockayne observed, his voice holding genuine warmth. "The Gwalior artillery was always said to be extremely good but your fellows put them to shame. Or possibly it is *your* presence that is responsible for their accurate shooting; it was not so apparent in our recent battle for Cawnpore, with your juniors in command."

Phillip mopped his heated face. "My juniors are not to be

faulted, sir," he defended. "These guns are being used now as they are supposed to be used." He gestured to the specially affixed sights and went into technical details. "Employed as light field-guns—as, I understand, they *were* being employed in your recent battle—they are awkward to manoeuvre and excessively slow. Captain Peel did have them up in the attacks on the Lucknow mutineers' positions but this was when they were required to breach fortress walls, to enable infantry to carry them with the bayonet. Sir Colin was determined to move fast and there was no alternative—we *had* to get into the Residency. But"—he shrugged—"we put double crews on each heavy gun and depended as little as possible on bullocks and native drivers. Both are unreliable under fire. They—" He broke off, eyes narrowed and watchful, sensing rather than hearing the sound of oars. Muffled oars, coming from the opposite direction from that in which, a few minutes ago, his guns had been sighted. There was nothing to be seen on the dark surface of the river and, apart from a few isolated rifle shots from the fort, little to be heard.

Vaguely uneasy nevertheless, Phillip crossed to the far side of the bridge but the Marine sentry posted there shook his head emphatically when questioned. "No, sir, nothing's stirring. Seems to have gone very quiet all of a sudden, sir."

"What's wrong, Commander?" Colonel Cockayne asked as he, too, peered into the blackness. The moon was partially obscured by cloud, its reflected radiance dimmed to a dull, faint glimmer. "You don't imagine they'll send a raiding party, do you? Because you can dismiss the idea—they won't risk it at night. In any case, they know we've got heavy guns here by now and they'll expect them to be guarded."

"I thought I heard a boat," Phillip said. "But I must have imagined it. The sound was coming from upstream and . . ."

The reverberating roar of several guns, opening in unison, drowned his voice. The batteries which had originally been firing on the bridge had changed their positions, he realised, as the Colonel gripped his arm and pointed. Roundshot thudded against a large, flat-bottomed boat thirty yards from where he was standing but it was too dark to see how much damage had been done and, intent only on returning the enemy fire, he ran back to his own gun.

"They're still on the far side of the canal, sir," little Lascelles told him eagerly. "But one, at least, is in one of those walled enclosures that run down to the river's edge. They must have knocked part of the wall down. May I open fire, sir?"

"Yes, carry on, Mr Lascelles," Phillip told him crisply. "But take your time—accuracy is more important than seeing how many rounds you can get off." Garvey's gun had already opened and he left them to it, clambering back on to the parapet of the bridge in order to spot the flashes and endeavour to pinpoint the batteries' exact positions. A shell whined overhead, its fuse spluttering, and more roundshot struck the water upstream of the bridge—the rebels had a howitzer, his brain registered, and six—no, seven—guns, well spread out, three to his left on the canal side, four between the still smouldering Assembly Rooms and the river bank to his right. If they made anything like good practise, he thought grimly, then the bridge was done for—its flimsy, floating base would be smashed to pieces long before dawn. Fortunately they were *not* making good practise, most of their shots continuing to be well wide of their target but . . . A muffled explosion over to his right sent him scrambling back to the island.

Garvey's men were cheering triumphantly and he saw, as smoke and a single tongue of flame rose skywards that a well aimed—or lucky—shot had hit one of the rebels' ammunition waggons, imprudently parked in a garden enclosure running down to the river bank. There must have been a second close beside it for, even as he stared at the running figures silhouetted against the blaze, another waggon was caught in the conflagration and this, too, blew up with a dull roar.

"Well done, my lads!" Phillip shouted. "Well done indeed, Mr Garvey!"

He did not discourage the cheering; the rebels, by this time, were well aware of their presence on the bridge, and his men had worked hard—they deserved the chance to vent their feelings. From the piquet of the Rifle Brigade on the Oudh bridgehead and from that of the 88th, on the Cawnpore side, the cheers were echoed and re-echoed with heartening enthusiasm and he found himself smiling, for, heaven knew, they had had little enough to cheer about during the past three days. A defiant roar from the Gwalior cannon and the bursting of a shell from the howitzer, unpleasantly close, put an abrupt end to the cheering; Lascelles' gun had not ceased fire and Garvey's crew needed no orders to bring their weapon back into action. The duel was resumed and Phillip was about to cross to Lascelles's position when a hoarse shout from Colonel Cockayne sent him back to the bridge parapet at a run.

"Look!" the cavalryman invited, a note of fury in his voice. "For God's sake, look at that, Commander!"

He pointed and Phillip, following the direction of his upraised hand, saw that there were ten or a dozen swimmers in the water, their dark heads clearly visible as they struck out frantically for the Oudh bank. He saw something else as well— the body of the Marine sentry who had been posted on the parapet, which lay spreadeagled across the thwarts of one of the boats forming the bridge. The man was dead, his throat cut from ear to ear and hideously gaping, his Enfield lying uselessly beside him. Beyond him, moving gently with the pull of the current, a native riverboat with a straw-thatched awning had been wedged between two of the anchored craft which supported the bridge.

It was obviously this which the swimmers had used to convey them across the river and which they had now abandoned but . . . Why, in heaven's name, *had* they abandoned it? There were hardly enough of them to have constituted a raiding party and the fact that the unfortunate sentry had seen—and presumably challenged—them was not sufficient reason for them to kill him, unless . . . Phillip tore off his jacket and sword-belt, his heart thudding as the awful truth dawned on him. Deaf to the Colonel's startled questions, he precipitated himself into the water. A few swift strokes took him to the abandoned boat, and as he dragged himself on to its deck, he saw the faint gleam of an ignited length of fuse. To allow themselves time to escape, the raiders had used a slow match of quite exceptional length, he realised thankfully; it was hissing its way very slowly across the damp deckboards and he had no trouble in extinguishing it with his booted foot.

The worst danger averted, he took his time removing the two kegs of powder from beneath the thick straw awning and dumping them, one after the other, into the murky river water. Satisfied, as he watched the bubbles rise from the saturated powder, he set the boat adrift and clambered back to the bridge. The *Shannon*'s Marines and the men of the bridgehead piquet were blazing away with rifles at the fugitive swimmers but, Colonel Cockayne told him regretfully, without hitting of them, and Phillip could not find it in his heart to share his regrets when the raiders finally gained the bank and vanished. True, they had brutally murdered the Marine sentry but it had been a bold, well-planned attempt to destroy the bridge and, in carrying it out, the rebels had displayed more courage than the Colonel, at any rate, had given them credit for. Wisely, however, he refrained from saying so, and warded off congratulations on his own exploit with a wry, "Well, it was either them or us, sir, and when I realised what they were up to, there wasn't time to delegate the job to anyone else."

Two of the Marines brought up the body of their dead comrade and, while this was being taken back to the fort for burial, he instructed the others to try and sink the drifting bomb vessel. A few rounds of accurate Enfield fire caused it to settle and start to fill with water but, ironically, it was a round-shot from one of the enemy batteries which sealed its fate, bringing cynical cheers from those of the *Shannon* party who witnessed the incident. All the men were in good heart, even the weary, sweating gunners; they were unable to silence the batteries opposing them—now augmented by another four howitzers—but they were holding their own, drawing fire from the fort and forcing the rebels to withdraw from their river-bank positions to others at longer range.

Shortly before dawn, Midshipman Lightfoot, Phillip's galloper, made his appearance, with Captain Baird and some other members of the Commander-in-Chief's staff. They brought the welcome news that Brigadier Hope Grant had left camp with the cavalry and horse guns, with which he would cross the river to Cawnpore, in order to clear the way for the Lucknow convoy, with the heavy guns following with all possible speed. Baird continued on, to acquaint General Windham with this information and Lightfoot, surrounded by eager questioners, told them that Captain Peel had reached Mungalwar with the *Shannon*'s siege-train at a little after 2 p.m.

"The Captain is waiting only to obtain fresh gun-cattle, sir," he said to Phillip. "He instructed me to tell you that he will be at the bridgehead by sunrise, and he will be obliged, sir, if you would remain in your present position to cover General Hope Grant's crossing." His instructions carried out, Lightfoot added, less formally, "I saw your sister and the children when they reached camp. They were bearing up pretty well, sir, although they didn't get in until an hour after our siege-train."

"Did you speak to them, Mr Lightfoot?" Phillip asked.

"Only to ask how they were, sir, as I thought you'd want to know. Conditions were a bit—well, chaotic at the camp, with guns and stores mixed up with the sick and the women and children. They were streaming in all night and there were hardly any tents up for them because the baggage train was still on the road. The wounded have had a very bad time of it indeed, sir, and I fear many of them won't live to reach Cawnpore. Captain Peel sent me to look for Mr Salmon and he seemed in a poor way, so the Captain had him moved to our section of the column, with the rest of our wounded men. He said we could best look after our own, sir. And Mr Salmon certainly agreed!"

Poor young Nowell Salmon, Phillip thought, recalling the action which had resulted in his being hit twice in the thigh, during the battle for the Shah Nujeef at Lucknow. Peel had fought his guns right up against the formidable walls of the mosque and the Naval Brigade had suffered its worst casualties in consequence. But they had breached the wall, although this fact had not been discovered until a sergeant of the 93rd Highlanders had crept up to it, in darkness, seeking a way in.

"Sir . . ." Acting-Mate Garvey was at his elbow. "Shall I permit the spare guns' crews to break their fast?"

Phillip nodded. It was a timely suggestion; the men had dry haversack rations with them and the grog cask, in the charge of a quartermaster, had accompanied them, made fast to a limber. With two crews on each gun, they could eat in relays. "Very well," he assented. "Carry on, Mr Garvey—and make sure you take something yourself." But the boy still looked concerned and he asked, smiling, "Is anything worrying you?"

Garvey reddened. "We haven't shaved, sir," he said apologetically, rubbing the soft stubble on his smoke-blackened chin. "And if the Captain's due here at sunrise, I thought—"

"I don't imagine," Phillip told him gently, "that the Captain's own party will have had time to shave this morning, Mr Garvey, so I fancy that on this occasion he'll overlook it."

The men had barely consumed their meagre fare when one of Sir Colin Campbell's aides rode down with an order for the *Shannon* detachment's two guns to take up a new position on the Oudh bank, preparatory to a full scale bombardment. Brigadier Hope Grant's advance guard made its appearance while this move was still in progress and, with it, Captain Travers's heavy battery, which unlimbered to the left of the bridgehead and began at once to exchange fire with those of the rebels on the Cawnpore side of the river. With dawn now grey in the sky, the arrival of a large body of guns and horsemen had not passed unnoticed by the enemy and, as the leading squadron of cavalry descended the slight slope to the bridgehead and dismounted, they redoubled their efforts to dispute the passage. Roundshot plunged into the river on both sides of the swaying boats, and shells screeched overhead but—miraculously—the bridge remained undamaged. When, punctually at sunrise, William Peel trotted up at the head of the *Shannon*'s siege-train, Sir Colin Campbell waited with ill-concealed impatience until he had brought his guns into action and then ordered the cavalry and horsed guns to advance.

Brigadier Hope Grant, a wiry, be-whiskered man in a sand-coloured cotton dress uniform and the faded blue Lancer's forage cap he always wore, led the way across. The head of the column gained the Cawnpore bridgehead, to be met by a galling fire of musketry from the burnt-out buildings and overgrown garden enclosures bordering the canal but, preceded by dismounted cavalry skirmishers and two troops of courageously handled Horse Artillery, they drove the rebels back, gunners and riflemen in the entrenchment giving them telling support.

Standing to the rear of his belching gun, Phillip watched, glass to his eye, as the Lancers remounted their horses and, led by a squadron of scarlet-turbanned Sikh cavalry sowars, the column reformed and passed in front of the entrenchment to the accompaniment of prolonged cheering from its defenders. After a brief cannonade, they crossed the canal and then, in open order, swung right-handed to make for the flat plain to the south of the city. There he lost sight of them but he knew, from the ADC from whom he had earlier received his orders, that they would take up a position facing the city, their right resting near to the entrenchment, their left on the Old Dragoon Lines, close to the Grand Trunk Road.

There was still a good deal of firing on the Cawnpore side but Sir Colin Campbell, fuming with impatience, galloped over the bridge with his staff to establish his battle headquarters in the fort. The rebel batteries on the Bithur road side of the fort continued their efforts to destroy the bridge and impede the crossing of reinforcements but now they, in turn, were outgunned and by mid-afternoon all had been silenced or withdrawn out of range, battered into temporary submission, at least, by the sheer weight and accuracy of the British bombardment.

At a little after 4 p.m., Captain Peel ordered the *Shannon*'s guns to cease fire and the men, worn out by their exertions, obeyed the order thankfully. Too exhausted to eat, most of them gulped down their evening grog ration and lay down on the churned-up ground beside their guns, to snatch what sleep they could before being called on to return to duty. Fighting off an almost overwhelming desire to follow their example, Phillip was standing with William Peel at the road verge when word came that the main body of the Lucknow convoy had left the Mungalwar campsite to begin the crossing.

"Thank God!" Peel said, his voice unexpectedly charged with emotion. "I must confess, Phillip, that there have been moments during the past two days when I began to fear that we had rescued the Residency garrison, only to bring an infinitely worse fate upon them!"

"I too," Phillip admitted gravely. "If those Pandy gunners over there had worked their guns even half as well as our men did, I shudder to think what might have happened, sir. And if General Windham hadn't defended the entrenchment so gallantly . . ." He thought of Harriet and her two small, helpless children and felt his stomach churn.

At half-past five, as the sun was sinking in a blaze of glory, a procession almost six miles in length started to wind its way along the dusty, rutted road towards the bridge—escorting infantry, bullock-drawn guns, women, children, and the sick and wounded, borne in country carts, carriages, on ammunition tumbrils, or in palanquins and *doolies*. A number of the women trudged bravely on foot, clutching their children by the hand, and behind them streamed the camp followers and native servants, the laden elephants and camels, spare teams of gun-cattle and horses, and yet more waggons, piled high with the paraphernalia of an army on the march.

They came slowly and wearily past the now silent guns,

a motley crowd of soldiers in faded uniforms and civilians in tattered clothing, armed with a variety of weapons from sporting rifles and old fashioned Brown Bess muskets to the latest pattern Enfields. Only the men of the Relief Force looked like soldiers, the 93rd Highlanders—Sir Colin Campbell's favourite regiment—in tartan and feather bonnets, stepped out proudly behind their pipers, matched by the tall, bearded men of the Punjab Infantry and the scarlet-clad 53rd, whose fifes and drums were playing them in. But the clouds of dust stirred up by their passing were so thick that it was well nigh impossible to recognise individual faces among the crowd, and Phillip watched in vain for a glimpse of Harriet, his throat tight as the groans and shrieks of the wounded rose above the steady tramp of marching feet and the rat-tat-tat of the drums.

Moved to pity by their plight, the *Shannon* seamen roused themselves and, with Peel's permission, went among the *doolies,* handing out plugs of chewing tobacco and even precious pipes and cigars, recklessly parting with what remained of their rations to the sorely tried sufferers in their jolting, airless conveyances. All through the night, the passage of the convoy continued, the bridge bathed in moonlight; next day, so congested had the route become, that thousands were still waiting to step on to the floating roadway which would lead them into Cawnpore and it was not until six o'clock on the evening of the 30th November that the last baggage waggon and the rearguard reached the opposite bank of the river.

Garvey's two guns returned to the entrenchment during the morning but Phillip remained with the siege-train and made the crossing late that evening, riding with William Peel at its head, to take up their position facing the south side of the city, in support of Greathed's Brigade, which had occupied the Generalgunj. The women and children, who had reached

Cawnpore at midnight on the 29th, had originally been accommodated in the Old Dragoon Lines but had come under fire
from a strong force of the Nana's levies, which had compelled
a move to the safer surroundings of an infantry barrack nearer
to the entrenchment. Here a forest of tents was rapidly set up
and, despite the melancholy spectacle of ruined cantonment
buildings, devastated gardens, and the stark remains of
General Wheeler's ill-fated entrenchment close by, the children, at any rate, were soon romping merrily, their ordeal—
if not forgotten—at least in temporary abeyance.

Phillip found his sister, at last, on the morning of the 1st
December, sharing her tent with two other women and a sickly
baby, but she was in good heart and full of praise for the efforts
made to lessen their discomfort.

"We are given three good meals a day, Phillip," she told
him. "Tea with milk and sugar, fresh bread . . . if you only
knew what that means to us, after the Residency fare!" Tears
shone in her eyes but she brushed them away. "We are accustomed to being fired on, so attacks on the camp do not alarm
us as they might have done six months ago . . . and we are
well guarded. Our own men of the 32nd are entrusted with
our safety and the Cavalry are on constant patrol. Besides,
there are your guns. It was largely thanks to them and to your
gallant seamen that the bridge was preserved, I was told." She
laid her hand on his and Phillip looked down at it, shocked to
see how thin it was. Harriet, smiling, denied that she or her
children were in need of anything.

"Dear Phillip—we have our lives, have we not? I have lost
my beloved husband, and the children their father, and poor
little Baby is among Lucknow's dead . . . but we are here, we
are safe! What more could I ask? True, the journey here was
exhausting and fraught with anxiety, but we accomplished it

without suffering any hardship. And, since our arrival here, we have been shown nothing but kindness. The soldiers come and take the children to play—they make them presents and there is promise of a band concert before we leave. The officers shower us with the most generous hospitality. We are fortunate, Phillip, compared with many others."

Her courage was magnificent, Phillip thought, humbled by it. She had endured so much, yet she was undefeated, determined to make light of her hardships.

"Have you heard," he asked her, "for how long you will stay here?"

She shook her head, with its cropped hair—now, to his distress, touched with grey. "Not definitely, no. But until we are safely on our way to Allahabad, Sir Colin Campbell cannot attack the rebels and drive them from the city, can he? So obviously he will want to be rid of us as soon as he can. I have heard a rumour that we shall set off in two or three days."

"You'll go to Calcutta, to Graham and Catriona?" Phillip urged. "They have a house there and they will, I know, welcome you with open arms."

"Oh, yes," Harriet agreed. "I've written to Graham—mail, I believe, is to go out before we do. It's odd, is it not, that it has taken a mutiny and a war to enable me to see both my brothers after so many years? How I wish that . . ." she broke off, biting her lower lip in a vain attempt to still its sudden trembling and Phillip knew that she was thinking of their younger sister, Lavinia, whom neither of them would see again.

"Graham's agent has keys to his house," he began. "If he should be at sea when you reach Calcutta, you—"

She seemed not to have heard him. In a low, controlled voice, she said, "I went to see the—the place General Wheeler's garrison defended and I was . . . oh, Phillip, I was utterly appalled! What could have possessed an experienced officer of his repute to attempt to defend such a place? The buildings were riddled with shot, much worse than any in the Residency, and they say the walls—before they collapsed—were built of mud and only four feet high. There was no shade and the hospital was a burnt-out shell . . . and they say that almost four hundred women and children were besieged there. Women and children, Phillip—and they held out for three weeks! I . . . it breaks my heart to think what they must have suffered, and poor darling little Lavinia among them."

"It breaks my heart also," Phillip professed.

"Did you—did you see the house they call the Bibigarh?" Harriet asked. "The one where they were murdered?"

He inclined his head reluctantly. "Yes, I saw it. I wish I had not. I don't advise you to go there. You—"

Harriet shivered. "Don't worry, I shall not. Seeing that ghastly entrenchment was enough. But we could not avoid seeing it—they brought us right past it, after we crossed the river, and in the moonlight it . . . it was a shock, when I realised what it was. It made us all thoroughly miserable."

"I'm sure it must have," Phillip agreed, tight-lipped. Hoping to distract her thoughts, he talked of the future, questioning her as to her immediate plans. "You'll go home, will you not, Harriet, you and the children? You'll be given passage from Calcutta, I imagine, but if there should be any delay, Graham could arrange matters for you. Catriona's guardian is a ship owner."

"There will be nothing for us to stay here for now," Harriet said. "Yes, we shall go home. It will be good to see England again and darling Mamma and Papa—better for the children, too, than this climate. I believe we are to stay in Allahabad for a week or two, to enable us to—to recover. Perhaps you will be able to take a few days' leave, to visit us there?"

"I'll see what can be done," Phillip promised. "Now about money, Harriet—will you permit me to give you what you need?"

She smiled and patted his hand. "Dear Phillip, that is kind of you. We have nothing, of course, the children and I, save the clothes we stand up in and even those are gifts. We lost everything in Sitapur, when poor darling Jemmy's regiment mutinied." She had never spoken of Sitapur or of her husband's death but now, in a few brief and heartbroken words, she told him what had happened and Phillip listened, sick with pity. "They hacked him to death in front of me—Jemmy's own men, his trusted Havildar-Major among them! But then, almost as if they were ashamed and regretted what they had done, they promised that they would take me and the children to safety . . . and they kept their word. They protected us and took us to the Lucknow road in the carriage, with the Ayah and Sita Ram, Jemmy's orderly. But there they had a change of heart and they abandoned us, without food or water. They took the carriage and they made poor, loyal Sita Ram go with them. Ayah was afraid and she fled to her village but she found us again when we were nearly mad with thirst and the people of her village *sold* us water. We wandered about for hours in the jungle, searching for the river . . . it was barely half a mile away but we did not find it for hours, Phillip. I don't know why."

"It's very easy to lose your bearings in jungle," Phillip consoled her.

"I felt so helpless," Harriet said brokenly. "The children were depending on me but I could do nothing, nothing. Sometime during the following morning, we met a wounded

Eurasian clerk, on a horse. He was making for Lucknow and he told us that almost all the rest of our people in Sitapur had been murdered—or had fled, like we had, blindly into the jungle. He said we would probably encounter some of them but we didn't. The only ones I . . . found were dead, they had been tortured and murdered. People I knew well, a young couple I had taken tea with only a few days before. Their bodies were left near a village and at first I thought the villagers had murdered them, until the headmen gave them decent burial and took us in. Without thought of reward, Phillip, that good old man and his people cared for us and kept us hidden and, when the sepoys had left the area—on their way to Delhi, I suppose —the headman took us to Lucknow by boat. Not only us but others, who were in hiding nearby . . . and he risked his life to smuggle us through the city to the Residency. And Jemmy's faithful orderly, Sita Ram, came with us. He served in the garrison and he's with us now, still trying to care for us, because he says he gave Jemmy his word that he would do so."

Harriet looked up, her eyes bright with tears but this time she made no attempt to brush them away. "They are a strange race, Phillip—they can breed men like Sita Ram and that old headman, Mahee Singh, and a woman like Ayah, who was terrified, yet gave me back a ring I'd given her, so that I could hire a boat to take us to Lucknow. And . . . all the rest, the betrayers, the murderers, treacherous deceivers like the Nana. I've lived out here for almost twelve years, yet I don't feel that I know or understand them—least of all the sepoys. Jemmy's men *loved* him and he loved them—there was trust and respect between them."

"There was in many of the sepoy regiments, Harriet," Phillip said, his tone carefully neutral, lest he hurt her. "Officers trusted their men and were betrayed."

"As Jemmy was," Harriet conceded sadly. "And yet, you know, after they had murdered him, the native officers carried his . . . his poor, broken body into our bungalow and set it on fire. The Subadar told me that it was to be his funeral pyre, so that his . . . his soul might find release and he said—with genuine feeling, Phillip—'The Colonel Sahib was a good man. Had he been willing to lead us to Delhi, we would have followed him gladly.' Do you wonder I find them hard to understand?"

"No, my dear, I don't." Phillip took his watch from his pocket, studied it and sighed. "I'm sorry, Harriet, but I shall have to go. I'd hoped to see the children, though. Are they likely to be long?"

"I don't know," Harriet answered regretfully. "They went, with about twenty others, to a picnic some of the attached Native Infantry officers got up for them. It's not very far away —as you know, we're restricted to the camp area. I let them go because, poor little souls, it's been so long since they had any fun. If only I'd known you were likely to visit us, I'd have kept them here. They're both longing to see and talk to their Uncle Phillip. We could go and look for them, if you like." She hesitated. "What *is* the time?"

"Eleven-thirty. But I—"

"Couldn't you stay?" Harriet pleaded. "Colonel Cockayne promised he would bring them back before noon."

"Cockayne?" Phillip echoed. "The Irregular Cavalry Colonel from—where was it? Ghorabad, I think. He was with us on the bridge for a while. Do you know him?"

Harriet nodded. "He told me . . . and he was singing *your* praises, Phillip. He said you were a most efficient and courageous officer." She smiled. "Colonel Cockayne was a friend of Jemmy's—not a close friend, but they used to shoot together.

His regiment was in Sitapur before being posted to Ghorabad, and last cold weather the Colonel came to stay with us, so that he and Jemmy could go on *shikar*. Agnes Cockayne and their daughter came with him—Agnes is a darling, rather quiet and mousey, I suppose you'd call her, but a darling. And the daughter, Andrea, is a beauty . . . you'd hardly expect her to be, with such ordinary-looking parents, but she really is one of the loveliest girls I ever saw in my life. But now, alas, they—"

"Now," Phillip put in, recalling the Colonel's impassioned outburst, "they are both under siege by the rebels in Ghorabad, I understand? The Colonel escaped." Harriet, he saw, was frowning as he repeated the gist of the accusations he had heard being hurled at Sir Colin Campbell. "I confess," he added dryly, "that it would have taken more nerve than I've got to beard Sir Colin as Cockayne did—the Chief doesn't take kindly to criticism from his subordinates! And Cockayne didn't mince his words."

"All the same, I can sympathise with him," Harriet defended. "Poor man, he is heartbroken and close to despair. He risked his life to come here, imagining he had only to ask and he would be given British troops to save the Ghorabad garrison but, of course, that wasn't possible. We in Lucknow were given first priority." Her slender shoulders rose in an expressive shrug. "But perhaps, once we are safely in Allahabad and Sir Colin has cleared Cawnpore of rebels, the Colonel will get his troops. I pray that he may. The Ghorabad people have been defending themselves in a small fort outside the town for over three months, in conditions which are a great deal worse than we endured in poor Sir Henry Lawrence's Residency. My heart bleeds for them, Phillip."

"I know, Harriet, my dear," Phillip offered awkwardly. "I know how you must feel." Tactfully, he changed the subject, bringing the conversation back to Graham and their parents and the prospect of her returning to England. The children were delivered to the tent by Colonel Cockayne, who exchanged greetings and then hurried on, with the plea that he had other children to return to their mothers. The picnic had evidently been a great success; little Phillip, his shaven locks starting to grow again and clad in a freshly laundered white sailor suit, was bubbling over with excitement, full of the games they had played and the pony which one of their hosts had allowed him to ride. Already he was changing, Phillip realised thankfully, learning to laugh again and to think and behave as a child. Augusta, small and still looking very fragile, could talk only of the wonders of the repast set before them and then, quite suddenly, the colour had drained from her thin little face and she had rushed from the tent, wailing that she felt sick and that her stomach pained her.

"It's all right," Harriet said, when the crisis had been dealt with and the child tucked up in one of the tent's two *charpoys* to sleep off her indisposition. "They're simply not accustomed to rich food and Augusta has had two bad bouts of dysentry. I shall be thankful when I can take them home, Phillip. Home, to England's green and pleasant land . . . imagine it! I hope they'll send us soon." She clung to him tearfully as he took his leave, begging him to take care of himself. "Dearest Phillip, it has done my heart good to have had even this brief glimpse of you, after so many years. I shall pray for you, dear brother, and wait eagerly for news of you. God bless you, Phillip!"

Phillip did not see her again before the convoy left for Allahabad, under a strong escort, on the night of 3rd December. Each day prior to their leaving, the rebels had cannonaded the camp and, in a furious attack on the lines occupied by the 93rd Highlanders, six men were wounded, including their gallant Commanding Officer, Colonel Ewart, whose left arm was shattered by a roundshot. A field battery— whether by accident or design—ranged for several hours on Sir Colin Campbell's own sleeping tent and those of his staff, causing some casualties and considerable damage. Unable to do more than hold the rebels at bay until free of the restraint imposed by the presence of the women and children and the wounded, the Commander-in-Chief bided his time, making plans for the attack he would launch as soon as the convoy was safely on its way.

Misconstruing this as weakness, the Gwalior rebels made frequent raids on out-lying piquets and subjected the British camp to almost incessant bombardment, sending fire rafts down river in an unsuccessful attempt to burn the Ganges Bridge. The *Shannon's* guns and rocket-tubes were kept busy, in the entrenchment and in the occupied Generalgunj area of the city, striving to keep down the enemy's fire. At all costs, Sir Colin Campbell was determined to prevent any pursuit of the convoy and a heavy attack on his left flank—aimed at regaining control of the Allahabad road—was met and vigorously repulsed on 5th December, in an artillery duel lasting over two hours.

Word reached him that evening that the convoy had reached the railhead at Chimi, 45 miles from Allahabad and, presuming it now to be out of danger, Sir Colin issued orders for his force to assume the offensive the following morning.

CHAPTER THREE

The *position* occupied by the Gwalior rebels was a strong one and Sir Colin Campbell considered it carefully before calling a conference of his senior officers. Studying the reports brought in by spies and those obtained by personal reconnaissance, he weighed up the possibilities, aware that his own inactivity and the trouncing General Windham had suffered at their hands had left his enemy confident of victory. With newly arrived reinforcements, he had five thousand infantry, six hundred cavalry and thirty five guns, including the *Shannon*'s powerful twenty-four-pounders. The rebels outnumbered him by five to one but . . . he smiled a trifle sourly. The initiative was with him—he could choose at which point to attack them.

Their left, he saw, checking his maps, contained the whole of the old cantonment area, from whence they had launched their final and most dangerous assault on General Windham's entrenchment and Brigadier Carthew's ill-fated piquet. The tree-clad ground was cluttered with ruined bungalows and burnt-out public buildings; these, and the two ravines, which cut deep into the river bank between the city and the entrenchment, afforded cover for whole regiments of infantry, with supporting guns, and were strongly held. An attack in that direction would be costly and he dismissed the idea of it, as he had dismissed Windham's suggestion that he make a frontal attack on the city. That was where they expected him to attack, undoubtedly. The Gwalior infantry had occupied the houses and bazaars in the centre of the city for days now; with snipers posted on the rooftops and the narrow, winding streets barricaded and defended by guns, it would take a much larger force than he had at his disposal to drive them out.

Their right, however, might well prove vulnerable. It extended from the west side of the city almost to the Grand Trunk Road, following the line of the canal and taking in the brick kilns, where Windham and Walpole had fought their rearguard action. Two miles to the rear, on the open plain bordering the Calpee road, the Gwalior Contingent's camp was pitched, with that of the Nana's forces on the east—or river—side of the city, a further two miles distant across the plain. If he could drive a wedge between them, taking advantage of the open ground, on which native troops seldom fought well, whilst holding their reserves in the city, then . . . The Commander-in-Chief's expression relaxed. He said, when he had dictated his orders with his accustomed attention to detail, "Send for the Brigade Commanders and I'll acquaint them with the plan of attack."

Captain Peel, returning from the conference on the evening of the 5th December, was enthusiastic as he issued his own orders.

"Sir Colin's plan of attack is delightfully simple, gentlemen," he informed his assembled officers with smiling confidence. "We strike camp at seven tomorrow morning, sending our baggage to the riverside under guard. At nine o'clock General Windham is to open a heavy bombardment from the fort, to create the impression that an attack is impending from his position on their left and centre. When the bombardment is well under way, our attacking columns will advance against their right, forming up to the rear of the old Cavalry Lines, where they will be masked from the enemy's observation. Our Brigade will remain in the Generalgunj, mounting a bombardment of the brick kiln position, here." His finger jabbed at the map spread out on the table in front of them, as he went into precise detail of the units involved and the positions they would take up. Then, his smile widening, he added, "Sir Colin intends to fall on their main camp—here, on the Calpee road—and the advance is to be made with all possible speed, the cavalry and horsed guns making a detour to their left and crossing the canal by the bridge—here—so as to threaten the enemy's rear. We are to advance with the main infantry attack, crossing by the bridge fronting the brick kiln position, once it has been cleared by our skirmishers . . . and, if our practise has been good enough, there should not be much left to clear."

There was a murmur of eager assent and Peel went on, "Gentlemen, I have assented to a request from General Windham that Mr Garvey's party shall remain to assist in manning the fort's batteries. For the rest, since the Commander-in-Chief desires our guns to be handled like field-guns—that is how we will handle them. Double crews on each gun, Mr Vaughan, if you please, with drag-ropes in case our gun-cattle fail us, and the rifle companies in support. There will be no hanging back—our guns will be up, wherever they're needed, or by heaven, I'll know the reason why!"

"They will be there, sir," the *Shannon*'s First Lieutenant assured him. "You need have no fear on that score."

"I haven't," William Peel returned. "I'm only making sure you know that we've been given carte blanche, my dear fellow, and the opportunity to show the Army what we can *really* do! Goodnight, my boys—good luck and God go with all of you tomorrow."

At 9 a.m. the following morning, General Windham opened his batteries and was promptly answered by the enemy. For two hours the artillery duel continued, whilst the assault force—hidden from view by the city wall and its surrounding buildings—formed up in continuous columns to the rear of the old Cavalry Lines. At 11 a.m., when the bombardment slackened, the infantry deployed along the line of the canal and started to advance, the *Shannon*'s guns coming into effective action on the left, as Brigadier Greathed's infantry attacked the enemy on his front with a sharp fire of musketry.

Waiting, with the Commander-in-Chief's staff, Phillip watched through his Dollond as the attack developed. The Rifle Brigade, under Walpole, with a detachment of the 38th, rushed the bridge over the canal on Greathed's left, and moved forward under the shadow of the city wall towards the brick kilns. The high, grassed-over mounds which covered the kilns concealed a large force of enemy infantry and a number of field-guns and, when the two remaining British Brigades, under Brigadiers Adrian Hope and Inglis, took ground to the left and wheeled into three parallel lines fronting the canal, a heavy fire was opened on them from the kilns.

Peel's twenty-four-pounders, Longden's mortars, and Bouchier's and Middleton's field batteries replied, subjecting the kilns to a merciless pounding and, under cover of their fire, the two brigades completed their formation. Preceded by the 53rd and the 4th Punjab Rifles, in skirmishing order, Hope's Brigade began to advance, with Inglis's in support.

Sir Colin Campbell, who had also been watching through his field-glass, sent an aide galloping across to warn the cavalry and horsed guns to make their detour. He said gruffly to Phillip, "Away and tell Captain Peel to give the infantry the best support he can, Commander. And you may stay with him." He smiled suddenly, the smile lighting his lined, rather austere face to what, for a fleeting moment, was boyish eagerness. "I fancy the tartan may welcome the sight of me at their head for the last hundred yards!"

He put spurs to his horse and Phillip, galloping off obediently on his own errand saw, out of the corner of his eye, the old Chief take his place in front of the line of Highlanders of the 42nd and 93rd, which was advancing in the wake of the skirmishers. Even above the din of battle, the cheers which greeted his unexpected appearance could be heard quite clearly, echoing from man to man.

Feeling oddly uplifted, Phillip rode on, to find William Peel with two of his guns already limbered up.

"One of them should suffice to get us across the canal," he said. "We can't move them all at light infantry speed!" Grinning, he gestured to a single twenty-four-pounder, its double crew of seamen at the drag-ropes. "But that should give them an unpleasant shock, I think. Right, my lads! Put your backs into it . . . all together now—heave!"

Slowly the great gun moved forward into an inferno of fire. Grouped in their hundreds about the high mounds of the brick kilns, rebel infantry fired from cover, the gunners on their flanks sending over a storm of shot and shell. As the leading skirmishers approached the bridge over the canal, they were halted by withering volleys of musketry, but pressing on, they drove back the sepoys who opposed them, only to be driven back themselves when the well-masked supporting guns swept the approaches to the bridge with grape. They took cover. Then, as Bouchier's guns unlimbered and opened fire on their left, they made a second attempt to carry the bridge, Sikh and Irishman fighting shoulder to shoulder in the choking smoke, but were again hurled back by an impenetrable curtain of fire.

Shouting at the pitch of his lungs for them to make way, Peel led his single gun up to the bridge. Phillip's horse went down under the most murderous fire he had ever experienced. He picked himself up, bruised and dazed, hearing from somewhere over to his right, the skirl of Highland pipes and full-throated cheering, both drowned, an instant later, by volleys of rifle fire. Without conscious thought, he seized the end of one of the drag-ropes as the seaman who had been hauling on it took a charge of grape in the stomach and fell to the ground. With Peel's tall figure just visible through the smoke ahead, a private of the 53rd beside him, they manhandled the great gun over the bridge.

"Action front, my boys!" the *Shannon's* Captain yelled. "Let 'em have it!"

The twenty-four-pounder opened with dramatic effect and, inspired by its presence, the main body of the British infantry pressed forward, many of them fording the canal. Resuming their line of formation on the other side, they advanced on the brick kiln position with the bayonet, cheering as they went, and the defenders abandoned the mounds and ditches they had held and fled in panic. All along the line of attack, it was the same story. Lieutenant Young, the *Shannon's* Gunnery Officer, came up with the second gun and both limbered up to join in the pursuit of the fleeing rebels. As bullocks were being yoked to them, Midshipmen Kerr and the diminutive Clinton received permission to mount their howitzers on the crest of one of the mounds, from which they shelled a force of rebel cavalry and horsed guns, attempting to slip out from the west side of the city to go to the support of their defeated infantry.

A Royal Artillery officer galloped back to Captain Bouchier, whose smoking field-guns had just ceased fire and Phillip heard him shout to the battery commander, "Come on, George! The Pandies are bolting like the devil—you don't want to miss the hunt, do you?"

William Peel, overhearing him, too, threw back his head and gave vent to a bellow of laughter. "Well, *we* don't want to miss it, do we, boys? Look lively there and get those bullocks moving, for pity's sake, or we shall be left behind!"

"We'd do a lot better without them cows, sir," a big gunner's mate suggested, with wry frankness, as the first team started to move reluctantly forward under the prodding of the drivers' goads. "With respect, Captain, sir, they need a fire under 'em to make the sodding things put their backs into it . . . but we don't. Just you say the word, sir, and we'll catch up with them skirmishers again, quick an' lively!"

Peel, waxing impatient, duly "said the word" when the Gwalior Contingent's camp was sighted, and the great guns, propelled with a will by their crews, reached its boundary as the Sikhs and the 53rd were clearing it of its last remaining occupants. So rapid had been the advance that the rebels had been taken completely by surprise. Everywhere there was evidence of this, from the *chupatties* left heating on a score of bivouac fires to the strings of gun-cattle still tied beside their ammunition tumbrils and the sick and wounded, abandoned where they lay.

When Sir Colin Campbell rode in at the head of his Highlanders, it was to prolonged and hearty cheers but he waved them sternly to silence. "We've not finished the job yet," he reminded his commanders. "It's only two o'clock, which leaves us another four hours of daylight, so let us use them to advantage." Leaving the 23rd Fusiliers and the 38th Regiment to hold the captured camp, he directed his Chief of Staff, General Mansfield, to move round the north side of the city with the Rifle Brigade, the 93rd and two field batteries, to cut off the rebels' line of retreat by the Delhi road. Brigadier Inglis, with the remainder of his Brigade and the 42nd was sent along the Calpee road to rendezvous with the Cavalry and Horse Artillery and perform a similar service to Mansfield's.

"Be so good," the old General requested Captain Peel, "as to despatch two of your field-guns, with your Marines, to cover the Fattehpore road. Captain Bouchier's Battery will continue the pursuit to prevent the enemy making off with their guns and I should be obliged if you would give him support with yours until the cavalry come up, Captain Peel. There's no need," he added, with a faint smile, "for you to keep up with the skirmishers this time—although to say that I appreciate the zeal and energy with which, this morning, your gallant sailors have impelled and worked their guns is an under-statement. Now, however, we have Pandy on the run and haste is not *quite* so necessary."

Phillip, on a borrowed horse, rode back to direct Midshipman Kerr to take his battery to the Futtepore road; Lieutenant Young and Midshipman St John Daniels, with two more field-guns and the rocket-launchers, were detailed to accompany General Mansfield's force, and the remaining brigades continued the pursuit. Bouchier's battery led for two miles, checking only to spike abandoned enemy guns; then some of the rebels made a stand and the British gunners swiftly unlimbered and went into action at grape range, the *Shannon's* seamen again hauling up their ponderous twenty-four-pounders to give supporting fire, as the 53rd and the 64th advanced menacingly in line. Brigadier Hope Grant was with the battery and it was he who finally called a halt, when a cloud of dust on the left flank heralded the belated arrival of the cavalry, whose detour—due to mistaken directions from their native guide—had delayed them for almost an hour.

Sir Colin Campbell ordered them to take over the pursuit, which he led in person and Phillip, resuming his role as naval liason officer, had the exhilarating experience of joining a spirited cavalry charge, as the 9th Lancers and the Sikhs of Hodson's Horse and the Punjab Cavalry detachments spread out across the plain in extended order, eager to make up for the tardiness of their arrival.

The demoralised rebels did not attempt to try conclusions with them and the retreat became a rout, as wounded, guns, and equipment were abandoned and the panic-stricken survivors lost all cohesion, intent only on escape. It was dusk when the chase ended on the banks of the Pandoo River, fourteen miles from Cawnpore. Thirty-four guns had been captured, the camp of the Gwalior Contingent, with its tents and supplies, was in British hands and, by now, General Mansfield's force was almost certainly in a position to threaten those rebels who had remained in the city, in addition to cutting them off from all chance of reinforcement from the Nana's camp outside. Expressing his satisfaction at the outcome of the battle, the Commander-in-Chief ordered the column to re-form and retrace its steps. It was midnight when they reached the camping ground which had been selected at the junction of the Calpee and Grand Trunk roads and, since no tents had yet been brought up, the weary men bivouacked on the ground.

No word was received from General Mansfield until the following morning, when it was learnt that he had fired for some time on bodies of rebels retreating along the Bithur road. Being himself attacked by enemy gun batteries in the old cantonment area, he had been compelled to break off in order to reply to them and, when dusk fell, he had posted strong piquets and had then also bivouacked for the night. Under cover of darkness, the remaining rebels evacuated the city and, on the morning of 7th December, two squadrons of cavalry, sent in to reconnoitre, reported Cawnpore entirely clear of enemy troops.

A column under Brigadier Hope Grant, consisting of cavalry, infantry and horse artillery, was despatched towards Bithur in the hope of intercepting the Nana's force and those of the Gwalior troops who had eluded Mansfield the previous night. Learning that the Nana had passed the night at Bithur and then beaten a hasty retreat, with his troops and guns, to a ferry some miles up river, Hope Grant trailed him for thirteen miles and then halted, continuing the hunt at first light. A further thirteen-mile dash brought him to the ferry, to find a large rebel force on the point of embarking their guns, preparatory to crossing into Oudh. Grant attacked them at once with his cavalry and artillery and, after a brisk engagement, captured all fifteen guns and sent the survivors fleeing in confusion, the Nana leading the retreat into Oudh.

When the column returned in triumph to camp with their captured guns, a brief period of rest was decreed and William Peel suggested that Phillip might take a few days' leave in order to visit his sister in Allahabad.

"They'll be sending the women and children to Calcutta before Christmas, I imagine," he said. "And you'd like to bid them farewell, would you not? You had very little opportunity even to talk to that poor sister of yours while we were on the march—so take this chance while you've got it, Phillip."

"I should like to very much, sir," Phillip admitted. "If you're sure—"

"That there will be nothing doing here?" Peel finished for him. He smiled. "It's unlikely, my dear fellow. The Chief's next objective is the restoration of our communications with Delhi and the Punjab, and to do that he says will require what amounts to a re-conquest of the Doab . . . that is the whole area between the Jumna and the Ganges. He intends, as the first step, to occupy Futtehghur, which is a town on the Ganges opposite Agra that he believes to be of great strategic importance. But before he can move from here, he's got to wait for the carriage he sent to Allahabad with the women and the wounded to be returned to him, and he's also planning to link up with another British column from Delhi. There'll be nothing much doing for us until the end of the month and we shan't be short of officers or men—as you know, our fellows are being relieved of their garrison duties in Allahabad and I've sent for them to join us. The first party should be here within a day or so—Wilson, Verney, and eighty Jacks. Accompanying them, as a volunteer, believe it or not is a Post-Captain by the name of Oliver Jones!"

"A Post-Captain?" Phillip echoed, in some surprise. "Is he to join the Brigade, sir?"

Peel shook his head. "We should be a trifle top-heavy if he did . . . no, he's attached himself to Her Majesty's 53rd, I understand, and is only by coincidence coming up here with young Wilson's party. A wing of the 53rd is on its way, too, to reinforce the regiment."

"Then presumably Captain Jones is on half-pay?"

"So I gather, yes." Peel's quick smile was amused, but it held a measure of relief. "Fortunately he's junior to me by a couple of years and a lot further down the Post-Captain's list.

When I was first informed of his impending arrival, I feared he might be vastly senior and tend, perhaps, to stand on his rank. We're a happy ship's company, Phillip, and I would not want anything or anyone to interfere with my Shannons—least of all a volunteer."

"*I'm* officially a volunteer, sir," Phillip reminded him. William Peel clapped him affectionately on the shoulder.

"Why, for God's sake, so you are!" he agreed with mock dismay. "And, if I recall the circumstances in which you joined us—you're officially on sick leave, are you not?"

"That, too. I—"

"My dear Phillip," Peel put in forcefully. "You are very much one of us and I don't intend to lose you. On your return from Allahabad, you ought possibly to apply for a medical board, so as to keep the record straight and avoid any official complications over your pay. But it can wait till then." He searched among the papers on his camp table. "There's a convoy of wounded going by road and rail to Allahabad tomorrow morning—you can travel with that and return with our second party. No date has yet been fixed for their departure but I'd like them here before the end of the month. You and Henry Wratislaw can bring them up."

"Aye, aye, sir," Phillip acknowledged. "And thank you very much indeed. I appreciate your consideration."

"You've more than earned it, my dear fellow," William Peel assured him. He found what he had been searching for among his papers and handed over several letters addressed to Lieutenants Hay and Salmon. "Be so good as to deliver these to our invalids, will you please? Ted Hay won't be fit to return to duty for a while, I'm afraid, but Nowell Salmon might be, by the time you start back—although I shouldn't encourage him. Tell them both that I'll send for them without fail before we tackle the re-conquest of Lucknow."

There were various other personal commissions and messages, and Phillip set off for Allahabad next morning with his valise bulging. It was a slow journey to the railhead, with over a hundred sick and wounded from the last action, in addition to a similar number from the Lucknow garrison who had been delayed by lack of carriage. But Chimi was reached by noon on the third day and the rest of the journey to Allahabad, in a crowded open rail-truck, took only two hours. Harriet and her children were staying as guests in the spacious bungalow of one of the military surgeons—an old friend—and already Phillip was able to see an improvement in her health and that of the children, which greatly relieved his mind on their account. A letter from Graham arrived for Harriet during his stay, informing her that he and Catriona were in Calcutta and anxious to receive them.

"We sail for England in the Lady Wellesley *during the third week in January,"* Graham wrote. *"And I can give you and the children passage, if you can expedite your departure from Allahabad. If not, my house will be at your disposal for as long as you may require to use it and I will arrange with the Agents for your passage in one of our sister ships."*

"It would be wonderful to take passage in Graham's ship," Harriet said wistfully. "It seems half a lifetime since I saw him. He wasn't at my wedding, of course, and . . . Papa *has* forgiven him, has he not? They are on good terms again at last?"

"Indeed they are," Phillip assured her. "And you will love his wife, Catriona. We must make certain that you are in Calcutta in time to sail with them." He made every effort on her behalf and was able to escort her, with the two children, on board the first of the river steamers engaged by the Indian Government to transport the Lucknow survivors to Calcutta, satisfied that they would reach their destination at least a week prior to the *Lady Wellesley*'s date of departure.

The *Shannon*'s two wounded officers, Edward Hay and Nowell Salmon, were also comfortably accommodated and making good progress, the latter now able to walk with the aid of a stick but neither was, as yet, fit to return to duty. Consoled by Captain Peel's promise, which Phillip passed on to them, they offered no more than bantering complaints when he and Henry Wratislaw prepared to march the remainder of the *Shannon* Brigade to Cawnpore, on the day following Harriet's departure. Thirty sick and wounded men were left with the two young officers in Allahabad, and a hundred and thirty fit and eager bluejackets paraded, long before dawn, to escort a train of ammunition waggons and two 24-pounder rocket-tubes to add to the already formidable armament of the Brigade.

The journey, made partly by rail and in company with fresh drafts of infantry, was uneventful and the detachment reached camp at Cawnpore on the evening of the 23rd December, having caught up with the convoy of transport waggons for which Sir Colin Campbell had been waiting.

"We're under orders to march on Futtehghur," William Peel said, when Phillip reported to him. "Now that the necessary carriage has arrived, there's no reason to delay. Brigadier Walpole left with a column for Bewar five days ago and he's to rendezvous with us and a column from Delhi, under Colonel Seaton, at a place called Mynpooree—fifteen miles from Futtehghur—in approximately ten days' time." He went into more precise detail and then said, smiling, "You can, of course, come with us if you wish, Phillip—but I've had a *very* pressing request for your services elsewhere."

"For *my* services, sir?" Phillip echoed, brows lifting in surprise.

Peel nodded. "In addition," he went on, his tone a trifle dry, "I have received a communication from Captain Cooper Key, Senior Naval Officer, Calcutta, and my immediate superior. He has been ordered to rejoin Admiral Seymour's Flag in China, with the *Sanspareil,* and he's somehow got wind of the fact that I have a convalescent Commander who, he considers, must—if fit for duty—be surplus to my requirements. Technically, Phillip, in view of Jim Vaughan's impending promotion to the same rank as yourself, it would seem that I have."

Phillip eyed him uncertainly. "The—er—the surplus, Commander, would, I take it, be posted to the *Sanspareil?*" he suggested.

"Very probably—she's not sailing until mid-January. But it's not a posting you would welcome, is it?"

"No, it's not, sir," Phillip admitted feelingly.

William Peel rose to refill both their glasses. "On the other hand, my dear fellow," he observed. "You haven't yet passed a medical board and, as I mentioned, I've had a very pressing request for your services . . . on detached duty, away from the Brigade."

"Not, I trust, to command General Windham's batteries in the fort, sir?" Phillip qualified.

Peel's blue eyes lit with an amused gleam. "No, I'm giving that command to two of our young gentlemen—Kerr and Clinton—who will remain here with 78 Jacks at the Major-General's specific request. *You* are wanted to assist in a rescue attempt which, by the sound of it, may be something of a forlorn hope, I'm afraid. It's a task for a volunteer, Phillip— or rather for volunteers. If you take it on I can let you have

two of our field-guns, with a mid and thirty men—but you'll
have to volunteer them. I thought, however, that you might
prefer it to the possibility of being ordered back to China."

"I should, sir—infinitely!" Phillip assured him, without hesitation.

"Then you had better seek out Colonel Cockayne of the
Irregular Cavalry and tell him so," William Peel advised. "He'll
be overjoyed."

"Ah, of course!" Comprehension dawned and Phillip
grinned his relief. "Colonel Cockayne has prevailed upon the
Commander-in-Chief to send a force to endeavour to rescue
his garrison at Ghorabad—is that it, sir?"

"That's it," the *Shannon*'s commander confirmed. "Sir Colin
has promised him two hundred and fifty British troops and a
squadron of Sikh cavalry. He was offered a half-battery of
Madras field artillery but he particularly asked for two of our
guns, under *your* command. He appears to have a very high
opinion of you—he was with you and Garvey at the Bridge of
Boats, was he not, the night we came in from Lucknow?"

"Yes, he was. He—"

"What impression did you form of him? Your party will be
under his command, you know, and very much dependent on
him—he's the man with the local knowledge."

Phillip considered the question, a thoughtful frown creasing his brow. His sympathies were all with Colonel Cockayne,
whose single-minded determination to rescue his stricken garrison compelled both sympathy and admiration but—apart
from the little Harriet had been able to tell him—he really did
not know a great deal about his future commander. There had
been the incident with Sir Colin Campbell, of course . . . he
repeated this to William Peel, adding wryly, "Cockayne is no
respecter of persons, at any rate, and I should say he's a brave

man—he'd have to be, to tackle the Chief like that! For the rest, I don't know, sir."

"Frankly, nor do I," Peel confessed. "Ghorabad is—what? About fifty or sixty miles east of here, in hostile country, and the force Cockayne's been offered is small enough, in all conscience. You'll have to proceed with caution, Phillip."

"I will, sir," Phillip promised. He hesitated, still frowning. "I suppose you wouldn't consider giving me one of the twelve-pounder rocket-tubes in place of a gun, would you, sir? Ghorabad is on the Sye River, I believe, and it occurred to me that it might be possible to mount an attack from boats, as we did at Fatshan. I brought you two 24-pounder tubes from Allahabad and—"

"My dear fellow!" William Peel clapped a hand on his shoulder in warm approval. "Of course you may take one of the rocket-tubes and I will not require you to sacrifice a gun— although I'm afraid I cannot let you have any more men. Thirty's the most I can spare and I have to remind you, they must be volunteers. The Chief is expecting considerable resistance at Futtehghur and our siege-train will almost certainly be needed at full strength." Again he went into details concerning Sir Colin Campbell's plans for the occupation of Futtehghur and the Doab, adding pensively, "Sir Colin is hoping that he will be able to retake Lucknow by the end of March, Phillip. In the meantime, he intends to send out relatively small forces to subdue the surrounding countryside and punish the rebel chiefs and landowners, so as to clear the way. Hope's Brigade and Hope Grant's Cavalry are at it now and, once Futtehghur is secured, he talks of subduing the Rohilcund. Our Jacks and their guns are in great demand and I've had to agree to letting detachments go with these punitive expeditions, little as I like splitting up the Brigade. But I'll

want all my detachments back for the advance on Lucknow
. . . including yours, however your forlorn hope may have
fared. You understand, do you not?"

"Perfectly, sir," Phillip assured him. He made his report on
the *Shannon*'s sick and wounded in Allahabad and Peel brought
him up to date on recent happenings in Cawnpore during his
absence.

"There was a rumour that the Nana had hidden a vast
hoard of treasure in one of the wells at Bithur," he said. "And
at Brigadier Hope Grant's request, I sent Jim Vaughan and
Walter Kerr, with a party, to assist in pumping it out and
removing the loot. Unhappily they could make no headway
against the spring by which the well is supplied and all they
found was a small silver goblet, which Petty Officer Devereux
managed to dredge up with some sort of homemade grappling
iron. Sly old devil that he is, Devereux was endeavouring to
hide it when one of the bluejackets spotted what he was at
and threatened to report him. You know Devereux's habit of
swearing in very bad French when anyone annoys him? Well,
he was at it hammer and tongs when Jim Vaughan overheard
him and demanded to know what he'd said. Quick as a flash,
the old reprobate answered, 'Why, sir, I was just making the
remark as 'ow it blows werry 'ard in the Chiny seas!' Now, of
course, his remark has become the Jacks' favourite excuse for
talking out of turn!"

Phillip laughed, visualising the veteran petty officer's
sparsely covered red head and his scarred and wrinkled face,
with its habitual expression of injured innocence. A fine seaman, Tom Devereux had joined the Navy as a boy of ten and
was one of the wits of the *Shannon*'s lower deck to which—
when deprived of his rank for insobriety—he frequently
returned. Although Devon born and bred, he liked to claim

Gallic ancestry and was known as "Frenchie" Devereux.

"How about the Post-Captain, sir—Captain Oliver Jones?" he asked curiously. "He'd left Allahabad before I arrived, so presumably he turned up here, as expected?"

"He did indeed!" William Peel answered with relish. "A capital fellow, riding a very dashing charger equipped with a brand new set of white leather saddlery. He dresses for military campaigning in a frock coat, with top boots, spurs, and corduroy breeches, and carries all his current needs on his person or attached to his horse by means of wonderfully contrived leather straps. They include a drinking flask, a revolver case, a present-use pouch, a reserve pouch, and a cased Dollond, plus the most formidable-looking sword, curved like a native *tulwar* with which, according to the 53rd's CO, he has already given a good account of himself! But he's remaining with the 53rd pro tem—I suspect because he imagines they're more likely to see action than we are. Between ourselves, Phillip, I've made no attempt to convince him to the contrary and he's gone off as a volunteer ADC with Brigadier Hope, to scour the countryside for the Nana."

"He's unlikely to be given a posting to China, then?" Phillip suggested, with mild sarcasm.

Peel shook his head. "No—Captain Jones is on half-pay and has come out here at his own expense for what he himself is pleased to describe as a 'lark.' His attitude to war is, to say the least, a trifle light-hearted but I've no doubt he will learn that it's pretty grim business before he's much older. I advised a visit to the Bibigarh, but I don't think he took my advice. He missed seeing the Lucknow column, of course, which might have given him pause for thought . . . and if he'd been here when General Windham was under attack by the Gwalior rebels, I don't imagine he would have regarded *that* as much of a lark. It was a deuced near run thing, Phillip—even Sir Colin admits it now, although he blames Windham for not adhering strictly to his orders. But I hear he's apologised to Brigadier Carthew."

They talked for a little longer and then, when Jim Vaughan, the *Shannon*'s First Lieutenant, joined them, broke off for the evening meal. When this was over, Phillip went to the fort in search of Colonel Cockayne and, learning from him that his small force was complete and ready to march within the next 24 hours, agreed to accompany him and went to volunteer the thirty bluejackets William Peel had promised. He had no difficulty in obtaining the men he wanted, the first to step forward being the veteran petty officer, Thomas Devereux. Midshipman Lightfoot, hearing a rumour that something was afoot, arrived breathless with the plea that he be permitted to join the party, and his own numbers complete, Phillip reported the fact to Colonel Cockayne.

CHAPTER FOUR

he Colonel was in his tent, a map of Oudh spread out before him and a beaker of whisky in his hand. Hospitably, he poured another for his visitor and invited him to seat himself. With the aid of the map, he indicated his proposed route, pointing out likely camp sites and the point at which he had decided to cross the river.

His voice was slurred and Phillip realised, to his surprise, that his new commander had evidently been drinking heavily. But Cockayne held his liquor well; an occasional hesitation and one or two incorrect map references were swiftly corrected and, putting down his lapse as a lone celebration after weeks of anxiety, he thought no more of it. The Colonel knew every inch of the country his force was to cover and he drew a useful sketch map of the city of Ghorabad, at Phillip's request, tracing the course of the Sye River on whose banks it was situated and marking in the position of the fort, in which the British garrison had taken refuge, and the palace of the local Rajah, Newab Abdul Ruza.

"Abdul Ruza is a Muslim, Commander Hazard," he said, offering the sketch for Phillip's inspection. "And he's been engaged in fermenting rebellion for a long time, in association with the Moulvi of Fyzabad, whose name you may have heard. The Moulvi is one of the most powerful of the rebel leaders in Lucknow and the Newab is one of his most fanatical recruits. His palace, as you can see, is on the right bank of the river . . . here, on the east side of the native city. He has his own *zamindari* levies, matchlock men, and a few brass cannon, and his palace is constructed for defence, as they all are, with loopholed walls and two stone-built watch-towers."

"How about the fort?" Phillip enquired. "Is that well constructed, sir?"

Colonel Cockayne expelled his breath in a long-drawn sigh. "Originally it was, yes, but it was allowed to fall into disrepair. We patched it up as well as we could but we hadn't much time before the native garrison mutinied. Also there was a . . ." He hesitated, and then added reluctantly, "there was a difference of opinion between the Commissioner, John Hardacre, and myself. Actually, he's quite junior in the Civil Service and his Army rank was only that of Captain, so I . . . I over-ruled him. It was a military decision, in any case, you understand."

"To defend the fort do you mean?" Phillip prompted, when he fell silent.

Morosely Colonel Cockayne refilled his beaker. "For you, Commander? No . . . oh, very well, then. And yes, it *was* my decision to defend the fort. Hardacre wanted to fortify and provision his Residency—it was in better repair, admittedly, but in my view indefensible. One of those long, rambling single-storey houses with a flat roof and a low mud wall surrounding it. Besides, it was too far from the river. The fort's right on the river-bank and I decided that, if we weren't able to hold out, we could at least try to make our escape down river by boat, after the rains."

"Was that how you made your escape, Colonel?" Phillip asked, when his companion again lapsed into silence. His question sprang from no more than idle curiosity and

Cockayne's angry reaction to it took him completely by surprise.

"The devil take you, sir, what business it is of yours how I made my escape?" the cavalryman demanded. The beaker crashed down on the small camp table, its contents spilling on to the outspread map. Phillip grabbed it quickly, shaking the moisture from it, as two bloodshot eyes bored furiously into his. "We march at first light tomorrow morning, Commander Hazard," Cockayne informed him, with drunken dignity. He issued orders in a brusque stream and added, after a pause intended to add weight to his words, "You understand, sir, that *I* am in command. I shall require no advice from any subordinate officer and I shall offer no explanation for any action I may take, unless I see fit to do so. I had hoped, I confess, to confide in you . . . I was a friend of your late brother-in-law and of your sister, Commander Hazard, and having witnessed the excellent work you did with your guns on the Bridge of Boats, I . . . oh, well, it's of no consequence. I give you goodnight, sir!"

Somewhat taken aback, Phillip replaced the map and came to attention, offering a formal and noncommital response. Colonel Cockayne waved a hand in dismissal and, turning his back, picked up the storm lantern from his table and, by its flickering light, appeared to be searching for a fresh bottle of whisky. Phillip did not wait to ascertain whether or not his search was successful, but during the three-mile ride through the darkness to the Naval Brigade camp, he had much to occupy his thoughts—not least the uneasy fear that his decision to join the Ghorabad relief force might prove to be one he would later regret. It was manifestly unfair to pass judgement on a man when he was in his cups but . . . Harriet, he recalled, had been a trifle reticent about the Colonel, emphasising the fact that he had not been a close friend of her husband's, as if she knew something not entirely to his credit which she had been reluctant to repeat—even to him. On the other hand, she had entrusted her children to his care and had spoken warmly of his wife and daughter, so that . . . Phillip sighed, aware that it was too late to alter his decision.

William Peel was still up when he reached camp, but looking so tired that he contented himself with a brief report of the instructions he had been given and, after warning his party that reveille would be at 3 a.m., he repaired to his own tent to pack his few essential belongings and snatch a short catnap before the time for muster.

At dawn, when the column formed up preparatory to recrossing the Bridge of Boats into Oudh, Colonel Cockayne was his normal friendly self. His greeting was pleasant, his orders courteously delivered and he appeared to have no recollection of the strange little scene he had created the previous evening, as he expressed approval, in flattering terms, of the naval party's turn-out.

"We will halt at sunrise, gentlemen," he told his assembled officers. "To enable the men to break their fast but thereafter I propose to call only two short halts. We have 65 miles to cover and I should like to make eighteen or twenty today, when we shall have the benefit of a good road, which is regularly patrolled. I am aware that tomorrow will be Christmas Day but I regret that I can permit no celebrations, not even of Divine Service. To effect the rescue of the Ghorabad garrison, it is essential that we move with all possible speed, giving the enemy no advance warning of our presence. For this reason, I have required you to travel light, without tents and with the minimum of native servants and camp followers. At night every man will sleep with his rifle at his side, and strong

piquets are to be posted. On the march, the cavalry will skir-
mish ahead of the column and a detachment will act as baggage guards. Well?" he studied their faces. "Any questions,
gentlemen?"

"Are we to make no observance of Christmas, sir?" someone asked. "For the sake of the men's morale, sir, surely we
could—"

Cockayne cut him short. "Do you imagine, sir, that the garrison we are on our way to relieve will have cause—or even
the means—for celebration? We are soldiers and we have battles to fight. We'll celebrate when we have won them." He dismissed the officers to their units and, placing himself at the
head of his squadron of blue-turbanned Sikh sowars, led the
way to the Bridge of Boats.

It was not until they made their first halt at sunrise that
Phillip was able to obtain a clear idea of the composition of
the column. The infantry, he realised consisted of small
detachments, the majority newly arrived as reinforcements for
the regiments forming the garrison of Cawnpore and those
which had served in the Lucknow Relief Force. A few of the
officers and NCOs were veterans, judging by their suntanned
faces and faded uniforms, but the rest were young soldiers,
who had plodded wearily and silently along and who now
flung themselves full length on the dusty ground, too jaded
and dispirited to build bivouac fires on which to cook their
meal. He eyed them pityingly, contrasting their demeanour
with that of his own cheerful bluejackets who, their ration
meat already boiling away under the supervision of the two
mess cooks, were larking about the grog limber, where Petty
Officer Devereux was preparing to dole out their tots.

The young soldiers, of course, were not yet acclimatised
or fighting fit. After the long voyage out from England, con-

fined in over-crowded and unhealthy conditions below decks
in a troop transport, most of them had been despatched up-
country by *dak* and bullock carriage, rail or river steamer—
some even on foot. Now, with scarcely a pause, they found
themselves being marched into hostile territory with every
prospect of engaging in battle with an alien and ruthless foe,
of whom they would have heard only the most horrifying sto-
ries . . . small wonder if they were apprehensive, poor young
devils, Phillip thought. And their officers would be of little
help to them at this stage since they, too, were young and
inexperienced. The highest ranking that he could see were two
Captains, neither more than twenty-four or five; the rest were
of subaltern rank, pink-cheeked boys, who held apart from
their men, talking in drawling voices among themselves as
they waited, in varying degrees of impatience, for their servants to bring them their food.

"I fear that Colonel Cockayne has had rather a high pro-
portion of *griffins* and unseasoned recruits foisted upon him,"
a voice with a strong Scottish accent observed softly from
behind him. Phillip turned, recognising with pleasure a Native
Infantry Captain named Crawford, who had been attached to
the 93rd Highlanders during the attack on the Sikanderbagh
at Lucknow. "It is something of a relief to find you and your
splendid sailors here, Commander," Crawford added. "At least
we know that our artillery will be well served!"

"I'm equally relieved to find you," Phillip confessed, "I
trust in command of a detachment of the 93rd?"

The other shook his head regretfully. "Alas, no—I am on
my own, apart from my invaluable orderly, without whom
campaigning would be a misery." He gestured to a tall, fine-
looking Highlander, who was talking to a group of young
soldiers seated on the ground nearby. "Collins has eighteen

years' service and was in the 'Thin Red Line' at Balaclava . . .
a truly splendid fellow. I told him to mix with these new boys
of ours and try to put some heart into them."

"An excellent idea," Phillip said. He took out his flask and
offered it, but again the Native Infantry officer shook his head.
"No, thanks—I'd better attend our CO. I volunteered to act as
DAQ to the force and Colonel Cockayne is a stickler for his
staff pulling their weight! I'm in his black books already
because I advocated waiting for a day or two, in the hope of
improving the quality of the troops allocated to us. I even
offered to intercede with poor Colonel Ewart, before they
carted him off to hospital in Allahabad, in the hope that he
would give us a company of Highlanders . . . but Cockayne
wouldn't listen."

"Why on earth not?" Phillip questioned, more than a little
shocked.

"Oh, he's like that—always has been." Crawford shrugged.
"He acts on impulse and doesn't take kindly to advice. I believe
you were there when he blasted off at the Commander-in-
Chief, were you not?"

Phillip grinned, "I was indeed—and I shan't forget it in a
hurry! Look, my friend, you might as well eat, even if you
won't share my flask. Our cooks are ready and they're not bad
hands at preparing ration beef." Crawford accepted a plate of
the appetizing stew and they settled down to eat beneath the
shade of a gnarled and multi-rooted banyan tree growing at
the roadside a few yards away. Midshipman Lightfoot brought
them coffee and Phillip brushed aside his companion's thanks.
"Captain Peel subscribed to the belief that sailors march best
on well-filled stomachs, even if the Army doesn't, and we
employ cooks to prepare our food. It's a better system than
yours, I venture to suggest. Our cooks ride on the grog-limber

and aren't too exhausted by a long march to fulfil their func-
tion when a halt is called. And we pool our rations, so that
each man gets a fair share."

"Judging by the excellence of this," Crawford conceded,
mopping up the remains of his stew with unconcealed satisfaction, "you're right. But I can't see Colonel Cockayne permitting many halts of this duration, once we leave the road."

"He's a strange fellow, the Colonel. He'd be well advised
to pamper these young soldiers a little, if he wants to get the
best out of them," Phillip observed.

"I can tell you he won't, Hazard. Rather the opposite. He'll
drive them till they drop."

Phillip's brows lifted. "You astonish me! Tell me, have you
known him long?"

"Yes, for a good number of years. I once served in his regiment—and in Ghorabad—but I . . . that is, I transferred to the
Oudh Infantry." There was an odd expression in George
Crawford's dark eyes, almost of anger, but it faded and he
added, smiling, "I also know his wife and daughter, which is
really why I'm here. I . . . well, not to put too fine a point on
it, I'm deeply attached to Colonel Cockayne's daughter. If it
hadn't been for this infernal mutiny, I should have declared
myself to her but as things are"—his smile vanished—"I can
only pray God that the poor, sweet child is still alive."

The lovely daughter Harriet had spoken of, Phillip
thought. He studied his companion's lean brown face with
renewed interest, liking what he saw. Crawford was in his mid-
or late thirties, as so many of the Honourable Company's captains were, his thick dark hair already tinged with grey but he
was a credit to his profession, intelligent and certainly not
lacking in soldierly virtues. At the Sikanderbagh, he had been
one of the first through the breach at the main gate and Colonel

Ewart had singled him out for praise for the heroism he had displayed in twice risking his life to bring out wounded men. Yet it seemed, from the hints he had let drop, his attachment to Colonel Cockayne's only daughter had been formed in spite of some early differences between himself and the Colonel. To have transferred out of the regiment suggested a certain incompatibility, to say the least—or perhaps Cockayne had not welcomed the younger man as a prospective son-in-law.

Phillip frowned, as Crawford said bitterly, "The Ghorabad garrison are in dire straits. In my view, it will be a miracle if even half of them have survived."

"Then there *is* reason for Colonel Cockayne's haste?" Phillip suggested.

"Yes, there is every reason, although a couple of days would have been neither here nor there. With seasoned troops, we could have made up for the delay."

"In that case why—"

"My dear Hazard, Colonel Cockayne's conscience is tormenting him," Crawford returned thickly. "It gives him no rest . . . and there is reason for that, too." He rose, setting down his plate and the mug of coffee, only half finished, as if he had forgotten about them, and went on, his voice harsh with pain. "If you thought the Lucknow garrison suffered it will, I fear, bear no comparison with the suffering those poor souls in Ghorabad have had to endure. When the mutiny broke out, about sixty British women and children and roughly the same number of non-combatant civilians—mostly Eurasians— took refuge in a crumbling mud fort, built fifty years ago, with a handful of British officers and NCOs to defend them. I don't know how many but I do know that the mutiny was a bloody affair, in which many of the regimental officers were murdered by their own men before they could reach the fort. The wretched place lies on the opposite bank of the river from Cantonments and the Civil and Native Lines, you see, and they never got there. The Residency would have been much nearer and I believe some of them tried to defend it but Cockayne—"

But Colonel Cockayne had chosen to defend the fort, on his own admission, Phillip recalled. Assailed by sudden doubts, he interrupted anxiously, "They are still holding out in the fort, aren't they?"

"There's no way of knowing that until we get there," George Crawford told him. "The Colonel insists they are. I . . ." he seemed about to say more but bugles were sounding an end to the halt and the men starting to shuffle reluctantly into line, so instead he excused himself and hurried off towards the head of the column, leaving Phillip decidedly uneasy. The march was resumed and, in one respect at least, Crawford's forecast of Colonel Cockayne's intentions proved accurate. Only two brief halts were called and the unseasoned young soldiers began to fall out in increasing numbers. Some, too exhausted to care what punishment might be in store for them, ignored their sergeants' admonitions and abandoned their rifles and accoutrements by the roadside, to limp sullenly on without them, whilst others simply collapsed. The waggons following in the rear, compelled to wait in order to pick up men and weapons, dropped so far behind that, at the first halt, they were out of sight and the second had to be prolonged, to enable them to make up some of their lost ground.

Phillip found his guns and waggons held up and, in an attempt to curb his party's impatience, told Devereux to initiate some singing. The seamen, who were in the habit of thus enlivening the tedium of long marches, joined in with enthusiasm, roaring the chorus of their favourite Rifle Brigade March, "I'm Ninety-Five," with unrestrained gusto, which brought up the lolling heads of the detachments to their front and rear. Some of the older soldiers joined in and, to the accompaniment of a drummer and two fifers of the 88th, other regimental tunes and even a Christmas carol were added to the bluejackets' repertoire. Morale had improved noticably when an ensign of the 34th, acting as aide-de-camp, cantered back with an order from Colonel Cockayne that the singing was to cease.

"We are about to leave the road," he announced self-importantly. "And the Colonel does not consider it desirable that hostile villagers should receive warning of our approach."

From the ranks of the 88th immediately to his rear, Phillip heard a defiant Irish voice raised in protest. The protest was blasphemous but good humoured, and a more experienced officer would either have ignored it or replied in kind. The plump faced young ensign, however, rounded on the culprit furiously. "Place that man under arrest!" he commanded. "I'm charging him with insubordination!"

He put spurs to his horse and trotted off before the detachment commander could remonstrate with him, a few derisive cheers speeding him on his way. "Sir"—Midshipman Lightfoot kneed his bony countrybred to Phillip's side—"I know that fellow . . . he was at school with me. His name's Highgate, Benjamin Highgate. We used to call him 'Bulgy Benjy,' sir."

"Did you now?" Phillip eyed him gravely, controlling an impulse to smile at the appropriateness of the schoolboy nickname. "It's a pity they didn't teach him better manners at your seat of learning, Mr Lightfoot."

"Oh, he was kicked out, sir," Lightfoot returned, with conscious smugness. He grinned. "For bullying. He doesn't seem to have changed much—but I'm surprised he's only an ensign. His father's in trade, sir, and disgustingly rich. I'm sure he could have afforded to buy Benjy a Captain's commission if he'd wanted to."

"Perhaps it is just as well he didn't," Phillip said. He was reminded briefly of Captain Lord Henry Durbanville and felt his throat tighten at the memory. It was a long time since he had thought of that strange young man but undoubtedly the resemblance was there, and he found himself hoping that someone would have the opportunity to cut Ensign Highgate down to size before he did any serious harm.

The sun went down and, as the march continued over rough, open country and no halt was called, more and more young soldiers fell by the wayside. Even some of the veterans were grumbling now and not a few of them were limping; the laden waggons could take no more of the stragglers and those who had collapsed had to be assisted by their comrades. Discarded equipment littered the ground and Phillip ordered his seamen to pick up as much as they could but, with his limbers piled high and the weary gun-cattle swaying in their traces, the rear of the convoy came virtually to a standstill. Petty Officer Devereux reported two of the bullocks down in front of the leading gun and Phillip, left with no choice but to delay the column, told him to replace both teams with the only slightly less jaded reserve animals. Predictably, while this was being done, Ensign Highgate came cantering back to ascertain the cause of the delay.

"I am to inform all commanding officers of detachments," he stated, pulling up midway between the naval party and that of the 88th, and shouting to make himself heard, "that any man who abandons his rifle in enemy territory is to be put on a charge and will receive 25 lashes before the march is resumed tomorrow morning!"

Phillip, his temper already strained, felt a choking anger

rise in his throat as the significance of this announcement slowly sank in. Native troops could not be flogged for any misdemeanour, he was aware, but British soldiers—and seamen—were still subject to such punishment although, in practice, floggings were seldom ordered for any but major military crimes. To threaten young soldiers with it, when they had been compelled to make a forced march without adequate training, smacked of sadism or worse. Ensign Highgate, as a mere messenger, could scarcely be blamed for issuing the threat but . . . his tone curt, he called the boy to him.

"*What* did you say?" he demanded.

The plump young ensign eyed him insolently. He repeated his announcement word for word and was about to add to it when Phillip cut him short.

"Presumably Colonel Cockayne gave you that order, Mr Highgate?"

"Of course he did. I am his aide-de-camp and the Colonel sent me to—"

"To deliver it to each detachment commander in person, not to shout it aloud?"

"Well, I . . ." the boy reddened. "The Colonel said that the men should know that they would be punished if they continued to behave in such an unsoldierly fashion, and I thought . . . that is, I supposed—"

"Clearly you have not carried out the duties of an aide-de-camp before," Phillip said coldly. He outlined these in brusque detail, conscious of Midshipman Lightfoot's delighted grin as he did so. "You have no authority of your own to issue orders. When conveying an order from the Column Commander, you should state from whom it has come, giving to the officer for whom it is intended the respect to which his rank entitles him."

"I don't understand," Highgate blustered, still very pink of face. "I have shown no disrespect, sir, I—"

"Have you not?" Phillip snapped. "I am a Commander in the Royal Navy, Mr Highgate, and that is the first time you have seen fit to address me—correctly—as 'sir'."

"I beg your pardon, sir," the ensign said, with some show of contrition. He, too, had now seen Lightfoot's amusement and had evidently recognised his one-time schoolfellow. "I— er—that is, Commander Hazard, sir, I have an order for you from—er—from Colonel Cockayne."

"Anticipating that order, Mr Highgate," Phillip put in, "perhaps you will be so good as to return to Colonel Cockayne at once. Inform him, if you please, that my gun-cattle are exhausted. When I have yoked up fresh teams, I will endeavour to close the column but I fear it will be dark before I can do so. Where does the Colonel intend to make camp, do you know?"

"He—er—two miles on, sir, I believe."

"Very well. Deliver my message to the Colonel, if you please."

Young Highgate rode off obediently, pausing to salute before putting his horse to a canter. The short respite enabled the men of the rearguard to recover and, although it was, as Phillip had anticipated, quite dark before the guns and the rear of the column reached the camp site, they came in in good order, each man marching with shouldered rifle. Colonel Cockayne was not in evidence and Phillip, having parked his guns and ammunition waggons and posted guards, decided against approaching him. He ate a belated evening meal and wrapped himself in his cloak against the night chill, preparatory to getting what sleep he could on the iron-hard ground but scarcely had he lain down than Petty Officer Devereux was shaking him apologetically back to wakefulness.

"It's the Colonel, sir—he wants to have a word wiv' you, sir."

"Very good." Controlling his annoyance, Phillip got to his feet and strode over to where Colonel Cockayne was standing, warming himself beside the glowing embers of the naval party's cooking fire. His face was in shadow but it was evident, from the curtness of his greeting that he, too, was annoyed.

"You wish to see me, sir?" Phillip said, refusing to be provoked. He moved away from the fire, out of earshot of his men. The Colonel followed him, bristling.

"Yes . . . I'm given to understand that you expressed disapproval of an order I issued to detachment commanders, concerning punishment for men who abandoned their rifles on the march?"

Phillip shook his head. "I expressed no disapproval of the order, Colonel—only of the manner in which it was conveyed by your aide-de-camp. Ensign Highgate chose to shout it within hearing of my bluejackets, instead of delivering it to me, as he should have done. Taking it that he was inexperienced in his duties, I pointed out to him how an order should be delivered."

"Damme, Commander Hazard, you sent the boy back with a deuced insubordinate answer!" Cockayne accused.

Phillip repeated his headshake. "My message was simply a statement of fact, sir. Possibly due to his inexperience, Ensign Highgate may have delivered it to you in an insubordinate manner. All I intended him to do was to inform you of the state of my gun-cattle and the fact that, until I had yoked reserve teams, I could not continue the march. I—"

"You implied criticism of the length of the march, Commander."

"I implied only that I could not haul guns with worn-out

beasts, sir. That is a regrettable fact, which it was my duty to report to you, since the rear of the column was delayed in consequence." Somehow, Phillip managed to contain his rising anger. Catching the strong smell of alcohol on Cockayne's breath, he added quickly, "If that's all, Colonel, I'd like to get some sleep. I presume that we shall march out at first light and that your decision *not* to hold Divine Service still stands?"

"Your presumption is correct," the Colonel confirmed. "Although so many officers have requested it, that I've agreed to say a general prayer before we move out. But that," he added vehemently, "will be *after* we have made an example of four of those miserable specimens who lost their rifles in spite of my warning. I've been given scum, not fighting men, Hazard—boys who have never heard a shot fired by the enemy. But I'll make them fight, never fear."

Phillip recoiled. "By flogging them—on *Christmas Day,* sir? Surely that will only serve to—"

Cockayne did not allow him to finish. "Yes, by flogging them, if I have to, to serve as an example to the rest. Damme, sir, do you question my right to punish them—on Christmas or any other day?"

"No, not your right, sir. Rather the wisdom of adopting such measures with unseasoned troops."

Phillip had been at pains to speak reasonably but the Colonel brushed his arguments aside as if he had not heard them. "By noon tomorrow we shall be in striking distance of the village of Betarwar. It's walled and loopholed, as they all are, with watch-towers and a wet ditch running round it. I'll want you to bombard the place with your rockets, to soften it up and, if possible, set it on fire before we go in with the infantry. Your guns will have to move faster than they did today, Hazard, and—"

"But, Colonel . . ." Phillip was shocked out of his self-imposed caution. "I understood that we were to regard the relief of the Ghorabad garrison as a matter of extreme urgency. If we waste time attacking rebel villages along the route, will that not increase the danger to the Ghorabad people? We shall lose half a day, at least, and risk losing men, when we can ill-afford to lose either." He would have said more, thinking bitterly of the fate of General Wheeler's garrison at Cawnpore, but Cockayne waved him impatiently to silence.

"The safety of the Ghorabad garrison is of as much concern to me as to any man in this column," he pointed out coldly, "since my wife and daughter are among them."

"I know that, sir. It was simply that I—"

"*I* am in command, Hazard, and I am not bound to explain my orders or my decisions to you. But"—the Colonel shrugged and again Phillip caught the whiff of spirits on his breath—"I shall do so on this occasion, since you appear to doubt their wisdom. These unseasoned troops of ours will have to be bloodied and taught to fight . . . well, they shall learn their first lesson tomorrow and victory will give them heart. At Ghorabad, they will have to face five or six thousand rebels, including Company mutineers—but at Betarwar only a few hundred *zamindari* warriors with flintlocks will oppose them, so that victory is assured. Oh"—as Phillip bit back an exclamation—"do not let that trouble your conscience, Commander. Betarwar is a hot-bed of treason, as I have very good cause to know . . . and the chief of this area is a brother of Abdul Ruza. A blow struck against him is also a blow against the Newab who, when he hears of it, may well be tempted to lead a force to avenge his brother. If he does, we shall meet him in open country instead of behind fortified walls, which will be to our advantage. Even if he fails to do so, his brother's fate will undoubtedly give him pause and—"

"His brother's *fate*, sir?" Phillip put in. "What exactly do you mean to do to the Newab's brother?"

"I shall hang him," the Colonel answered, without hesitation. "Together with the other *budmashes* of his village, all of whom are known to me and all of whom richly deserve to die for their treachery. Well . . ." he was smiling now, his temper completely restored. "I've given you my reasons, Commander Hazard, and I shall count on your co-operation. We will move off at first light and I shall require your guns in position for the attack on Betarwar by noon. That's all, I think . . . goodnight."

Phillip returned to his out-spread cloak. He was tired but for some considerable time, sleep eluded him. There was, he was forced to concede, a certain logic in Colonel Cockayne's decision to attack the rebel village before proceeding to Ghorabad. An easy victory for the young soldiers would undoubtedly improve their morale, give them the confidence in their fighting abilities which they lacked but . . . He sighed. There was something more behind the decision, he was convinced, although as yet he could not have said precisely what it was. A personal element, perhaps, on Cockayne's part—the thinly concealed desire for personal vengeance? There had been an odd note in his voice when he had spoken of Betarwar as *"a hot-bed of treason"* and . . . what else had he said? *"As I have very good cause to know . . ."* Surely that suggested a personal motive for launching a punitive raid on the village, rather than an altruistic one?

Phillip was tempted to seek out George Crawford, in the hope of setting his mind at rest but then decided against it. There was little enough of the night left now for sleep—his questions would have to wait until morning.

The bugles sounded reveille only a few minutes, it

seemed, after he had fallen asleep. He rose, shaved, and washed after a fashion and then heard the call for assembly, which was followed by the twitter of Devereux's boatswain's pipe. "Hands to witness punishment!" the petty officer bawled. "All hands lay—" Phillip interrupted him.

"Who gave that order?" he demanded.

"Frenchie" Devereux met his gaze blankly. "The Colonel's aidey-camp, sir," he answered, his voice as expressionless as his weatherbeaten face. "I thought as 'ow you knew about it, sir, seein' as the Colonel was talkin' to you las' night. There's four poor sodger-boys gettin' the cat for lettin' their bandooks— their rifles, I mean, sir—go adrift. The aidey-camp said as we was to muster wi' the sodgers and, you bein' still asleep, sir, I sounded the call."

So Cockayne's threat had been no idle one, Phillip thought savagely, and very little time had been wasted on any drum-head courts martial—whatever trial the men had been sub-jected to must have taken place before the reveille or, perhaps, the previous evening. "Very well," he acknowledged, realising that Devereux was still waiting for his answer. "Carry on, Chief."

"Aye, aye, sir." Petty Officer Devereux repeated the pipe. The bluejackets mustered and were marched off by Midshipman Lightfoot to form up on the left side of a hollow square facing a four-wheeled baggage-waggon, beside which Colonel Cockayne stood waiting, arms folded across his broad, white-clad chest. In the half-light of early morning, his face was impassive and he displayed no emotion when, the sur-geon's cursory examination completed, the four prisoners, clad only in shirts and trousers, were marched forward under escort to hear their sentences read.

All four were young, Phillip saw, their backs—when the

shirts were removed—white and unmarked. Although clearly apprehensive, they stood stiffly to attention and each, in turn, took his 25 lashes in stoical silence. Cut free from the waggon wheel by one of the drummers who had administered the flogging, the last of the four slid unconscious to the ground, but the other three were able to resume their shirts and their scarlet jackets without assistance and march back to the ranks of their own regiments, apparently without having suffered any serious ill-effects.

The Colonel, true, at least, to his promise, read a short prayer. Then the bugles sounded and immediately afterwards, formed up in line of march, the column set off across flat, cultivated country, with a cavalry screen spread out in front of the leading infantry detachment. They proceeded in an easterly direction, their plodding feet raising a thick cloud of choking dust from the narrow, rutted cart-track they were following.

A short halt was called at sunrise, sufficient only for the hasty consumption of uncooked rations, but word of the impending attack had leaked out and there was little grumbling on this account, the young soldiers seemingly eager to face their baptism of fire. The advance continued and although from time to time a Sikh cavalry sowar rode back to report, the countryside appeared to be deserted and entirely devoid of menace.

The village of Betarwar was sighted a little before noon and George Crawford rode forward with a cavalry escort to reconnoitre. While the rest of the column enjoyed a welcome respite Phillip, in response to an order from Colonel Cockayne, brought his guns and the rocket-tube into position under the cover of a *tope* of mango trees. The village was very much as the Colonel had described it and, subjecting its loopholed walls to a careful inspection with his Dollond, Phillip saw that they were manned by, perhaps, a hundred armed villagers, the muzzles of their long-barrelled flintlock muskets clearly visible through the loopholes. The fields in the immediate vicinity—under stubble and offering no cover—were empty, even of domestic animals. The inhabitants of Betarwar had evidently seen the cavalry skirmishers a considerable time ago and taken refuge behind their defensive walls, with their beasts and . . . there would be women and children among them. Phillip lowered his Dollond and glanced enquiringly at Colonel Cockayne.

"Should we give them some sort of warning, sir?" he suggested. "A shot over their heads and a call to surrender?"

The Colonel gave no sign of having heard him. His own glass to his eye, he was watching George Crawford and his reconnaissance party over to his left and the sudden sharp crack of a single musket brought his head round. The shot, fired ill-advisedly or, perhaps, inadvertantly, struck the sand a good fifty yards short of the group of horsemen; they wheeled and retired without haste, trotting easily towards him, Crawford with an arm raised as if to signal something. No other shots were fired at them but, waiting only until they were clear of the target area, Cockayne turned to Phillip and ordered curtly, "Open fire with your rockets, Commander Hazard!"

"Now, sir? Without calling on them to—"

"Now, I said, sir!" Cockayne flung at him angrily. "I want that village set ablaze. You can open a breach in the walls with your nine-pounders once it's well alight."

Phillip had no choice but to obey him. Hissing skywards and then curving down on to the rooftops of Betarwar's clustered houses in a shower of sparks, the rockets did their deadly work with swift efficiency. One after another, the straw-thatched roofs burst into flames and soon the whole village was an inferno, great clouds of choking smoke covering it like a pall. The villagers replied with a single ancient cannon mounted to the right of the main gateway but, although of heavy calibre, it was so inexpertly served as to be useless. Advancing to close range with his two 9-pounders, Phillip and his gunners came under musket fire but this, too, was ill-aimed and ineffective. It took him barely fifteen minutes to smash two wide breaches in the mud wall and put the village cannon out of action, a lucky shot having blown up the stored powder with which it was being supplied.

The infantry deployed and, led by Colonel Cockayne in person, advanced with fixed bayonets on the shattered wall, to vanish into the smoke, cheering as they went. Phillip waited, sick at heart. Mutiny and treason had, he knew, to be punished but this ruthless slaughter of guilty and innocent alike had more in common with vengeance than it had with justice. Even in Lucknow, with hundreds of British lives in jeopardy, Sir Colin Campbell had issued orders that no retribution was to be exacted from the townsfolk by his victorious troops—and none had disobeyed those orders. Sepoys and native landowners, taken in armed revolt against the British Raj, were liable to the death penalty, it was true—but never without trial. Yet here . . . he felt bile rising in his throat as sounds of the unequal battle reached him faintly across the intervening fields of stubble. To Lightfoot, who expressed boyish pride in the good practise their guns had made, he snapped a crisp order to check the reserve ammunition and then added, relenting, "The men may as well cook dinner, Mr Lightfoot. We look as if we'll be here for sometime yet."

Half an hour later, George Crawford rode out of the blazing village, with the news that it was about to be vacated. "It's a bloody shambles, Hazard," he said, his face grim and pale under its coating of dust and smoke and sweat. He slid stiffly from his saddle, accepting Phillip's offer of a swig from his flask and gulping it down thirstily. "Thanks . . . I needed that, by God I needed it!" He returned the flask, his hand shaking visibly. "Cockayne said he wanted to blood his young soldiers— well, by heaven, he's done it! Let 'em loose with the bayonet in there and they don't know any difference between mutineers and harmless peasants. It's enough that they all have black skins."

"*Why?*" Phillip asked, tight-lipped. "I thought all he wanted to do was save his people in Ghorabad."

Crawford sighed. "He let slip, last night, that he sought help from the Betarwar villagers after his escape from Ghorabad and they refused—beat him up, he told me, and robbed him."

"Yes, but—"

"I know, I know," the staff officer said wearily. "He's waging a personal vendetta. But he can claim justification for today's attack—our unseasoned troops had to be taught their business. And virtually all these Oudh villages *did* turn against us, Hazard—British fugitives were maltreated, many of them were murdered, including women and children, without mercy. The Moslem *talukdars* and their retainers gave active support to the siege of the Lucknow garrison and both they and the Hindu *rajwana* fought against poor old General Havelock's column. They prevented him reaching his objective in August. Retribution *is* long overdue."

"But Colonel Cockayne is supposed to be commanding a relief force," Phillip pointed out. "Sir Colin Campbell gave him these troops on the clear understanding that he would use them for that purpose, did he not? Certainly it was on that understanding that *I* volunteered to serve with him. I didn't volunteer to slaughter women and children, whatever the colour of their skins, and we're descending to the level of murderers if we do it. To the level of Pandy murderers, Crawford, and at a time when Christians preach peace and goodwill to all men!"

"I'm not defending Cockayne," Crawford qualified. "Only saying that he can justify what he did here today, if he's ever required to . . . and he hasn't finished, you know. He intends to hold a ceremonial execution."

"Of the Newab's brother, d'you mean? When?"

"Now, I believe—after an even shorter trial than the men who were flogged were given last evening." George Crawford sighed and moved reluctantly to his waiting horse. "It's a hell of a way to spend Christmas Day, isn't it? But . . . I'm a member of the court, so I had better go and get it over with."

"You can't stay and eat with us?" Phillip invited.

"Alas, no." Crawford pointed to where a small procession was emerging from the smouldering wreckage of the main gate of the village. "I see the prisoner and escort are on their way. But, as I said, the trial isn't likely to take long and I don't particularly want to witness the hanging . . . may I come back and take you up on your hospitable offer?"

"Of course, my dear fellow," Phillip assented readily. "I'll wait for you."

As George Crawford had predicted, the trial was quickly over; within less than half an hour, he returned, an anxious expression on his good-looking face. He ate his meal of naval stew in virtual silence and Phillip, sensing that something had occurred to upset him, tactfully refrained from pressing him for an explanation. Below them, as they sat under the shade of the grove of trees, preparations for hanging were swiftly completed and the troops, with the exception of sentries and a cavalry piquet, formed up once more in a hollow square, facing the tree which had been selected to serve as a gallows. No general assembly bugle call had been sounded and Phillip kept his party with their guns, feeling no obligation to send any of them down to witness the barbaric ceremony, since he had not been ordered to do so.

To the roll of drums, the *talukdar,* his hands pinioned behind him, was half-pushed, half-lifted to a waggon positioned beneath the tree and the dangling rope was looped about his neck. He was too far away for Phillip to see the expression on his face but he stood stiffly erect, showing no obvious sign of fear and then, in response to a shouted order, the horses harnessed to the waggon were whipped into motion. Moments later, a twitching body was suspended from the tree and, after a few convulsive jerks, it was still, a limp figure in a stained white robe, which distance robbed of much of its horror.

"Well, that's that," George Crawford said resignedly. "The fellow was guilty all right, so his death doesn't weigh unduly on my conscience. And he had a fair trial, for all it wasn't a lengthy one. But . . . he said something during the trial that worries me, Hazard. He may have been lying—it's on the cards that he was because he knew damned well what was going to happen to him. Only—" he broke off, frowning.

"What *did* he say?" Phillip prompted.

"He said that the Ghorabad garrison had surrendered to his brother, the Newab, and that the survivors were being held as hostages."

"Oh, my God!"

"Yes . . . one thinks of General Wheeler's garrison and that ghastly house where the Nana's poor hostages were murdered,"

Crawford said bitterly. "And it doesn't bear thinking about, does it?"

Phillip shivered. "No. No, it does not. I—" Aware of his companion's tension, he thrust the unwelcome memory to the back of his mind. George Crawford, of course, was frantic with anxiety for the girl he hoped to marry, the Colonel's young daughter Andrea but . . . He said, his tone deliberately sceptical, "You admit that the fellow might have been lying. What was Colonel Cockayne's reaction? Surely he—"

"He wasn't there," Crawford answered uneasily. "*I* was acting as president of the court martial and the other members were all Queen's officers, who don't understand Hindustani. I told the interpreter to keep his mouth shut, of course, but . . . dammit, I shall have to tell Cockayne, shan't I?" He hesitated, a small pulse at the angle of his jaw beating agitatedly. "Keep this in confidence, Hazard, won't you?"

"Naturally I will. Is there more?"

"Unhappily there is. You see, Hassan Khan claimed that the Ghorabad garrison surrendered quite a long time ago." Crawford spread his hands helplessly. "That's what sticks in my throat, Hazard."

Phillip stared at him in shocked surprise. "I don't think I understand . . . for God's sake, *how* long ago? What are you suggesting? That Colonel Cockayne knew they'd surrendered before we left with this relief column?"

Crawford inclined his head reluctantly. "He must have known, if Hassan Khan is telling the truth. He . . . devil take it, he insisted that the Colonel made his escape some hours *before* the surrender!" Reminded of Colonel Cockayne's strange outburst when he himself had asked about his escape, Phillip drew in his breath sharply. Crawford added, with distaste, "The fellow accused Cockayne—or tried to, until I silenced him—of running out on his own people. Of running out on his wife and daughter, for heaven's sake! Could you believe that of him?"

Could he, Phillip asked himself, *could* he in all honesty? Slowly he shook his head. "No," he said. "I could not. Dammit, that was Hassan Khan's interpretation of his actions. Cockayne has always said that he escaped in order to seek aid for the garrison—and he did just that, even if his pleas for British troops fell on deaf ears until now. He even braved Sir Colin Campbell's wrath to get them."

"Yes, that's true." George Crawford got to his feet and started to pace restlessly up and down. Finally, as if reaching a decision, he came to a halt facing Phillip. "Please understand, Hazard, there's no love lost between Colonel Cockayne and myself but I'm making no accusations—I'm simply telling you what the prisoner said. He offered no proof. He admitted he wasn't in Ghorabad at the time but his statement was made with death staring him in the face. What possible motive could he have had for making it, if it wasn't true?"

Phillip frowned. "Hatred, perhaps," he suggested. "The desire for revenge . . . I don't know."

Crawford sighed. "He was undoubtedly full of hatred—and with reason, of course. His people slaughtered and his village set on fire, himself facing an ignominious death—oh, yes, I freely concede that he was motivated by hatred. And therefore he might have been lying but—it puts me in a devilish difficult situation, doesn't it? I mean, I owe Colonel Cockayne my professional loyalty, whatever differences were between us in the past, and yet I—"

"You're wondering whether or not to tell him of the prisoner's accusation—the personal allegations the fellow made against him?"

"Yes, I am," the Native Infantry officer confessed. "Because if it's true, as heaven's my witness, I cannot let it rest there. I—"

"If it's true," Phillip told him, with conviction, "we shall very soon find out, my friend."

"Find out? How shall we find out? Cockayne won't tell us!"

"No, possibly not. But we shall know within the next day or two whether we are a relief column or a punitive force, shall we not? And we shall know whether or not the Ghorabad Fort is still in British hands."

George Crawford looked relieved. "Yes, you're right," he agreed. "All the same, it's my duty to report the statement Hassan Khan made to the court. Colonel Cockayne is in command—he has to be told that the Ghorabad garrison may have surrendered."

"Yes, that much he must be told," Phillip said. "Or you would be failing in your duty without a doubt. But if you'll take my advice, Crawford, you'll leave it at that."

"*Can* I leave it at that?"

"I think you'd be wise to, my dear fellow. To repeat the unsubstantiated accusations of a condemned rebel can only do irreparable harm. If Hassan Khan was lying, the Colonel will never forgive you for giving credence to such damaging allegations against him. Had others heard and understood them, it would be a different matter—then he'd have to be told. But as it is—" Phillip shrugged. "It's up to you, of course."

"Yes. Thank you—you've offered me sound advice, Hazard, and I'm grateful." George Crawford's expression relaxed. "I have a personal stake in all this, as you know, and I wasn't seeing things objectively. I'll go and report to the Colonel at once, I . . . dear God, I pray that Hassan Khan *was* lying! Because if that poor child is in the Newab's hands I . . ." He broke off, teeth clamped fiercely on his lower lip in an effort to recover his composure. "Thanks again, Hazard. I'll see you when we make camp."

He remounted and rode off. Phillip watched him go, a thoughtful and somewhat anxious frown creasing his brow, but he was permitted little time for reflection. The bugles sounded, Ensign Highgate trotted over to request him courteously to limber up, and within half an hour the column was heading eastwards, leaving the smouldering ruins of the village of Betarwar to be swallowed up in the dust of its passing.

CHAPTER FIVE

Permission to sing on the march was given and, swinging along at ease with pipes lit, the men took advantage of this unexpected relaxation of the stern discipline which had hitherto been enforced on them . . . although, significantly perhaps, their repertoire of songs included no Christmas hymns.

But the young soldiers' morale had greatly improved. They had come through their baptism of fire, had struck a blow against the enemy and suffered only minor casualties, and now they marched with their heads held high, brave in their newfound manhood, their earlier weariness and resentment forgotten, and the Colonel's praise still ringing in their ears. Even those who had been sickened by the bloodshed kept their feelings to themselves, fearful of ridicule and hearing the word "Cawnpore" repeated by their comrades and shouted aloud by some of their NCOs. They had, they told each other, avenged the hideous massacre of their countrymen and women at the Suttee Chowra Ghat and the still more terrible butchery of the poor innocents in the Yellow House, the appalling evidence of which they had all seen with their own eyes—however brief their sojourn in Cawnpore—and few questioned the justice of what had been done in Betarwar.

In that respect at least, Colonel Cockayne had been right,

Phillip thought, but . . . He glanced about him uneasily, listening to the raised voices, when the singing stopped.

"An eye for an eye," he heard a grim-faced corporal exclaim. "That's what the Bible says, don't it? The sods got what they deserved—we didn't do nuffink to them that they didn't do to us. What if it is Christmas Day? It makes no odds. And them as says there was wimmin an' kids killed terday that shouldn't 'ave been—why, they've only ter pay a visit to that there Yeller 'Ouse in Cawnpore and they'd soon think different!"

"Aye, Corp, that's a fact!" a youthful private echoed excitedly. "We'll show them black swine what's what—just let us at 'em with the bayonet! An' when we've done with the men," he added boastfully, "they can give us the wimmin an' we'll show them, too! *I'll* show 'em, like I done today. Yellin' their bleedin' 'eads off, they was, begging us for mercy—but we shown 'em, didn't we?"

Petty Officer Devereux, trudging stolidly beside his leading gun, met Phillip's gaze and, removing his battered clay pipe from his mouth, spat his disgust expertly in the dust at his feet. "Mon Dieu, sir, to 'ear them young roosters crow," he observed cynically. "You'd imagine they'd just taken on the 'ole Pandy army and the Nana with 'em, instead o' beatin' the tar out o' a bunch of miserable native peasants armed wi' pea-shooters. Any case, we done their work for 'em with our rockets—they 'adn't nuffink more to do than go in an' mop up. And—Cawnpore or no Cawnpore—there wasn't no call to let 'em loose on the wimmin an' bairns, was there, sir? Leastways I don't think so, if you'll pardon me speakin' frankly, sir. It's simply lowering ourselves down to their level, in my 'umble opinion. There wasn't much noblessy oblige about today."

These were exactly his own views, Phillip thought wryly.

Colonel Cockayne could have raised his men's morale without permitting the excesses which, it was becoming evident, he had permitted. Even seasoned and highly disciplined troops should not be allowed to run wild and, in the case of these raw boys, to induce over-confidence could have fatal results.

"Let us pray that it will not be necessary to repeat what happened today, Chief," he answered, keeping his voice low.

"Aye, sir." The petty officer's tone was flat. "That—and the floggings. But I've got a nasty feeling that it's what we're 'ere for—again speakin' freely, sir. And our lads don't like it, any more than they liked not 'aving Divine Service this morning . . . Christmas Day, sir! Why, even in the Black Sea, with the decks and rigging frozen, the Navy 'eld Divine Service on Christmas Day, didn't they, sir?"

"Yes," Phillip agreed, remembering. "Aboard every ship of the Fleet. But we're under military command, Devereux and—"

"Some command, sir, if you'll pardon the liberty," Devereux put in resentfully. He, too, lowered his voice as he went on, "Oates says as they raped some o' the wimmin back there an' then burnt 'em alive in the huts. Like animals, sir, not British sodgers. But they was egged on, Oates says."

Oates was a long-serving able-seaman, Phillip recalled, whom William Peel had disrated from petty officer for insubordination and drunkenness on the voyage up river from Calcutta. He was better educated than the majority and the men listened to him . . . "Oates wasn't there, was he?" he asked.

"Oh, no, sir," Petty Officer Devereux denied. "But 'e's bin talkin' to some o' the sodgers. 'E says they was allowed to break open chatties o' that there arrack an' drink as much as they could hold when they went into the village. An' you know what Oates is about drinkin' ever since Captain Peel took 'is rate off 'im, sir. Fanatical 'e is, why—"

"Yes, I know, Chief. I'll have a word with him before we make camp."

"Aye, aye, sir." Devereux knocked out his pipe, and, after a searching glance at Phillip's face, managed a grin. "No call ter let our lads get down 'earted, though, is there, sir? Will we gie 'em 'Shenandoah' an' a chorus or two o' 'Way Down Rio' to perk their spirits up?"

"Yes, by all means," Phillip assented with relief. "Carry on, Chief."

His own spirits remained low, however, despite the lustily rendered choruses, and they reached their lowest ebb when the column made camp at dusk and George Crawford sought him out. "Well?" he asked anxiously. "Did you tell Colonel Cockayne that his Ghorabad garrison may have surrendered to the Newab?"

"Yes, I told him." There was an edge to George Crawford's voice and his dark eyes held an angry glint. "He pooh-poohed the mere suggestion—insists that his intelligence reports confirm that the fort is still in British hands."

"Intelligence reports? Where's he getting them from?"

"I don't know—he doesn't confide in me, simply says he's getting them. I can only suppose the Punjab Horse collect them."

"They could be correct, I suppose," Phillip said, without conviction. "But surely, as DAQ you—"

"I am no longer serving in that capacity," Crawford put in wearily. "My loyalty is in question, Hazard, so I've been relieved of my duties."

"Relieved of your duties?" Phillip stared at him in disbelief. "Your loyalty in question, for God's sake! Did you tell him all that blasted *talukdar* said at his trial? Surely you didn't mention the personal accusations he made, did you?"

Crawford shook his head. "No, no—I took your advice. But I could not, in all conscience, endorse the Colonel's proposed plan of action, Hazard . . . either as a soldier or as a man. And that, it seems, constitutes disloyalty. If I hadn't left him when I did, I believe he would have had me placed under arrest."

"Dear heaven, has he taken leave of his senses? Or . . . dammit, was he *drunk?*"

George Crawford shrugged despondently. "No, he was perfectly sober. As to his sanity, I honestly don't know. But this I can tell you . . ." He hesitated and then burst out explosively, "he informed me that he intends to employ the same tactics as he used today—burning villages and putting their wretched inhabitants to death, laying waste to the countryside all the way to Ghorabad—in the belief that he can thereby induce the Newab to come out and fight him!"

"I see." Phillip was conscious of a sick sensation in the pit of his stomach. The implications were clear, he thought grimly but, in view of George Crawford's personal involvement he, too, hesitated for a moment before putting his thoughts into words. Finally he said, at pains to keep his voice steady, "But if he does that and the garrison *are* being held as hostages, he'll be placing their lives in even greater jeopardy, will he not? Another day of ruthless, indiscriminate slaughter such as we had today would be more likely to induce the Newab to order their execution than to spare them—whether or not he comes out to fight."

"Precisely," Crawford was making a valiant effort to keep his feelings under control. "And I tried to tell Colonel Cockayne so—I begged him to make certain that the garrison are still holding out before committing himself. I even volunteered to

lead a small party of cavalry to the outskirts of Ghorabad—
now, tonight, so as to resolve all doubts, but he wouldn't listen. It was then that he relieved me of my duties. He . . . in
God's name, Hazard, you'll have to do something! In the name
of humanity you must—I've done all I can. Those poor, unfortunate people must be saved if it's humanly possible—we *cannot* have another Cawnpore!"

His face was a white, stricken mask in the dim light and
Phillip studied it with deep concern before replying to his
appeal, aware of the mental torment the older man was
enduring but striving, in spite of this, to assess the situation
dispassionately. All his earlier doubts regarding Colonel
Cockayne's motives had returned full force to plague him
but . . . Cockayne was in command. It was not for any subordinate officer to question his orders, as the Colonel himself
had made abundantly clear. He did not act without careful
thought; that, too, he had made clear, and his information as
to the present state of affairs in Ghorabad—however it had
been obtained—was probably more reliable than the claims of
a dead *talukdar* who, watching his village burn, might well
have lied in bitterness and malice.

"Hazard, you are next in seniority to Cockayne," Crawford
pointed out. "He's a Lieutenant-Colonel, so your rank is equivalent to his, is it not?"

"Yes," Phillip conceded unwillingly. "But what of it? Mine
is a naval rank—I'm not permitted to interfere with the military command in a mixed force and in this I—"

"But your Captain Peel assumed command of a mixed
force at Kudjwa, surely?"

"Only because the military commander was killed and the
greater portion of the force consisted of the *Shannon*'s seamen
and Marines. There's no precedent for it." They were treading

on dangerous ground, Phillip thought uneasily. George Crawford was over-wrought, carried away by the force of his own emotions . . . understandably so, since the girl he loved was in Ghorabad and he was beside himself with anxiety on her account. He laid a sympathetic hand on the other's arm. "My dear fellow, you know I'll do anything that lies within my power—" he began and then, sensing that his companion expected more than platitudes and vague promises, added quickly, "I doubt whether Colonel Cockayne will listen to me either but, if you wish, I'll try to talk to him. I might at least be able to ascertain the source of his intelligence reports, assess their reliability and—"

"I fear you'll have to do more than talk," Crawford warned. "But if you could even prevail on him to hold his hand until we are quite certain that the Ghorabad garrison have not surrendered, it would be an immense weight off my mind. I'm still more than willing to take a reconnaissance party there so as to make certain—tell him that, will you please? And go to him now, Hazard, I beg you. He can hardly relieve *you* of your duties."

"Now—before he's eaten? Would it not be wiser to wait until he's had time to cool down?" Phillip sighed ruefully. "If he's still in a towering rage when I try to tackle him, it won't exactly help our cause, will it? Besides, I need to know a few facts, arguments I can put to him, so that he'll have to listen."

George Crawford gestured to the darkening sky. "There is very little time, my friend. God knows what is happening now in Ghorabad but . . . I don't suppose half an hour will make much difference. What is it you want to know?"

"Well . . ." Phillip hesitated, considering. "As a naval officer, Crawford, I'm woefully ignorant of military strategy and Indian Government policy. But let's suppose the garrison *are* still holding out and Colonel Cockayne contrives to draw the Newab into the open . . . could he justify the tactics he proposes to employ? The burning of native villages, the wholesale slaughter of peasants and their families?"

"If he had to face a court of enquiry, you mean?"

"Yes. In similar circumstances, a naval officer would have to explain his actions to the satisfaction of Their Lordships. Could Cockayne explain his?"

"If they were successful, I suppose he could—yes." Crawford shrugged. "Sir Colin Campbell would not approve but there's quite a considerable body of opinion out here which maintains that all the Oudh landlords and peasants are rebels in arms against us and that, so far as they are concerned, retribution should be harsh and bloody. The Newab is a proscribed rebel with a price on his head—therefore any punitive action taken against him or his people would, in the present climate of opinion, probably meet with official approval . . . always provided that it was successful. But—"

"Do you think the tactics Cockayne intends to employ can possibly be successful?" Phillip put in. "I'm asking for your professional opinion, Crawford—personal feelings apart, you understand?"

"I understand." Crawford was calmer now, although he was still sweating profusely and he muttered an apology as he mopped his face with a sodden handkerchief. "I'm bound to admit that such tactics *could* succeed, since there's no certainty in this kind of campaign. But in my view, they could easily lead us into the devil of a mess and frankly, Hazard, I fear they will. The Newab only has his levies in Ghorabad—the Pandy regiments are reported to be in Lucknow—and, in normal circumstances, he'd probably defend himself but no more. A series of savage attacks on his villages would, as Cockayne claims, almost certainly bring him out, but they'd also bring out every *zamindari* force in the area, bent on retaliation—the Newab could double his effective force, treble it even, in a few days. If he decided he was strong enough to attack us, the chances are that *he* would choose the battleground or set an ambush for us. And with raw troops like these . . ." He spread his hands in a despairing gesture. "Caught in an ambush or in the open, without much warning—good Lord, Cockayne could find himself in very serious trouble! He could lose more than half of them before he had even got them deployed and into position. Your guns and rockets and our Miniés and Enfields would probably gain us eventual victory but our casualties would be appalling. These *zamindari* levies are not to be despised, you know. They fight bravely—better than the Pandies, in many instances—and they have both cavalry and guns. And they know how to use them."

"Yes, I know that. I was at Kudjwa with Captain Peel," Phillip confessed. "And they fought like tigers—it was the sepoys who gave ground. But carry on, please—I didn't mean to interrupt you. What—again in your professional opinion—ought Colonel Cockayne to do in this situation, apart from despatching a reconnaissance party to Ghorabad? What would *you* have done, if you'd been in command of this force?"

The Native Infantry Officer frowned. "That's a hell of a question, isn't it? I'd have left Betarwar severely alone, for a start, of course." He sighed. "This is a small force, Hazard. But it's highly mobile and perfectly adequate for the purpose for which it was intended . . . that is, for a rapid advance on Ghorabad to rescue the garrison and then an equally rapid return to Cawnpore. That's what I should have done and what, in my opinion, Cockayne should endeavour to do now . . . whether the garrison surrendered months ago or are still holding out in the fort. No punitive forays—there are other ways of building up morale. Nothing calculated to stir up any hornets' nests on the way, just a three-day slog to reach his objective. He could have done it, too. If it hadn't been for the attack on Betarwar today, I believe that we could have reached Ghorabad unmolested."

"Could we? Do you honestly believe we could, Crawford?"

"Yes, in all honesty I do," Crawford asserted. "The Oudh peasantry have seen their Pandy allies defeated at Lucknow, at Bithur more than once and again, very recently, at Cawnpore. They've seen the writing on the wall and I fancy they would have let us alone—from expediency, if nothing else—if Cockayne hadn't made up his mind to stir them up. But if he persists in his avowed intention, if what was done today at Betarwar is repeated elsewhere, then the consequences could be disastrous, in my view. Certainly to the poor unfortunates at Ghorabad and very possibly to ourselves . . ." He talked on, giving technical details, but Phillip scarcely heard him, his brain suddenly racing, drawing conclusions which—even half an hour before—he would have dismissed as outrageous.

It had all started at Betarwar, he thought. It had begun with Colonel Cockayne's decision to give his unseasoned troops a taste of action—a decision which, at the time, even George Crawford had believed he could justify—only the troops had been allowed to go too far. Allowed or . . . damn it, *encouraged* to commit excesses? There was a bitter taste in his mouth as he recalled the scenes he had witnessed—for all they had been at a distance—and the boastful utterances of some of the young soldiers. Seaman Oates had said that they had been permitted to break open the villagers' supply of arrack and, if that had been so, who had given them permission? Cockayne had been there, he had led them into the blazing village in person. If he had not authorised the breaking open of the casks, he must have known who had done so, which—since he had apparently made no attempt to countermand the order—suggested that it must have been given with his tacit approval.

Drinking by European troops, before or after any action, had always been severely discouraged by responsible commanders. It led to rapine and murder and was particularly likely to do so now, when the men were inflamed by tales of the atrocities committed by mutineers. Sir Colin Campbell, well aware of the danger and determined to prevent excesses, had imposed harsh penalties for the looting of captured alcohol and even William Peel, who disliked flogging, had ordered the lash on more than one occasion for seamen found guilty of stealing liquor of any kind while on active service. Why then, why the devil had Colonel Cockayne permitted it?

Unless . . . Phillip drew a quick, uneven breath. *Unless he had wanted the village of Betarwar reduced to a shambles—unless he wanted the Oudh peasantry to ignore the writing on the wall, so that . . . no, no, it was impossible!* He said, in a shaken voice, "Crawford, if we *had* marched straight to Ghorabad and left Betarwar alone, do you think that the Newab might also have seen what you referred to as 'the writing on the wall'?"

George Crawford looked startled. "I don't think I follow you. The Newab is a proscribed rebel, as I told you, with a price on his head. He knows he can expect no mercy from the Indian Government or the military authorities. He—"

"But suppose he had been offered terms?"

"Offered terms—by Colonel Cockayne, do you mean?"

"Yes," Phillip confirmed. "His life for the surrender of his hostages. Or, if the garrison are still holding out against him, in exchange for the raising of the siege—do you think he might have accepted? With our forces at his gates and only his own levies to defend the city, the writing on the wall would have been pretty clear, even to him, would it not?"

"Good God!" Crawford was still visibly taken aback. "Such a possibility hadn't occurred to me. I suppose he *might* have accepted, in those circumstances, if he had been offered terms. But he won't now, not after what was done at Betarwar. Devil take it, Hazard—Cockayne hanged his brother!"

"Yes," Phillip echoed grimly. "Cockayne hanged his brother and let our troops run wild in the village. He went there for that specific purpose—he told me so himself—and now you say he intends to serve every village between here and Ghorabad in the same manner! *Why,* man . . . *why?* Tell me that, if you can!" It was as much an appeal as a question and he waited, willing his companion to offer an explanation that would dispel his doubts and feeling the sweat break out on face and brow as he waited.

George Crawford continued to stare at him blankly; then comprehension dawned and he said, with evident reluctance, "To make it impossible for the Newab to accept terms, I can only surmise—to force him to stand and fight. Because— dammit—because Cockayne wants to make a battle of it! He wants revenge and a glorious victory which will redound to his credit, no matter how many lives it costs. I . . . Hazard, I don't want to believe ill of Colonel Cockayne or of any British officer; it goes against the grain. And we don't know that he was empowered to offer terms for the Newab's surrender, do we? But . . . my God, if Hassan Khan was telling the truth, if he *did* desert the garrison, then—"

Then only a glorious victory could restore the Colonel's

reputation, Phillip thought. A glorious victory and . . . perhaps a dead garrison. He looked at George Crawford and saw his own unhappy fears mirrored in the older man's eyes.

"I *don't* want to believe it, before heaven I don't!" Crawford's voice shook. "But it fits or it's beginning to—except that his wife is there . . . his wife and Andrea. Surely no man worthy of the name would risk *their* lives—no, it's unthinkable!"

"Unless they are already dead," Phillip said flatly. "And Cockayne is aware of it."

Every vestige of colour drained from George Crawford's face. For a moment he could not speak. Then he bowed his head in bitter resignation. "That appears to be the only explanation, does it not? The only logical explanation for his failure to march straight to Ghorabad. Unless, of course, he *is* going out of his mind. That has to be a possibility, Hazard."

"Alas it does," Phillip agreed. "Well"—he sighed, not relishing the prospect—"I suppose I had better find him and do what I can to persuade him to think again about tomorrow's plan of action. You'll wait for me?" He gestured towards the naval party's hospitably glowing camp fire. "Our meal should be ready soon."

"Thank you," Crawford acknowledged tonelessly. "But I have no stomach for food. I . . . I think I'll have a word with the Subadar of the Punjab Horse. He may be able to tell me what intelligence reports have been brought in."

They separated and Phillip went in search of Colonel Cockayne. The column commander was preparing to dine, seated alone at the camp table beneath an awning of interlaced branches, his orderly busily turning a spit at a bivouac fire a few yards away, on which two chickens were roasting.

"Ah, Hazard! The very man I wanted to see!" The Colonel's greeting was affable and he appeared to have forgotten their

somewhat acrimonious exchange outside Betarwar that morning, as he waved a casual hand in the direction of the sizzling
chickens. "The spoils of victory! Come and share them with
me, won't you?"

Phillip hesitated. Like poor Crawford, he had little stomach for food, still less for the sharing of pillaged chickens with
the man who had ordered the sack of the village from whence
they had come but . . . making an effort to overcome his
instinctive feeling of distaste, he excused himself courteously,
if not entirely truthfully.

"Thank you, sir—I've already eaten."

"Then join me for a peg," Cockayne invited. He shouted
a brusque order and his native bearer came running from the
shadows, to set tumblers and a large, leather-covered travel-
ling decanter on the table in front of him.

"I only wanted to speak to you concerning tomorrow's
march, Colonel," Phillip began. "Not to interrupt your meal.
What I have to say is urgent but it will not take long and—"

"Nonsense, my dear Commander—you've time for a drink,
for heaven's sake! And by God you've earned one, after the
fine work your guns and rockets did today." His round, red
face lit by a beaming smile, the Colonel splashed whisky into
the tumblers with a lavish hand. "Help yourself to water if you
take it. Personally I never do—this is a Highland malt, too good
to drown, in my opinion." He savoured the whisky appreciatively, rolling it round on his tongue and then, as his orderly
approached uncertainly with one of the chickens, nodded him
to serve it. "You won't mind if I take my meal, since it's ready,
will you? I want to turn in reasonably early because we'll have
a hard day in front of us tomorrow. It's about twenty miles to
the Sye River as the crow flies but we shall have to go a few
miles out of our way in order to deal with two more of the

Newab's villages. They're both hot-beds of sedition like Betarwar, as you might expect, but they shouldn't delay us very long."

Conscious of a chill about his heart Phillip, his whisky untouched, attempted to speak but was waved imperiously to silence.

"Anticipating your question, Hazard, there'll be no serious problems for you if you simply do as you did today," the Colonel told him, attacking his chicken with relish. "H'm, this isn't bad, not bad at all . . . ah, where was I? Oh, yes . . . a preliminary bombardment with rockets, then when the place is well alight, advance and open up a breach with your nine-pounders. That's all you need do—the rest can be left to my infantry. They're improving, aren't they? There'll be no hold-ing them, now they've been blooded—they're raring to go."

"Colonel," Phillip said, unable to contain his impatience. "If you—"

"Have the courtesy to hear me out," Cockayne bade him sharply. "There's a *jheel* about half a mile to the south of the first village but, at this time of year, you won't have to make much of detour—the banks will be quite firm enough for your guns and I'll give you a cavalry screen. As I say, neither of the villages need delay us for long, they're only a few miles out of our way. Seven or eight, at the outside . . . here, I'll show you on the map." He reached for the map case on the table beside him, seeming so confident of the rightness of his decision that Phillip marvelled at his duplicity—if duplicity it was. But surely he *knew* what he was doing, knew the risk he would be taking if he attacked two more of the Newab's villages. Damn it, he *had* to know—this wasn't his first cam-paign! Unless, as George Crawford had said, he was going out of his mind . . .

"Is that what's worrying you, Hazard?" the Colonel asked, smilingly. "The delay?"

Phillip nodded, tight-lipped. "Indeed it is, sir. I don't understand why those villages need delay us at all. Would it not be advisable to press on to Ghorabad with all possible speed tomorrow?"

"If it were, don't you think I'd do so?"

"I am at a loss to understand why you do not, Colonel." Phillip braced himself as he saw the Colonel's smile abruptly fade. He would achieve nothing if he antagonised the column's commander, he knew, and he added, with restraint, "Surely, sir, the purpose of this force—its sole purpose—is to effect the relief and rescue of the British garrison at Ghorabad?"

"Certainly. That is precisely what it will do."

"With respect, sir, you appear to me to be more concerned with subjugation of rebel villages," Phillip countered, still keeping a tight rein on his temper. "We lost half a day's march today for that purpose and now you are proposing that we should waste most of tomorrow in the same manner. Every hour that we delay in going to their rescue must add to the danger of your people in Ghorabad. Are their lives not at stake? If they—"

"What the devil are you driving at, sir?" Cockayne demanded irritably.

"Permit me to explain, sir," Phillip requested. Speaking firmly but without heat, he advanced the arguments with which George Crawford had armed him and Colonel Cockayne listened, his meal congealing on his plate and all trace of his former affability gone. But he listened and it was not until Phillip mentioned the dead *talukdar*'s claim that the garrison's surrender had already taken place that, losing patience, the Colonel's smouldering resentment errupted into fury.

"Damn your insolence, Commander Hazard! You've been listening to Crawford's imbecile ramblings," he accused. "You've let him poison your mind with his lies!"

"I spoke to Captain Crawford, yes. But he—"

"No doubt he told you that I'd relieved him of his duties on my staff?"

"Yes, he did, sir," Phillip admitted. "He—"

"Did he also tell you that I threw him out of my regiment?" Cockayne questioned. He laughed, without amusement. "No, I'm sure he did not—it's not something he's proud of, I assure you. But I had good reason—the damned fellow started casting sheep's eyes at my daughter. For God's sake, she was only sixteen then and he's forty, with no money and no prospects and, to cap it all, he had a native woman in the bazaar whom he'd been keeping for years as his mistress! I couldn't be expected to tolerate that, could I? Or give his suit my paternal blessing. Damme, I didn't want him with this force. He was the last man I wanted—but he volunteered and Sir Colin Campbell appointed him to my staff without consulting me . . ." The tirade went on and Phillip tried vainly to stem the flow of angry words.

"And now," Colonel Cockayne flung at him, "the infernal fellow is trying to undermine your loyalty by telling you a pack of malicious lies! Devil take it, Hazard, don't you know better than to believe him? Don't you know better than to take the word of a condemned rebel? My garrison have *not* surrendered! They—"

"Sir," Phillip pleaded, "can you be certain of that?"

"Are you questioning my competence, damn your eyes?" the Colonel challenged wrathfully. "My fitness to command?"

Phillip remained silent, anxiously searching his face. What he saw there was not reassuring and his doubts concerning the Colonel's sanity added to his anxiety. But then, as swiftly as if it had never been, Cockayne's anger died. He had himself under control; his voice was steady, his tone dignified and reasonable as he went on, "Last night, when you questioned my orders, Commander Hazard, I paid you the compliment of explaining them in detail. I do not intend to do so again. I shall issue my orders and you will obey them without question. If you do not, I shall have no alternative but to place you under arrest, pending the return of this column to Cawnpore, when I shall report unfavourably on your conduct. Is that clear?"

"It is quite clear, sir," Phillip acknowledged. Aware that he was defeated, he made one final appeal. "Nevertheless, I beg you, sir, to order this column to continue its advance to Ghorabad without delay. With the greatest respect, I—"

"Your request is noted and refused," the Colonel returned coldly. "I do not require advice from a naval officer on matters of military tactics, Commander, so kindly refrain from offering it. And now oblige me by retiring."

Phillip saluted stiffly and turned on his heel. On his return to the naval party's bivouac, he found Midshipman Lightfoot waiting for him with a note.

"Captain Crawford asked me to give it to you, sir," the boy told him. "Before he left. The cooks have kept your meal hot for you, sir. Shall I fetch it?"

"I . . . no, thanks, youngster. Just some coffee, if there is any." Phillip hesitated. "You say Captain Crawford *left?*"

Lightfoot nodded. "Yes, sir,—on horseback. He was by himself—in fact, he asked me if he could leave his orderly with our party and I said he could. He's a 93rd man, sir, so I didn't think you'd mind. Er . . ." He gestured to the note. "I expect he's explained in that—Captain Crawford, I mean. He seemed a bit upset, sir—almost as if he'd received bad news . . . although I don't know where he could have got it from, out here, do you?" Warned by Phillip's glance, he restrained his curiosity and added quickly, "I'll get a hurricane lantern so that you can read the note, sir, and then I'll fetch your coffee. That is if you're sure you don't want anything to eat? It's jolly good, sir—fresh beef and—"

"Thank you, Mr Lightfoot, coffee's all I want." Fresh beef, Phillip thought . . . that, like the Colonel's chickens, had probably come from Betarwar. He suppressed a sigh and, when Lightfoot brought him a lantern, read the note.

"The cavalry have not brought in any intelligence from Ghorabad," George Crawford had written. *"And since I fear that you will be unable to induce our commander to change his mind or his orders for tomorrow, I am going to find out what I can of the present situation of the garrison.*

"I am going alone—I shall have a better chance that way, since I know the country and the language. If I should fail to return, you must, I am afraid, expect the worst."

"Your coffee, sir." Lightfoot was there, a steaming pannikin held carefully in both hands. "*Was* it bad news from Captain Crawford, sir?"

Phillip roused himself from his shocked contemplation of the note. "I'm not sure," he answered. "It may be, I'm afraid, but don't concern yourself with that for the time being, Mr Lightfoot. You cut along and get some sleep. Good night and—thanks for the coffee."

Young Lightfoot eyed him uneasily for a moment and then gave him a dutiful "Aye, aye, sir," and obediently returned to his place by the fire.

Left alone, Phillip sipped morosely at his coffee. It was twenty miles to the Sye River, he thought, and Ghorabad was a further three or four miles from the Bridge of Boats by which Colonel Cockayne planned to cross—Crawford could get there by daybreak, on a good horse, provided the bridge was still there and he reached it unchallenged. But he was taking the very devil of a risk and it was unlikely that he would be able to complete his self-imposed mission and rejoin the column until the following evening at the earliest—and even then he would need a good deal of luck. By tomorrow evening, if the Colonel carried out his plan to deal with the Newab's other two villages as he had dealt with Betarwar, the peasantry and the *zamindari* levies in the area would be up in arms and George Crawford would find every man's hand against him . . . as also would the column.

In a mood of black despair, Phillip sought for some way out of the impasse. Short of depriving Cockayne of his command, there was nothing he could do to alter the course of events, he decided wretchedly. He would lay himself open to arrest and a charge of mutiny if he even attempted to supercede the column's commander and, indeed, any failure to carry out his orders might well have the same result—had not Cockayne warned him that it would? So that . . . He shrugged resignedly. Unless and until the Colonel actually endangered the column or committed some act which would cast strong doubts on his sanity, his own hands were tied and he could only bide his time in silence, obeying whatever orders he was given.

Next day, the village of Morawah was attacked and set ablaze. The inhabitants put up only a token resistance and many of them took refuge in flight, but Colonel Cockayne despatched his cavalry in pursuit of those who had escaped the flames and himself led the infantry in a systematic slaughter of the unfortunates who had remained within their battered mud walls. Half a dozen of the men were dragged out from the shambles to be hanged, with the troops drawn up in their ceremonial square in order to witness the barbaric ritual.

But when the march resumed, there was no singing. The young soldiers marched in grim silence and only a few, reeling from the effects of the liquor they had been permitted to consume, expressed boastful satisfaction in their victory. By the time the second village had been similarly dealt with, there was a tangible uneasiness amongst the whole force and the NCOs could supply no answers to an increasing spate of questions concerning Ghorabad and their chances of effecting the rescue of the British garrison without further delay. The officers, for the most part, kept their own counsel, ignoring the questions or replying to them evasively. But the men's uneasiness began to spread to them also and, Phillip noticed, the youthful Captain Williams—acting as Chief of Staff in George Crawford's stead—was subjected to repeated demands for information by the detachment commanders, which he found it hard to satisfy.

"It seems the Colonel intends to make a forced march tonight, so as to reach the river by first light tomorrow morning," the baggage train commander confided, in aggrieved tones, trotting up on a lathered horse to join Phillip at the head of the guns. "Or so Tom Williams says. Have you heard anything definite, Commander Hazard?"

"No," Phillip confessed wryly. Whether inadvertantly or on instructions from Colonel Cockayne, Tom Williams had told him nothing.

"Well, I don't know about your gun-cattle, sir, but mine won't stand another five- or six-hour slog," Lieutenant Arbor said. He was a tough, grey-haired man of approaching fifty, promoted from the ranks, who had seen a good deal of active service and he sounded genuinely worried as he went on, "The cavalry have had a hell of a lot of chasing about to do—their horses ought to be watered and rested, if they're to be of any use to us tomorrow. Not to mention the men!" He swore in frustration. "My blasted Sikhs are rolling drunk and have been all day and a number of the Queen's splendid redcoats can barely stand up. They need a chance to get some solid food inside them and sleep it off—a forced march in darkness will just about finish them."

"There will be a moon," Phillip reminded him.

"I suppose that will help but . . ." Lieutenant Arbor hesitated, eyeing Phillip uncertainly for a moment. Then his feelings became too much for him and he burst out indignantly, "I hesitate to criticise our Commanding Officer but this whole damned march seems to me to have been badly mismanaged! I'm all for punishing rebels and mutineers, who richly deserve it, but what we've been doing for the past two days has been a waste of valuable time and manpower. These miserable villagers we've been butchering can hardly be described as a threat to the British Raj, can they? And in the meantime the Ghorabad garrison are still awaiting relief. I . . ." Again he hesitated. "I heard a rumour—God knows where it sprang from— that they may have surrendered. Apparently it came from the *talukdar* we hanged at Betarwar. Did you hear that?"

"Yes, I heard it. I—"

"Did you believe it, Commander?" Arbor pursued.

"It has to be a possibility, Mr Arbor." Phillip's tone was deliberately non-commital.

"Then God help the poor souls," Arbor said, with bitterness. "Because we shall probably be too late to do more than avenge them . . . if we ever reach Ghorabad." He turned in his saddle to look back at the seamen, plodding stolidly along beside their guns. "I congratulate you on the discipline you keep, sir. In this respect the Navy is an example to us all."

"We work our guns, Mr Arbor," Phillip told him smilingly. "That duty, thank God, has enabled us to avoid what the infantry have been called upon to do."

"I take your point," Arbor acknowledged. "And wish my baggage guards were not required to double as blasted infantry under our present commander!"

When he had gone back to the rear, Petty Officer Devereux drew level and Phillip dismounted, in order to walk beside him. "Something on your mind, Devereux?" he asked.

The petty officer nodded, his lined, leathery face unusually grave. "I over'eard a bit of what you and that officer were sayin', sir."

"Well?" Frenchie Devereux missed very little, Phillip thought and, with typical lower-deck shrewdness, usually drew the right conclusions. He had almost certainly witnessed George Crawford's departure the previous evening and—if he hadn't already guessed that officer's destination—would have made a point of pumping Private Collins, his 93rd orderly, until he obtained the salient facts. The two had been together throughout the day. "You've also been talking to Collins, have you not?" he suggested.

"Aye, sir," Devereux admitted quite readily. " 'E's an old sodger, sir, and there ain't no flies on 'im—knows what 'e's about, Collins does. And 'e reckons as there ain't no garrison at Ghorabad *to* rescue, not now—they've surrendered. Maybe a while ago—maybe before this 'ere column left Cawnpore. 'Is officer's gorn to find out for sure becos . . . well, for personal reasons, Collins says. There's a lady involved, I fancy—*cherchez la femme,* sir—"

"You haven't told our men any of this, have you?" Phillip demanded sternly.

The old petty officer eyed him reproachfully. "With respect, sir, I know better'n to do that. But they're not too 'appy about things, sir, an' that's the Gorspel truth. They know something's wrong . . . all that killin' in them villages, it ain't right, sir, not when we was sent out to relieve a British garrison. Collins reckons . . ." He paused, subjecting Phillip's face to a wary scrutiny and then added, his tone almost apologetic, "Sir, 'e reckons as we're in a rare mess and that it's Colonel Cockayne 'oo got us there. Meself—if you'll pardon me speakin' me mind, sir—*I* reckon the Colonel's well an' truly *derangey!*"

Phillip's instinctive reaction was to deny the suggestion. In the interests of continued good discipline, he knew that he ought to deny it but . . . Petty Officer Devereux was a good man and he was no fool. He might accept the denial but he would not believe it. He was worried, too, as many of the officers and NCOs were and, damn it, with reason.

"I didn't hear your last remark, Devereux," he admonished mildly. "And if I were you, I shouldn't speak my mind *too* freely."

"No, sir, I won't," Devereux assured him. "But we *are* in a mess, ain't we?" He jerked his straw-hatted head towards the rapidly darkening sky. "If we 'ave ter march all night, like Lootenant Arbor said, they could catch us in the open if they've a mind to, with the men asleep on their feet, sir, and them bloody gun-vaches of ours ready to drop. Why don't the Colonel wait till Captain Crawford gets back and can tell 'im what's goin' on in Ghorabad?"

"I imagine Private Collins can give you the answer to that question," Phillip returned. He added crisply, "When we halt, it will probably only be for a couple of hours. I want the guns ready for action at all times, double-shotted with grape and the crews closed up. See they get a hot meal and their grog, Chief, and chase up the bullock-drivers—those cattle must be properly watered and fed. On the march, if we should be attacked, stand by to unlimber and manhandle both guns when I give the order." He issued further detailed instructions and Devereux nodded his understanding.

"Do you reckon they will attack us on the march, sir?" he asked.

"It's possible," Phillip conceded. "But I think we've a little time in hand yet." It would take time, he thought, for the Newab to gather his forces in sufficient number to take the offensive. News of his brother's death and the attacks on the villages could only just have reached him and his *zamindari* levies had to be summoned from their toil in the fields, which would allow the British column a little leeway. Not much, but perhaps it would be enough; possibly that was what Colonel Cockayne was banking on and why he had decided on a forced march. An attack on the marching column was always on the cards, of course, and it was as well to be prepared for one, although the darkness would be as great an impediment to the attackers as it was to the column. His own guess was that the Newab would be waiting at the river, when—tired after their night march—the British troops would be most vulnerable to a sudden, swift assault. And if the Bridge of Boats had been even partially destroyed then . . . Phillip felt his stomach muscles tighten involuntarily.

They were approaching a low, wooded slope when the shrill notes of a bugle call broke into his thoughts.

"The 'alt, sir," Petty Officer Devereux announced thankfully.

"And it looks as if there's plenty o' firewood. Let's 'ope the black perishers give us time ter cook our meal, so as we can march on full stomachs at least!"

"Let's hope so." Phillip echoed his wry grin. "All right, Chief—carry on. You know what to do . . . Mr Lightfoot!"

Midshipman Lightfoot was at his side, alert as ever, but his young face unmistakably weary beneath its coating of dust and smoke. Taking pity on him, Phillip repeated the instructions he had given to Devereux and then dismissed him, himself supervising the parking of the guns.

Darkness fell and soon the bivouac fires were alight, glittering like so many fireflies as the men hacked brushwood and dry branches with which to feed them. They had halted beside a small wood, about half way across a flat, open plain which afforded no cover for an approaching enemy. Once the moon rose, they would be in no danger of a surprise attack—unless it came from the far side of the wood. Presumably Colonel Cockayne would post cavalry piquets to guard against that danger, Phillip told himself. He had noticed, as they approached it, that the wood was narrow—more a belt of trees running up and to along the crest of an undulating slope than a wood—but his guns were parked close to its lower edge and he decided to make sure that they were safely positioned whilst the cooks were at work on the evening meal.

He walked quietly and without haste, with only the occasional cracking of dry timber to betray his presence as he thrust his way through the closely growing trees, and he had almost reached the crest when, without warning, a dark shape rose out of the darkness to hurl itself upon him. He reacted instinctively, putting out an arm to ward off the attack and following this with a clenched fist, aimed at the white blur of a face. His fist connected; there was a grunt of pain and his assailant stumbled and almost fell, the dagger or sword with which he had been armed falling with a faint, metallic clatter against the bole of a tree. The man made the mistake of trying to retrieve the weapon and Phillip followed up his momentary advantage with a well-aimed boot, which precipitated his would-be attacker flat on his face.

He screamed out something incomprehensible in his own language and, anxious to take him alive so that he could be questioned, Phillip drew the pistol from his holster, intending to threaten him with it as, with his free hand, he attempted to secure a hold on the man's arm. But the fellow squirmed from his grasp and swiftly made off into the darkness, still yelling in his own language. He fired blindly in the direction of the sound; the next moment there was a pad of bare feet, coming from behind him and, as Phillip turned to meet this new threat, a musket exploded a few yards from him in a flash of orange flame. The ball creased the side of his head and he went crashing to the ground.

Dazed and shaken, he dragged himself up, in time to glimpse several white-robed figures running silently past him towards the crest of the slope and he blundered after them, in a vain attempt to intercept them. Reaching the edge of the trees, vertigo and lack of breath compelled him to end the futile chase. He sank to his knees, his head throbbing unmercifully and, as he waited for the vertigo to pass, the moon rose, bathing the slope below him in an unearthly radiance. Swaying like a drunken man, he clambered up again to cover the last few yards and once more glimpsed his ertswhile quarry—on horseback now—making off in the direction of the river.

There was something else, too, but his vision was blurred

and at first he did not realise the significance of what he was seeing. Then, as the dark, shadowy mass resolved itself into a considerable body of horsemen, he waited only to take stock of the ground across which they were advancing and, still swaying dangerously, started to retrace his footsteps towards the distant bivouac fires.

CHAPTER SIX

"**S**ir . . . Commander Hazard! Are you all right, sir?"
Midshipman Lightfoot's voice seemed to be coming
from a long way away but Phillip recognised it and struggled
into a sitting position. He felt curiously light-headed and his
vision was still blurred but, by the light of the moon which
now filtered through the trees, he saw that Lightfoot was not
alone. Lieutenant Arbor was with him, and Seaman Gates,
standing guard with his Minié, and behind him George
Crawford's big Highlander orderly, also armed. Both Oates and
Private Collins were peering anxiously about them and it was
Collins who spotted the long native dagger lying, half-hidden,
among the roots of a nearby tree. He picked it up with a stifled exclamation and Lightfoot asked, startled, "Were you
attacked, sir?"

"Yes." Gingerly, Phillip put out an exploratory hand to
investigate the throbbing pain which emanated from the right
side of his head. He withdrew his fingers, sticky with con-
gealed blood, trying desperately to remember what had happened, and what he was doing here. It was at this point that
the unknown assailant had hurled himself out of the under-
growth—it had to be, since the weapon he had dropped was
here but . . . there had been others with him, men in white
robes, one of whom had fired a musket at him at alarmingly

close range. He had fallen and . . . yes, damn it, he had tried to chase the men, had followed them to the edge of this patch of jungle and . . . memory returned.

"We heard a shot," Lightfoot was explaining. "And came to see what—" Phillip cut him short.

"Go up to the top of the slope," he bade the boy thickly. "You too, Arbor—now, don't wait for me. I don't think I imagined what I saw but we'd better make sure before sounding the alarm."

The two officers, catching his urgency, were gone for only a few minutes. When they returned, Phillip was on his feet. "They're there all right," Arbor confirmed grimly. "And advancing rapidly . . . no doubt with the idea that the column is making camp for the night and won't be expecting an attack. I couldn't make out a great deal but there must be several hundred *zamindari* cavalry and at least one sepoy regiment. The fellows who attacked you, Commander, were evidently spies, on their way to report back to the main body."

Relieved that his memory had not played him false, Phillip nodded. "Back to the guns, if you please, Mr Lightfoot," he ordered crisply. "And limber up. I'll be with you as soon as I've reported to Colonel Cockayne. Coming, Mr Arbor?"

Colonel Cockayne was finishing his meal when they reported to him. From his slurred speech and bloodshot eyes, it was evident that he had been drinking but, to his credit, as soon as the situation became clear to him, he did not hesitate and his orders were given with admirable clarity. Captain Williams and Ensign Highgate conveyed them to the detachment commanders and, leaving their bivouac fires still burning and their baggage and cooking equipment on the ground, the column moved out in order of detachments, to deploy and take cover in irrigation ditches and behind banks facing the camp site they had vacated. No bugles sounded, orders were whispered and the movement was made in virtual silence, Phillip's men manhandling their guns across the rough, sandy ground and taking position in the centre of the line of waiting riflemen.

They had not long to wait. Within fifteen minutes the cavalry piquets cantered back to rejoin the main body, with the news that a large force of enemy infantry had reached the crest of the ridge immediately above the camp site.

"*Zamindari* levies and a regiment of sepoys," Colonel Cockayne said, when the Subedar reported to him. His tone was harsh, his face, Phillip saw, oddly drained of colour, as he added, "We'll hold our fire until they reach the camp site. Their cavalry and four guns are on the road we were following. Range on them as soon as you see them, Commander Hazard, my infantry can deal with theirs."

"Very good, sir," Phillip acknowledged and Cockayne rode off to place himself at the head of his Sikh cavalry to the left of the line. Phillip stood by his guns, straining his eyes into the moonlit, misty darkness as, one by one, the bivouac fires began to flicker out. The rebels came down through the trees, moving like ghosts, with scarcely a sound, and all along the tensely waiting British line, the men held their breath. Then suddenly the silence was broken, a burst of musket fire heralding the arrival of the rebel infantry at the foot of the slope. To the thunder of galloping hooves, the *zamindari* horsemen charged down on what they had supposed to be a sleeping camp, and two of their guns—horsed six-pounders, judging by their speed and manoeuvrability—unlimbered to the left of the bivouac site, to open on it with grape and roundshot.

Phillip trained his gun on the flashes and opened in answer as, all along the British line, the Enfields and Miniés spoke.

Taken by surprise and caught in a deadly enfilading fire, the rebels were thrown into confusion. The sepoy regiment, which had been leading the way down the thickly wooded slope in skirmishing order, hesitated and then broke. Leaving a number of scarlet-jacketed casualties behind them, they fled precipitately for the concealment of the trees, meeting the descending *zamindari* flintlock men and bringing them to a temporary halt. But they came on again bravely, putting the sepoys to shame. From the edge of the wood, a number attempted to reply to the British fire; others, with reckless courage, even made a ragged charge, their cavalry supporting them but none got further than the smouldering bivouac fires. Phillip's gunners, working with speed and disciplined skill, met them with a hail of grape—young Lightfoot, in command of the second gun, leaping into the air with his cap held aloft when a rebel ammunition tumbril exploded with a dull roar.

The attackers were in full and panic-stricken retreat when Colonel Cockayne waved the line forward and led his eager Sikh cavalry in a spirited charge on the only six-pounder that was still firing. Hacking and slashing with their sabres, the sowars cut down the gunners and galloped on in pursuit of the fleeing rebels. Not to be outdone, the infantry detachments rose up from behind their improvised breastworks and dashed after them, their long bayonets gleaming. Within a few minutes, they were once again in possession of their camp site, deserted now save for dead and dying rebels and three abandoned guns, to which Cockayne added a fourth, his cavalry riding back with it in triumph half an hour later. Their blood-stained sabres and sweating horses bore witness to the success of their pursuit but the Colonel allowed them no rest. He praised their zeal and courage and then despatched them to scout in the direction of the Sye River, ignoring the pleas of their grey-bearded old Subedar to give them time to rest and water their horses.

"Now we can press on," he told his assembled officers. "*Now* we can relieve my garrison at Ghorabad—we've drawn the Newab's teeth, shown him what British troops can do and left him in no doubt of our intentions. The column will move out immediately, gentlemen. If we bestir ourselves, we can still reach the river crossing by first light."

"I've scarcely had time to attend to my wounded, sir," the column's senior surgeon protested. "And there are enemy casualties too. It is inhumane to leave them."

Colonel Cockayne eyed him contemptuously and, watching his face, Phillip was deeply perplexed by what he saw in it.

"Rebel wounded are of no concern to me, Doctor," he told the surgeon brusquely. "As to our own, it surely would not tax your skill too highly to place—how many? Not above a dozen, I swear—in *doolies* and attend to them at our first halt. You've no serious casualties, have you?"

"I've a man whose arm must come off, Colonel," the surgeon said indignantly. "And as a Christian, sir, I—"

Cockayne cut him short. "Take the arm off and follow on with the baggage train," he ordered. "But do not waste your Christian pity on wounded heathens—least of all on mutinous sepoys, my friend. Their lives are forfeit, in any case, and if they die here, they've saved us the trouble of hanging them." He waved a hand in dismissal. "To your posts, gentlemen."

"My God!" Lieutenant Arbor fell into step beside Phillip. "He's a strange fellow, is he not, Commander? If I ever saw hate in a man's face, I saw it in the Colonel's just then. It's as if he can't kill enough rebels to satisfy his craving for revenge. I might understand it if they'd butchered his garrison at Ghorabad but, according to him, they're still holding the Newab at bay. So it can't be that—what is it, I wonder?"

Phillip shrugged. "I don't know," he confessed.

"Did he thank you for your timely warning?"

"No. It must have slipped his mind. But—"

"Without it," Arbor said soberly, "we should have fared badly, instead of gaining a significant victory. But we're not home yet, you know."

Phillip glanced at him enquiringly. "What do you mean?"

"The sepoys who attacked us were from Lucknow. Look—" he bent over the body of a dead sepoy, indicating the number on the man's shako. "The 48th Native Infantry. The *ryots* may have been the Newab's men, there's no way of telling, but the 48th NI were never with him; his sepoys and sowars are all Oudh Irregulars. I'm afraid we haven't met the bulk of his force yet."

"Then we may almost certainly expect to meet them at the river?" Phillip suggested. They reached the first of his guns and he gave the order to limber up. Lightfoot stared at him in surprise but, recovering, passed on the order.

Arbor sighed. "If they intend to fight, I imagine it will be there or thereabouts. There's a sizeable village this side of it, where they might well make a stand. I've been there, though I don't remember much about it, except that it's protected by jungle—much thicker than that up there, where you were attacked—and with a stream running across the road." He drew a rough plan with the toe of his boot in the sand and Phillip studied it with interest.

"If they have heavy guns, we should have our work cut out to shift them from a place like that," he said thoughtfully. "Is there no way round?"

"Only through the town itself," Arbor told him. "Or by river . . . which would mean getting hold of boats." They discussed the possibility of an enemy stand, watching the weary bullock teams being whipped and prodded to their feet and yoked once more to the guns. The men were as tired as their reluctant beasts, Phillip thought and, calling Petty Officer Devereux over, ordered an extra issue of grog before moving off.

"There's nothing to stop the Newab making a bolt for it, of course," Lieutenant Arbor remarked. His voice lacked conviction, but he added with a cynical smile, "He'd be welcomed with open arms in Lucknow, if he brought his troops with him, because that's where the real battle will be joined and he probably knows it."

"But you don't think he will bolt?"

Arbor shook his head. "No. I think it has become a personal vendetta between him and our Colonel Cockayne . . . and the Colonel is largely responsible for making it into one, though God knows why. He wants to avenge what he regards as betrayal, I suppose. But a great deal—everything, perhaps—depends on whether the garrison are still holding out. If they are, the Newab might make a run for it . . . but we don't know, do we? I heard a rumour that George Crawford had gone to try and find out, but that may not be true."

"It is," Phillip said. "He left the column the night before last."

"Did he, by God!" Arbor's bearded lips pursed in a silent whistle. "I thought I hadn't seen him about. Did he go alone, Commander?"

"Yes, he did."

"With or without the Colonel's knowledge?" Arbor questioned shrewdly.

"Without, as far as I am aware," Phillip answered. "So I should keep it to yourself until he gets back."

"*If* he gets back! It was a foolhardy thing to do but"—Arbor sighed—"by heaven, I admire his guts! Mind, if anyone can get away with it, Crawford will. He knows this area like the back of his hand and he may even have friends in Ghorabad—native friends, I mean, who may still be loyal. He was stationed there with Cockayne's regiment, but as he may have told you, they had an almighty row and George Crawford got himself transferred. Gossip had it that the row was over a woman but I don't know any details, although I believe that most of the sympathy was for Crawford."

This was not quite the same as the story Colonel Cockayne had told him, Phillip thought wryly, but he let it pass. The bugles sounded and, breathing hard from his exertions, Midshipman Lightfoot reported the gun teams yoked and ready to proceed. The men were looking and sounding more cheerful since the issue of their extra tot of rum and Phillip nodded his approval.

"Well done, Mr Lightfoot. Carry on, if you please."

A seaman brought him his horse and Arbor prepared to rejoin the baggage train. "We'll be held up by that blasted sawbones," he said glumly. "But doubtless we'll meet at the next halt, Commander—if we're permitted one!"

He strode off and Phillip climbed stiffly back into his saddle. His head was still throbbing but the acute pain had become a dull ache which, if not pleasant, was at least endurable and, as the column resumed its march, he resigned himself to the discomfort and, after a while, dropped off into a doze, letting his horse find its own way. Once or twice the animal stumbled from weariness and he was jerked back to wakefulness, but for the most part he slept, hunched in his saddle, and when the first halt was called, he found—to his own surprise—that his headache had gone and he was ravenously hungry.

They had made only four miles, Ensign Highgate told him, but had been compelled to halt to enable the baggage train and the wounded to catch up. His indignation sounded like a reflection of his Commanding Officer's and Phillip suppressed a smile as the young aide-de-camp continued on his way, in order—as he had expressed it—"to acquaint Lieutenant Arbor with the need for haste." He would get very little change out of the tough, experienced Arbor if he took that tone with him but . . . to the devil with Ensign Highgate! No doubt he would learn sense in time . . . Phillip dismounted, thankfully stretching his cramped limbs. The men, he saw, without waiting for his order, had unlimbered and were standing by their guns, the cooks already at work brewing water for coffee and the bullock drivers attending to their exhausted charges under Midshipman Lightfoot's exacting supervision.

"Well done, Mr Lightfoot," he said again, as the boy came to report to him. "You can post a look-out on each gun and let the crews stand down. At this rate, it will be noon before we reach the river, and I don't think we're in danger of another attack—at least until we sight the bridge."

"Aye, aye, sir." Lightfoot sang out the order and the seamen raised a subdued cheer. "You're not looking quite so groggy as you did last night, sir," the midshipman observed. "Are you feeling better?"

"A great deal better, thank you," Phillip assured him. He smiled ruefully. "I rather think I slept most of the way here. However when I've had coffee and a bite to eat, I'll be as right as rain, don't worry."

"I'll see you get it right away, sir," Lightfoot promised. He hesitated and then added, "Ensign Highgate said the Colonel was most concerned about you when the attack started last night."

"Was he, indeed?"

"Yes, sir." The midshipman's tone was unexpectedly stiff. "According to Highgate, he was afraid that command of the guns would have to be entrusted to a schoolboy—if you weren't fit, I mean, sir. Those were his words and I—"

"And you took offence?" Phillip suggested.

Lightfoot avoided his gaze. "I did, yes, sir. Coming from Highgate, it was . . . well, an insult and he'd no right to say it."

Phillip laid a hand on his shoulder. The boy was almost as tall as he was and, he reflected, inwardly amused, there were not very many schoolboys of seventeen who could lay claim, as young Lightfoot could, to be fighting in his third campaign. "You may tell Ensign Highgate from me, Mr Lightfoot, that I would entrust not only these guns but an entire ship's company to your command . . . and without a moment's hesitation, if the situation demanded it."

"You . . . would you really, sir?" Lightfoot flushed with pleasure.

"You know damned well I would!" Phillip grinned at him. "You are an officer in Her Majesty's Navy with nearly five years' service behind you, are you not?"

"Yes, sir." Lightfoot returned the grin a trifle sheepishly. "I'll see about your coffee, sir, I . . . thank you, sir."

The first pink tinges of sunrise were in the sky by the time the naval party had broken their fast and, after satisfying his hunger and gulping down two mugs of scalding black coffee, Phillip lay back, his head pillowed on his clasped hands, to take advantage of the last chance of relaxation he would probably get all day. The baggage train, preceded by a small procession of laden *doolies,* had just made its belated appearance and the men, as well as their cattle, would have to be permitted time to eat and rest, however impatient Colonel Cockayne might be to press on to the river. He could count on another half hour, he decided, and let his heavy lids fall.

But in spite of his feeling of weary lassitude, sleep did not come. He was anxious about George Crawford's continued absence and his recent conversation with Lieutenant Arbor had increased his anxiety. Arbor's opinion of his brother officer had, it was true, been reassuring. *"If anyone can get away with it, Crawford will,"* the grey-haired baggage master had said. *"He knows this area like the back of his hand and he may even have friends—native friends—in Ghorabad who may still be loyal."*

All the same, he had condemned Crawford's self-imposed mission as foolhardy and had gone on to hint that relations between Colonel Cockayne and the man he had so arbitrarily relieved of his staff duties had been strained for a long time— strained to the extent that Crawford had been compelled to transfer to another regiment. And . . . Phillip stifled a yawn. Both men, on different occasions, had offered differing reasons for "the almighty row"—as Arbor had put it—which had blown up between them. The Colonel's had been the more damaging and certainly the more vindictive; of the two men, he himself liked and trusted Crawford. His feelings were instinctive; his doubts as to Cockayne's ability as a commander and even of his sanity were much more than instinctive, however, and they had grown with each passing day. Now others, veteran campaigners like Arbor among them, were beginning to harbour the same doubts, to ask the same questions concerning the Colonel's motives that he had asked and yet . . . He sighed in frustration, conscious that weariness was dulling his wits, preventing him from thinking clearly. There were some questions he hadn't asked, because he had taken the answers to them for granted and, he supposed, because he regarded George Crawford as a friend and—like Arbor— admired his guts. But . . . why the devil *had* Crawford embarked on his perilous and entirely self-imposed mission?

His devotion to the Colonel's daughter was the answer that

instantly sprang to mind . . . and the one he himself had taken for granted. Many brave men had risked—and even sacrificed —their lives to save the women they loved since the outbreak of mutiny among the sepoy regiments, and there could be no doubt that George Crawford was a brave man. He had implied that he still cherished hopes of making Andrea Cockayne his wife, despite her father's opposition to the match but . . . was that his sole reason for taking his life in his hands and going— in defiance of the Colonel's authority—to Ghorabad? *Could* it be, when he had had no means of knowing whether the unhappy girl was alive or dead? When . . .

"Sir . . . Commander, sir, there's a party of horsemen approaching the column and I think Captain Crawford is with them, sir!" Midshipman Lightfoot sounded excited and Phillip roused himself, conscious of a pang. Dear God, and he had doubted a brave man, he reproached himself—doubted or, at any rate, questioned his motives . . . He sat up, feeling the sun warm on his face. "Are you all right, sir?" Lightfoot asked uncertainly, offering his arm. "Permit me to—"

Phillip shook his head impatiently and jumped up unaided. "I am perfectly all right, thank you, Mr Lightfoot. Where is Captain Crawford?"

"Over there, sir." The midshipman pointed and Phillip took out his Dollond. With its aid, he was able to see George Crawford quite clearly. He was sitting hunched in his saddle, as if in the last stages of exhaustion, and with him were four native riders, one of whom had a square of white cloth attached to his lance-tip, which he was waving vigorously as a Sikh cavalry piquet cantered forward to intercept them. The Sikhs encircled the new arrivals, their commander saluting and, under their escort, Crawford and his party trotted up to the head of the resting column. A few scattered cheers greeted them, as the men recognized Crawford and word of his return spread; then the scarlet-clad figure of Ensign Highgate could be seen, as he thrust his way officiously past the little group which had started to gather about Crawford's companions and the cheers faded abruptly to silence.

"He did it, by Jove!" Lieutenant Arbor was beside him and Phillip turned, smiling his relief.

"He did indeed. Shall we go and find out what news he has brought?"

"Without a summons from the Colonel?" Arbor demurred. "We shall be unwelcome, I fear, but I'm prepared to risk that, if you are, Commander."

"I think, for what it's worth, I owe George Crawford my support, Mr Arbor," Phillip said. "The more so because I—"

"Hold hard, sir," Arbor warned. He pointed, a wry little smile curving his lips. "Here comes the man himself—and he's come to ask for more than your support, by the look of things. For God's sake, that young idiot of an ADC appears to be trying to arrest him!"

Phillip followed the direction of his pointing finger, brows lifting in astonishment. George Crawford, still on his horse, was riding towards them, Ensign Highgate trailing after him on foot with drawn sword, his plaintive protests unheeded. A soldier, with seeming casualness, thrust out a booted foot and Highgate tripped over it, to measure his length on the dusty ground. When he jumped up, the man had vanished and blank, unsmiling faces met his angry gaze as he looked about him for the culprit.

Crawford, taking pity on him, said quietly, "All right, Benjy—go back to Colonel Cockayne and say that I will report to him as soon as I've washed the dust from my person."

Benjamin Highgate recognised defeat. He saluted stiffly

and obediently went to deliver his message. When he had gone, George Crawford slid wearily from his horse. His orderly, the big Highlander, Collins, appeared from nowhere bearing a bucket of water and a towel, and he gratefully plunged face and hands into the bucket, sloshing the tepid water it contained over head and neck.

"God, that's better!" He towelled himself briskly.

"Coffee?" Phillip offered. "Or this?" He held out his flask.

Crawford raised a wan smile. "Both, if you can spare them. I might as well be hung for a sheep as for a lamb! John"—he recognised Arbor—"do me a favour, will you please? See to it that the men I brought with me are well treated."

"Of course," Arbor assented readily. "Damned well done, George . . . and good luck!"

"Thanks," George Crawford acknowledged. He gulped down the coffee Lightfoot brought him, eyeing Phillip unhappily over the rim of his mug as he drank. The coffee finished, he splashed in whisky from the flask and sipped it with slow deliberation. "I'm playing for time, Hazard," he said at last. "Putting off the moment when I must face Colonel Cockayne with the unpalatable truth. I thought I should feel some elation at proving him wrong but I don't. I just feel—oh, God, a terrible sadness. You've guessed what the situation is, have you not?"

"Yes, I suppose so," Phillip admitted. "If you had brought good news, you'd hardly be keeping it to yourself. I take it the Colonel was wrong—or misinformed concerning his garrison? They are *not* still defending the fort?"

"No, they are not." Crawford met his gaze squarely. "But some of them have survived and the Newab is holding them as hostages. I don't know how many or in what condition—I was unable to find out. But I have been given to understand that most of the women and children are alive and that he's prepared to bargain for them. They . . ." He hesitated and then went on painfully, "the whole garrison surrendered at the end of August, when word reached them that General Havelock had been forced to return to Cawnpore. They held out for as long as they could—presumably in the hope that Havelock would succeed in relieving Lucknow and would then send them help. But they never had a chance. That damned fort was indefensible! Nevertheless"—tears glistened unashamedly in his dark eyes—"they managed to defend it for over six weeks."

"And what of Colonel Cockayne?" Phillip asked.

George Crawford's mouth tightened. "It would appear that the Newab's brother told us the truth before we hanged him."

"Then he knew of the surrender?"

"He could not have failed to, if he was there. Or even if he escaped before it took place—damn it, he *had* to know!"

They were silent, looking at each other in dismay, both reluctant to put their thoughts into words. Finally Phillip said, "Then why deny it, in heaven's name?"

"Because he knew he would never have been given troops for any purpose whatsoever *excepting* the relief of a British garrison under siege—and a surviving British garrison at that," Crawford returned bitterly. "Sir Colin Campbell's first objective is to secure Futtehghur and the Doab, after which he intends to launch a full scale attempt to recapture Lucknow. Lucknow has always been his main objective, Hazard. Punitive expeditions into Oudh come much lower in his scale of priorities—he made that abundantly clear and I'm quite sure that Cockayne was aware of it. But that's what this has been, from the start, has it not—a punitive expedition? Whatever excuses Cockayne may have made."

"Yes, without a doubt," Phillip confirmed, with equal bitterness.

Crawford controlled himself with a visible effort. "Taking the most charitable view of Colonel Cockayne's behaviour," he said. "I imagine he must have convinced himself that the entire garrison were murdered by the Newab following their surrender and that he's become obsessed with a desire to avenge them. I've racked my brains for another explanation and I can't find one. I cordially detest the man, as you know, but I cannot believe that even he would have risked the lives of the survivors of the garrison if he had known that there *were* any survivors—not with his wife and daughter among them."

His reasoning made sense, Phillip thought. It was the only possible explanation—unless, as at times he had feared, the Colonel's sufferings had reduced him to madness . . . Out of the tail of his eye, he glimpsed a file of red-jacketed soldiers moving towards them, an officer at their head.

"What now, my friend?" he asked, gesturing to the approaching file. "You are about to be summoned forcibly to the Colonel's presence, unless I'm much mistaken. You said that the Newab was prepared to bargain for the lives of his hostages, didn't you? Have you proof of that?"

"I have." George Crawford had himself under stern control now. "I have brought back his proposals for Cockayne's consideration and, please God, his acceptance. The Newab's *vakeel,* Mohammed Aslam, came with me to vouch for his master's good faith and to implement the terms, if Cockayne agrees to them. He—"

"Are they such that he can agree to them?" Phillip put in.

"He *must* agree to them; it's our only hope of getting the hostages out of Ghorabad alive! But"—for all his rigid control, Crawford's hand was trembling, Phillip realised, as he felt it close about his arm—"I dare not trust myself to put them to him without your backing, Hazard. I can count on you, can't I?"

"I'll back you to the hilt, my dear fellow," Phillip assured him. "Needless, I hope, to tell you, I echo John Arbor's sentiments. You've done magnificently!"

"Thanks," Crawford acknowledged. "Let us make poor Williams's task easier for him, shall we?"

They moved towards the approaching file, curious eyes following them. Captain Williams, red of face but determinedly formal, brought his escort to halt. "I have orders for you to report to Colonel Cockayne immediately, sir," he announced, addressing Crawford.

"Or to arrest me if I don't, Alan?" Crawford challenged dryly. "Is that it?"

"I . . . yes, I'm afraid so, I . . ." Poor young Alan Williams's colour deepened. "The Colonel is in quite a state. You are holding up the column and—"

"Don't worry, old man, I'll make my report to him at once. Commander Hazard will accompany me, so you may dismiss your escort."

"I can't," Williams said wretchedly. "But we'll fall in behind you and the Commander."

The Colonel was seated at his camp table, with half a dozen of the column's more senior officers grouped around him, their faces tense and anxious. The gathering had all the formality of a field court martial and it was evident, when the column's commander launched into a series of angry accusations against his one-time Chief of Staff, that he, at all events, was virtually treating it as such. George Crawford, having saluted, listened in impassive silence to the charges being levelled against him.

"Well?" Cockayne demanded wrathfully. "Do you deny

having absented yourself from this column without permission and contrary to my orders?"

"Not contrary to your orders, sir," Crawford defended. "You had given me no orders. Furthermore, sir, you had relieved me of my duties and—"

"Damme, sir, that did not mean that you were free to desert the column!" Cockayne flung at him. "And most certainly not for the—devil take it, for the purpose of treating with the enemy, as you appear to have done. You've brought four rebels back with you, have you not?"

"Under a flag of truce, yes, sir," Crawford amended. "If I may be permitted to explain?" He spoke firmly, aware that he had the attention of the other officers. "As your former Chief of Staff, Colonel, I was uneasy about the reports you had received as to the exact state of affairs in Ghorabad. You believed that the garrison was still successfully defending the fort and that they—"

"And are they not, Captain Crawford? Damme, I—"

"Alas, sir, they are not. I made a personal reconnaissance— without your permission, I concede—although I had twice begged you to allow me to lead a party of cavalry to make a reconnaissance of the city, in order to ascertain the situation there . . ." In careful detail, George Crawford described what he had found. He avoided any mention of the exact date of the surrender, Phillip noticed with warm approval, and made no counter-accusations and, watching Colonel Cockayne's face, he saw some of the anger fade from it, to be succeeded by a look of stunned disbelief when Crawford spoke of the survivors. But he said nothing, sitting slumped in his chair as the younger man went on, "The Newab is holding them as hostages, sir. He is willing to release them, if you agree to his terms."

There was a murmur of excitement among the assembled officers and, when Cockayne remained silent, a Captain of the 82nd asked eagerly, "What are the Newab's terms? Has he told you what they are?"

"They are quite simple," Crawford answered. "And I have brought his *vakeel*—Mohammed Aslam, who is known to you, Colonel—to put the proposals to you. We can send for him if you—"

Colonel Cockayne broke his self-imposed silence. "In a moment," he said thickly. "Outline them, Crawford."

"Very well, sir." Point by point, George Crawford went over the Newab's terms, and Phillip listened, his hopes rising. They were fair; the Newab had, it was evident, seen what Crawford had once described as "the writing on the wall." He wanted his city left in peace and his own status restored; he was to be pardoned for his part in the rebellion, in return for which he offered to renew his oath of loyalty to the British Raj and to disband his levies, when peace and order were finally restored in Oudh. The hostages would be released unharmed; boats would be provided and a small party permitted to go, under arms, up river to escort them back to the column. As soon as the hostages reached it, the column was to withdraw and return to Cawnpore, and it would be unmolested, provided no further hostile action was taken against villages in the Newab's territory.

"What guarantee does the fellow offer," the 82nd officer pursued, "that our boat party will be unmolested when it goes to pick up the survivors of the garrison?"

"He will leave his son with us," Crawford told him. "And the *vakeel* will accompany the boats. I think"—he glanced, smiling at Phillip—"that Commander Hazard may be willing to take command of the boats. They are to be armed and—"

"I shall be more than willing," Phillip responded. "And I can mount a rocket-launcher in one of the boats . . . with your permission, of course, sir." Deliberately, he addressed Cockayne and the Colonel, after a momentary hesitation, bowed his head. He seemed to have aged and there was an odd, downward quirk to his mouth but he said nothing, leaving his detachment commanders to question and discuss the Newab's proposed terms. They did so, at some length but all, Phillip sensed, were immensely relieved—as, indeed, he was himself. The *vakeel* was summoned; George Crawford and John Arbor went over the terms with him in his own language, translating his replies for the benefit of those officers who did not understand Hindustani.

"I can see no reason why the Newab's offer should not be accepted, Colonel," Arbor said and there was a concerted murmur of assent.

"Our orders were to effect the rescue of the garrison, sir," another officer put in eagerly. "We weren't aware that they had been compelled to surrender, of course, but we shall assuredly be acting in the spirit of our orders if we bring the survivors safely back with us. This column need risk no further casualties and, above all, sir, we shall be avoiding another Cawnpore. It's fortunate indeed that these poor people weren't butchered out of hand."

They were all looking at the Colonel now, appealing confidently for his assent and Phillip, adding his voice to theirs, saw again the look of incredulity in his face. Perhaps Crawford *had* supplied the answer, he thought; perhaps, after all, Colonel Cockayne had believed his entire garrison to be dead . . .

"You realise the risk you will be running, Commander Hazard?" Cockayne demanded suddenly. "The Newab is quite capable of betraying you, if you take those boats into the city."

"I'm quite prepared to take the risk, sir," Phillip told him. "If my party are armed and we have the rocket-launcher, I fancy he'll think twice about attacking us—if he's even considering such a possibility. We've no reason to suppose that he is—and he has offered to leave his son with you as a hostage, has he not, sir?"

"True," the Colonel conceded but without conviction. He started to interrogate the *vakeel* in fluent Hindustani; the old grey-bearded Muslim answered his questions with quiet dignity, addressing him courteously by name. Their exchange was too rapid for Phillip to follow, but it was evident that they knew one another well and that there was a certain mutual respect—if, probably, little liking—between them.

"This man admits the killing of all the civilians who took refuge, against my advice, in the Residency," the Colonel said. "As well as that of a number of officers, who were shot down when endeavouring to reach the fort. But he claims that the mutinied regiments were responsible, not the Newab—and that, I regret to say, I know to be true. However, he cannot—or will not—tell me how many survivors the Newab is holding to ransom." He paused, fixing Crawford with an icy stare. "Did your personal reconnaissance reveal their number, Captain Crawford, by any fortunate chance?"

Crawford shook his head. "Alas, no, sir. But Mohammed Aslam gave me an assurance that the women and children were spared—as he did to you, when you questioned him just now. And he told me that they had been well treated."

"Yet he insists he doesn't know how many of them are still alive!" Cockayne retorted scornfully.

"Surely it doesn't matter how many, sir," young Alan Williams suggested. "I mean, sir, if only three or four of the poor souls are left alive, is it not our duty to endeavour to save them when the opportunity is afforded to us? God knows what they must have suffered in the Newab's prison!" He added diffidently, "And some of them are children, sir."

Again there was a concerted murmur of agreement and a spasm of pain flicked across the Colonel's round, red face as George Crawford said forcefully, "If we reject the Newab's terms for the release of those he is holding hostage, Colonel, he could order their deaths before we could get within sight of the city. And we should be powerless to prevent him. He—"

"Has he threatened to put them to death?" the 82nd Captain demanded, in a shocked tone. "*Has* he, Crawford?"

"Not in so many words, my dear Grayson. But the threat is implied in his offer of terms—that is the strength from which he is attempting to bargain with us."

Crawford turned to the *vakeel* and spoke to him in his own language; the old man nodded vigorously and then held out his hands in mute and moving appeal to the anxious group of officers surrounding him. The Colonel reproved him sharply and the Newab's envoy drew himself up affronted, to unleash a spate of words, whose meaning—although the actual words were unintelligible to most of the others—was nonetheless clear to them all. He started to move away and Captain Grayson, very white of face, laid a restraining hand on his arm, and returned with him to the Colonel's side.

"Surely, sir," he urged, "we must accept the Newab's terms; what choice have we? As Captain Crawford says, he is bargaining from strength. We cannot risk the lives of British women and children, and this fellow here"—he gestured to the old *vakeel*—"is well aware of it. I beg you to give him your assent, sir."

Colonel Cockayne eyed him with ill-concealed contempt.

"So you would allow a proscribed traitor to go unpunished,

in return for some vague promise that he will release an unspecified number of hostages—is that it, Captain Grayson? For heaven's sake, man, the whole story is probably a tissue of lies! The Newab betrayed us once and he'll betray us again. I know him, and he's not to be trusted. He—"

It was the most he could say without revealing his fear that the whole garrison had been slaughtered, Phillip thought. He met George Crawford's worried gaze and turned to face the Colonel.

"That has yet to be proved, sir," he countered.

"*Proved,* Commander Hazard?"

"Yes, sir. We don't know the Newab's intentions and we don't know how many of your garrison he is holding as hostages. I'm willing to put it to the test. Agree to the terms, Colonel, and permit me to take the boats up river. If the Newab does mean to betray us, he will have to show his hand when I reach the city, so you will have ample warning . . . and the Newab's son, as *your* hostage. What have you to lose, sir?"

"Are you offering me advice again, Commander Hazard?" Cockayne demanded unpleasantly. "You are a naval officer, for God's sake—what do you know of this country and its people? Damme, sir, I've had a lifetime's experience of them and yet *you* presume to tell me what I should or should not do in this situation! The decision is mine, sir, and mine alone, since I shall be called upon to bear the responsibility for your loss if you put your head into a trap. Your loss and that of the only experienced gunners this force possesses—do I have to remind you of that, Commander? Not to mention the freeing of a despicable traitor, who justly deserves to be hanged!"

Phillip drew himself up, as the *vakeel* had done a few minutes before. He was suddenly angry with this stiff-necked, arrogant Company's officer who, it seemed, wanted only to avenge his own real or imagined sufferings. Remembering the heartless butchery Cockayne had instigated at Betarwar and the two other ill-defended native villages, he said, with intentional harshness, "I'm offering a way out of an impasse, sir, and I'll leave you two guns' crews and my second-in-command, if you wish; they can be replaced by volunteers from your infantry. I . . ." He hesitated and then plunged in, his resolution hardening as he saw that the Colonel was about to argue with him, "In the name of humanity, sir, these hostages are British women and children—and your wife may be among them! Your wife and—"

Colonel Cockayne cut him short. "Very well, Commander Hazard, on your head be it. Make what arrangements are necessary with the Newab's agent; I wash my hands of responsibility for your safety or that of any volunteers who accompany you. It is evident to me, gentlemen," he added wearily, addressing the other detachment commanders, "that you are all—if I may say so in your ignorance—of a like mind to Commander Hazard in this matter. Am I correct in that assumption?"

There were no dissenting voices and Captain Grayson answered formally, "We are, sir."

"Then we will continue our advance to the river," Cockayne ordered. "Return to your detachments, gentlemen, and take post. The advance will be sounded in fifteen minutes. No, not you, Hazard"—as Phillip prepared to accompany the others—"I should like a word with you in private."

"Very good, sir." Phillip waited, hiding his impatience. When they were alone together, he realised that the Colonel's appearance and manner had undergone a startling change; the older man looked defeated and apprehensive and, as they discussed the arrangements for manning the boats, his voice had lost its customery hectoring arrogance. The various details of procedure settled, he appended his signature to the paper setting out the Newab's terms for the release of the hostages and proffered it, an odd little smile playing about his lips.

"Here you are. Let Mohammed Aslam take this back to his master. I warn you, it's probably your death warrant, Hazard—but you would have it, wouldn't you?"

"I'm sorry, sir," Phillip said stiffly. "But honestly I—"

It was as if he had not spoken. The Colonel went on, a bitter edge to his voice, "In view of which I shall tell you—in confidence—what I have never told another living soul. You are a man of honour, Hazard, however misguided . . . I can, I hope, trust you to respect my confidence, whatever may be the outcome of this affair?"

"Of course, Colonel," Phillip assured him. "But it isn't necessary. I'm not asking—"

"It will ease my conscience to tell you," Cockayne said. "God knows I have borne the awful burden of it alone for long enough. I've come near to breaking under the strain at times. I . . . you asked about my wife, Hazard."

"Colonel Cockayne, there's no need for you to tell me anything," Phillip began awkwardly, anticipating what was to come. "Believe me, sir, you—"

Again it was as if Cockayne had not heard him. His face had drained of its ruddy colour and the hard, bloodshot blue eyes held the unexpected glint of tears.

"My beloved wife is dead, Hazard. She died in my arms and at my hands." His voice was barely above a whisper and Phillip, appalled, had to strain his ears to hear it. "At her request, when we knew that we could hold out no longer, I put a bullet into her heart to prevent her falling alive into the hands of these fiends. A number of the others did the same. We . . . after what happened to the Nana's poor victims at Cawnpore, we dared not surrender them alive and . . . Sir Henry Lawrence had advised it, if the Lucknow Residency fell. Besides"—his voice rose—"we had all seen what the Newab did to those who tried to defend the Commissioner's house. He had them mutilated and beheaded in full view, outside our fort. Do you wonder that I want him to pay the penalty for his treachery, for the atrocities he committed when he believed that the power of the British Raj was waning?"

"I . . . no, sir, I do not," Phillip admitted honestly. This was worse, infinitely worse than he had expected, and he shuddered involuntarily, as a mental vision of the horrors the Ghorabad garrison had endured swam before his eyes. Poor devil, he thought, conscious of the stirrings of pity as he looked at Cockayne's ravaged face . . . poor, unhappy devil . . . what an intolerable burden of guilt and remorse he had been compelled to bear all these months since the surrender! God help him, it was a burden that would have broken most men . . .

"I escaped, thanks to the loyalty of two of my native officers," the Colonel continued bleakly. "They hid me in the city for weeks, at the risk of their lives, and when the mutinied regiments went to Lucknow, they procured a horse for me and smuggled me out. I got no further than Betarwar, where I was robbed and tortured, and then driven naked into the jungle to die . . . by the man I hanged, two days ago. I had no desire to live but . . ." He sighed. "I survived by a miracle and reached Cawnpore. Since then I have had only one thought, one ambition—to return here, with British troops at my back. I did not care what lengths I had to go to in order to get them; I was ready to perjure myself to Sir Colin Campbell. I . . . you realise I *did* perjure myself, don't you?"

"Yes, sir," Phillip said quietly. "I realise that and I can't blame you. But—"

"But you are still determined to take those boats to the city?" Cockayne accused. "Hazard, I believe I am the only survivor of the garrison. When you go—no, dear God, *if* you go—I tell you, in all sincerity, that the only hostages you are likely to have released to you will be the wives and children of Eurasian Christians . . . clerks' families and the like. Are you willing to risk your neck for them?"

"I cannot go back on my word now, sir," Phillip said. "And nor can you." He gestured to the paper in his hand. "We have to honour this, if there is the smallest chance of finding any of your garrison alive. Crawford is convinced that some of them were spared and the *vakeel* bears out his belief—he swore it, in front of us all, did he not?" Thinking of George Crawford, he added, "Your daughter, sir—can you be certain that she—"

"My daughter?" The Colonel stared at him blankly for a moment and then said, his voice charged with bitterness, "She, poor, sweet child, was with those who took refuge with the Commissioner in his Residency. I can only pray that her sufferings are long since ended." He paused, his frowning gaze on Phillip's face, as if hoping, even now, for a reversal of his decision. Receiving none, he took his watch from his pocket. "You'd better take post, Hazard—it's time we moved off. The boats are to be waiting for us at the river, I understand?"

"Yes, sir."

"Very well." Colonel Cockayne was himself again, brusque and autocratic. "Since you are still set on taking this dangerous gamble, you have my permission to ride ahead of the column with a cavalry escort, so that you may inspect them and arrange for the mounting of the rocket-tube. It will probably be dark before you can start up river and you won't be able to see much, so I advise you to keep in midstream until you reach the city. At the first sign of treachery, open fire with your rockets on the Newab's palace. It's on the east bank—I'll see you are provided with a plan of its location. Withdraw downstream when you have set it ablaze and I will bring the column in to storm the city from the west bank. Is that quite clear?"

"Quite clear, Colonel," Phillip acknowledged, his voice devoid of expression. "Will that be all, sir?"

Colonel Cockayne gave him a mirthless smile and held out his hand. "It is, I understand, a tradition of your Service that even its most junior officers are trained to act on their own initiative and accept the responsibilities of command in any situation? That's so, is it not?"

"It is, sir. But—"

"Then I shall pray, Commander Hazard," Cockayne said sardonically, "that you find your naval training adequate for *this* situation. I give you good day, sir!"

CHAPTER SEVEN

The city of Ghorabad was a ghostly vista of huddled buildings and loopholed walls in the wan moonlight, the silence broken only by the splash of oars as the three boats slowly approached their objective.

Standing in the bows of the leading boat, Phillip felt his stomach muscles tense as he looked about him. A few feet behind him, Petty Officer Devereux crouched, with Oates and the two loaders, Cole and Bustard, beside their long-barrelled rocket-launcher, which was mounted just forward of the single stubby mast. This was the largest of the boats the Newab had provided, with a crew of ten native oarsmen. All three were broad-beamed country boats, used normally to carry cargoes of rice and corn, with straw-roofed awnings covering two-thirds of their deck space. Steered by a sweep from a wooden platform in the stern, they were awkward to handle and, after some thought, Phillip had decided to retain their native crews, posting his own men, armed with rifles, to watch over them. He had been cheered by the spacious accommodation for passengers and by the fact that clean sacks and straw had been laid out beneath the awnings, in readiness to receive the released hostages in some degree of comfort. His own boat could take twenty-five or thirty, each of the others about half that number but Colonel Cockayne, when this was pointed out to him, had retorted cynically that the Newab was adept at deception.

For all that, he appeared to be keeping his side of the bargain. The boats had been waiting, when the British column reached the river and his son—a handsome youth of seventeen or eighteen—had appeared shortly afterwards with a small escort of *zamindari* horsemen, who had ridden back to the city, leaving the boy alone in the Colonel's custody. A little later, the old *vakeel* had returned, bearing the Newab's signature to the agreed terms, and he was with them now, squatting under the awning, apparently asleep, his long white cloak wrapped about his bony frame against the chill night air . . .

Phillip sighed. The only evidence of hostile intent on the part of the Newab and his people had been the destruction of the Bridge of Boats across the river and clearly Colonel Cockayne had expected this, since he had stated specifically that, if he attacked the city, he would do so from the west bank. According to the plan, there was a second bridge in the heart of the city itself which . . .

"There's the Newab's palace, over to your right, Hazard." George Crawford came to stand beside him. "I was instructed to make sure you knew its precise location."

"Thanks," Phillip returned dryly. "I can guess by whom." Nevertheless he made a careful survey of the sprawling building, with its twin watch-towers silhouetted starkly against the night sky and, as an added precaution, pointed it out to Devereux and the rocket-crew.

"The fort is beyond the palace," Crawford said. "Or it was—there's very little of it standing now, so I doubt if you can see it. And you won't see much of the old Cantonments either, or the Civil Lines. The Pandies set fire to them before they departed for Lucknow—as well, needless to say, as the Treasury, the *Cutcherry* and the Jail and all the other symbols of British rule. They were situated to your left, on the far side of the bazaar and the native city, with poor Hardacre's Residency beyond them again, between the Civil Lines and the city. The *ghat*—that is the landing stage—we're making for is the one these boats normally unload at, to the rear of the Subzee Bazaar on the west bank. We should see lights and some sign of activity there when we clear the walls."

Following the direction of his pointing finger, Phillip was able to make out the close-packed cluster of flat-roofed native dwellings which constituted the city, the monotony of its sky-line broken by a few domed mosques and the burnt-out shells of tall stone buildings which had once housed Ghorabad's British rulers and administrators. It looked dark and curiously menacing and there were few signs of the activity Crawford had predicted, when the landing stage came in sight about half a mile distant, ahead and to their left, a line of moored and deserted boats alongside it.

"Do you think," Phillip asked, lowering his voice so that the men behind him would not hear the question, "that the Newab *is* likely to betray us, Crawford?"

George Crawford drew in his breath sharply. "And I can guess by whom that question was prompted, my dear Hazard! In answer to it, however—no, I don't think he is. I should not have brought his proposed terms or urged their acceptance if I had believed that there was a serious risk of his breaking his word."

"I'm sorry," Phillip offered quickly. "I shouldn't have asked you such a question. Forgive me."

"Don't apologise, my dear fellow. My confidence in the Newab is based on his well-known desire for self-preservation."

Crawford laughed, with wry amusement. "He likes to be on the winning side—that was why he threw in his lot with the rebels initially. But now, as I suggested to you not long ago, I fancy he's seen the writing on the wall. If we win the battle for Oudh—as we shall—he knows that both his life and his lands will be forfeit. A pardon will suit him admirably . . . with that in his possession, he's playing safe. Also he let his Pandy regiments go to Lucknow and one thing I did find out is that he hasn't gathered the large force of *zamindari* troops I thought he would to defend the city. He probably hasn't more than twelve or fourteen hundred here at present. That state of affairs could change, I'm compelled to admit—it could change tonight."

"In which case," Phillip said, "he might still go back on his word?"

"He might," Crawford conceded. "But only, I think, if he's driven to it. Or . . ." He frowned. "If the Colonel's right and he *cannot* give us our women and children. I've had to steel myself to the possibility that they may all be dead, Hazard . . . and Andrea among them."

"Cockayne's convinced that none of them were spared. He told me we should be given Eurasian Christians, not British women and children."

"If any of *them* survived!" Crawford spoke grimly. "According to the *vakeel,* they were the first victims of the mutiny, poor souls—as they were in many other stations. Defenceless, living in or near the native city, neither wholly Indian nor acceptably British—if they weren't in the Company's service, nobody gave a damn for them. But . . ." He hesitated. "The Colonel talked to you this morning, didn't he, Hazard? I take it that what he told you was confidential?"

Phillip's gaze was on the landing stage. There were a few

lights there now, his mind registered, and men moving about the steps leading down to it, but no sign of any women or children. "A good deal of it was, yes," he confirmed. "And I gave him my word that I would respect his confidence. I can tell you, though, that you were right in some of the conclusions you drew. He *did* lie to get these troops and, as I said, he is convinced that the entire garrison perished months ago. He—"

"*Did* he desert them?" Crawford asked harshly.

Phillip turned to look at him. "No, I think not. He was here when they surrendered and he said his escape was contrived by two of his native officers. They kept him hidden in the city and then smuggled him out just before the Pandy regiments left for Lucknow. He said he got as far as Betarwar and—"

"For God's sake, Hazard!" George Crawford cut him short. "If he was here after the surrender, he *knows* what happened . . . and he's probably right about the Newab. The swine does intend treachery; he's trying to bluff us, to play for time. If that's the case, what the devil are you doing here? Why are you risking your neck in this—this forlorn hope—when Cockayne told you quite definitely that his people are dead? I don't understand you." His face was very white in the moonlight, his tone almost accusing. "You could have left it to me— I have a stake in this but you haven't. Dammit, man, you didn't even know any of them—you're a naval officer!"

Trained to act on his own initiative, according to Colonel Cockayne, Phillip reflected cynically and . . . what else had he said? *To accept the responsibilities of command in any situation*—well, perhaps there was something in that, after all. He had been too occupied with his preparations for the forlorn hope to analyse his reasons for deciding to embark on it, but he attempted to do so now, realising when he thought about it that most of them were rooted in his mistrust of Cockayne.

"For a start," he said, "I agreed wholeheartedly with young Williams. If only three or four of the poor souls are left alive, I think we have a duty to try to save them . . . even if they're Eurasian Christians and, as you put it, not acceptably British. None of us knows for certain whether or not the Newab's hostages are survivors of the garrison—even Cockayne must have doubts on that score. This is the only chance we've got to *be* certain and frankly, George, my friend"—he laid a hand on Crawford's shoulder—"I'd infinitely rather risk my neck than try to live with my conscience if I failed to take it. Besides, I had a sister in General Wheeler's garrison at Cawnpore and that, I believe, gives me a stake in this affair—in spite of the fact that I'm a sailor, not a soldier."

George Crawford eyed him in shocked silence for a moment; then he nodded. "What's the correct nautical expression—glad to have you aboard? Speaking from the heart . . . I'm damned glad, Phillip. Because there's something wrong, you know." He gestured to the landing stage. "I can't see anyone on that blasted *ghat,* except boatmen and coolies. If the Newab intends to release his hostages to us, it's time they were there."

"Give them a hail," Phillip suggested. "We're not very adequately lit; perhaps they haven't seen us."

The hail, in Hindustani, evoked only some shrill-voiced chatter from the natives on the landing stage and Crawford, after a brief exchange shouted across the murky water, shook his head despondently. "They say they know nothing of any memsahibs . . . and I believe them. They're scared out of their wits."

As if to prove the truth of his words, there was a mass flight up the steps from the *ghat.* At the head of the wide steps was a rambling wooden building, Phillip noticed—a storehouse or *godown* of some kind, with a flat roof. It lay deep in shadow and the fleeing coolies gave it a wide berth as they ran, tumbling over each other in their eagerness to escape into the narrow confines of the bazaar beyond. He took out his Dollond and subjected the *godown* to a careful scrutiny, as Crawford said, "Devil take it—there *is* something wrong! I'll question Mohammed Aslam."

The old *vakeel,* wakened from sleep and dragged unceremoniously from beneath the shelter of the straw-thatched awning by Crawford and his orderly, was gibbering with fear and, Phillip decided, as bewildered as they themselves were by the absence of his master's hostages.

"He says they should be here," Crawford translated angrily. "And he thinks there's just been a slight delay, because the Newab ordered them to be brought here when he received Cockayne's signed agreement to the terms. And," he added, his voice shaking, "he tells me now, damn his eyes, that they've been held in a rat-infested cellar at the Newab's palace . . . which means they have to cross the river and pass through the city to get here. He thinks that may be the cause of the delay and he's offered to go and make enquiries, if we put him ashore. What do you think—shall we let him go?"

Phillip studied the old man's face, seeing the fear which had suddenly replaced the bewilderment in his rheumy eyes and the spittle on his beard from the vehemence of his protests. He had been inclined to trust the dignified old native, to believe that he, at least, had spoken the truth but now . . . he shook his head. Every instinct warned him that the Newab intended to betray them and that his *vakeel*—if he hadn't suspected this initially—was only too well aware of it now. Or perhaps he, too, had been betrayed . . .

"No, we'll keep him aboard, George," he decided. "With a

pistol to his head, in the hope that his nerve will break and he'll tell us what his master is up to. But in case he doesn't, I'm going to take a party ashore to investigate that *godown* . . ." He pointed to the tall, shadowed building at the rear of the landing stage, measuring the distance with his eye. If he took the boat in without lights and landed his party at the extreme end of the *ghat,* it was just possible that they might circle round it without being observed. The other boats could act as decoys and come in to the support of his party if they were required. He turned to the rocket-crew. "I'm going ashore, Devereux. Haul off when we've landed. You know your target. Open fire on it at once if my shore party strike trouble. Oates, douse all lights and then take over the sweep and bring us in as quietly as you can. Steer for the end of the landing stage, under the shadow of that wall—see?"

"Aye, aye, sir." Oates was on his feet, alert and competent.

Phillip gave his orders crisply, directing the other boats into mid-stream. "Keep a guard on your boatmen and paddle in slowly," he called across to Grayson, who was in command of the nearer of the two. "Talk, make as much noise as you can and keep your lights burning. Come in at your discretion if you hear us open fire."

Grayson waved a hand in acknowledgement and George Crawford asked, his voice sharp with anxiety, "You don't think the women are in that *godown,* do you? Because if they are—"

"I don't know," Phillip admitted. "But it's certainly occupied and I propose to find out by whom. I'll take six men with me and try to surprise them."

"I'll come with you," Crawford said and, as Phillip hesitated, "For God's sake—Benjy can command the boat."

"Benjy?" He had forgotten Ensign Highgate, Phillip realised, but the boy was there, his plump young face pink with supressed excitement. "All right," he agreed reluctantly, wishing Highgate were Lightfoot. "No heroics, Mr Highgate. Your task is to set the Newab's palace on fire *if* my shore party comes under attack and you can leave Petty Officer Devereux to do what's required—understand? If we're not attacked, bring the boat in with the others on my signal."

"Very good, sir," Highgate said happily. "You can rely on me, Commander Hazard. Shall I"—he nodded in the direction of the old *vakeel*—"shall I guard the prisoner?"

Crawford relinquished his hold on the old man's shoulder. "You're welcome to him, Benjy. But treat him fairly; we don't know that he's betrayed us yet."

The boat glided in towards the darkened *ghat,* now seemingly deserted and Phillip, peering with narrowed eyes into the shadows, could see nothing calculated to alarm him. But there was neither sight nor sound of the hostages in the narrow streets behind the *godown,* there were no swaying lanterns or torches, no clattering escort . . . so either the hostages were still in the Newab's noisome cellars and he had no intention of releasing them or . . . he felt his throat tighten. Or else there were no hostages, no survivors of the Ghorabad garrison, not even the poor Eurasian Christians, and this was a trap, into which—against the advice of Colonel Lionel Cockayne—he was obstinately walking of his own volition. He shivered, finding the night strangely cold.

The men in the other boats were acting their parts admirably. He could hear the distant hum of voices, laughter and the splashing of oars and, out of the corner of his eye, could discern a lantern waving, as if someone were holding it above his head. And then, to his dumbfounded amazement, he heard something else—a single voice, a woman's voice, raised in song and coming from the darkness ahead. It was a faint sound, the singing not particularly tuneful and it was not until, hesitantly at first, other voices joined in the singing that he recognised it for what it was.

"O God our help in ages past . . . our hope for years to come . . ." Dear heaven, it was a hymn, an English hymn and English voices were singing it! Women's voices, children's . . .

"Phillip, do you hear that?" George Crawford gripped his arm and stumbled as the boat came alongside the landing stage with a grinding jerk. "You were right, by God, you were right—they're there, in the *godown!* They're alive!" He flung himself out of the boat, to stumble again and pitch forward face down on the uneven ground.

Phillip followed him, cursing under his breath, and helped him to his feet. "Steady, old man," he cautioned as the riflemen he had chosen stepped gingerly on to the crumbling stone landing stage. "They may have prepared a warm reception for us, so easy does it, my lads. Spread out and follow me. And not a sound out of any of you, understand? Mr Highgate, hold your boat here!"

Keeping to the shadows, he led his landing party up the steps towards the *godown.* It was smaller than it had seemed from the river and more dilapidated, with wooden shutters on its windows and a heavy, iron-bound door. The singing continued as they approached it, growing in volume as more voices took up the refrain and Crawford whispered eagerly, "Why don't you hail them? I can't see any guards. They've just been brought here and abandoned. Surely we should let them know we're here? Poor souls, they—"

"Quiet, for the love of heaven," Phillip besought him. "They know we're here; that's why they are singing. But we must take a look at the place first. We—" A high-pitched shriek froze the words on his lips and the singing ceased as suddenly as it had begun. A smell of burning assailed his nostrils and, an instant later, smoke and flames started to rise from the shuttered *godown*. Three men with lighted flares in their hands came running from behind the building, but they got no further than the top of the steps. "Let the swine have it!" Phillip yelled and four Enfields spoke almost in unison. "You—" he grabbed one of the riflemen by the shoulder and spun him round in the direction from which they had come—"call the boats in—all of them! Tell Mr Highgate to land his crew—look lively!"

George Crawford was ahead of him, running towards the building like a man demented, head bent, a cry on his lips. The *godown* was tinder-dry, and in a matter of minutes, was engulfed in flames, the shrieks and sobs which had been coming from it succeeded by an ominous silence. The men, without waiting for orders, were smashing the shutters with their rifle butts and tearing at them with their bare hands, oblivious to pain and danger alike. They had been only a few yards away when the fire had started. Had they been in the boats, Phillip's bemused brain registered, they would have been too late—much, much too late. But as it was . . . He gritted his teeth and hurled himself at one of the windows. As it was, they had a fighting chance.

The wood in front of him shattered, he drew a deep breath and clambered over it, to find himself in an inferno, blinded by smoke. Afterwards he could not have said how many pathetic, half-clad bodies he dragged out of the *godown's* blazing interior or how many of those he managed to carry to the comparative safety of the steps outside were alive or dead. Highgate's party came swiftly to their aid but, by the time the other two boats' crews joined them, the fire had sunk to smouldering quiescence and, with Grayson and Arbor, he staggered back into the burnt-out storehouse, aware that now they could expect to find only the dead and dying. Among them, to his stunned distress, they found George Crawford. The roof beams had collapsed, pinning him beneath the rubble, and when they freed him it was evident to all three of them that his injuries were mortal.

But he was conscious and, when they laid him on the steps, he whispered painfully, "Phillip, she is alive . . . Andrea is alive. I found her and . . . I brought her . . . out. I'd be . . . obliged if you could . . . ask her to come to me. It was . . . like a . . . miracle, finding her in the smoke. God guided me, I think, because . . . I could not see her face. But it . . . was Andrea, I'm . . . sure it was."

Phillip glanced at Arbor in mute question. The baggage-master shrugged helplessly. "They are the survivors of the British garrison all right—that's all I know. Shall we start taking them to the boats? We could be attacked if we linger here."

Phillip nodded and, sick with pity, went in search of Colonel Cockayne's daughter, calling her by name and only half expecting to find her. The withdrawal to the boats was, of necessity, slow; the women, many of whom were badly burnt, had to be carried or led, step by step, to where the boats were moored. But at least there was no sign of an impending attack and, leaving Arbor in charge of the evacuation, Phillip made a round of the sentries with Grayson and then returned, with a heavy heart, to where he had left George Crawford. By the faint glow of a lantern someone had placed on the steps above, he saw that a woman in a torn, smoke-blackened native sari was kneeling beside the injured man. She turned her head at his approach and he found himself looking into a thin, pale face from which all trace of youthful beauty and vitality had vanished. A livid weal circled her cheeks, swollen and bleeding, where the lash of a whip had left its unmistakable mark and he stared down at her, shocked into silence by this evidence of a cruelty he had hitherto only imagined.

"He is dead," she told him, gesturing to the still form which lay between them. Her eyes, sunk deep into the bones of her ravaged face, were very blue and empty of the tears he had expected, her voice flat and devoid of emotion as she asked, almost casually, "Who is he, please?"

Her composure and her seeming lack of womanly feeling took Phillip aback. But some of the Lucknow ladies, he recalled, had shown this same, oddly callous indifference to death. His sister Harriet had explained it, with brief bitterness, when he had asked her the reason. *"We often envied the dead, even though we loved them . . ."* He glanced again at the girl's scarred cheeks and caught his breath, seeking vainly for words which would soften the blow he must deal her.

"Don't you know him, Miss Cockayne?"

Andrea Cockayne shook her head. "I don't think so. A soldier insisted on taking me to him—a Highland soldier, who kept saying he needed me. But he was dead when I reached him and there was nothing I could do. Was he a friend of yours?"

"Yes," Phillip responded. He added gently, "His name is—was—George Crawford. He carried you out of the fire and he was in your father's regiment at one time. I believe that he—"

The girl got to her feet, cutting him short. "Oh," she said. "I remember now; my father disliked him for some reason. They quarrelled and Captain Crawford left the regiment. But . . . that was more than a year ago. I never saw him again and—I did not know him well. Poor man . . . I am so sorry he had to die like this. But he didn't carry me out of the fire. A sailor did. I . . ." She studied his face dispassionately. "I think it was you, was it not?"

"Was it?" Phillip's tone was stiff, for all the effort he made to control it. George Crawford had loved this girl, he thought. He had risked and lost his life for love of her, had for years dreamed of making her his wife but she, it seemed, had forgotten him, claiming that she had not known him well. Dear heaven, how vain had been his sacrifice! He looked down at George Crawford's dead face and anger momentarily transcended pity. He said, a distinct edge to his voice, "I have no clear recollection of that, Miss Cockayne. I was not searching for anyone in particular, but Captain Crawford was—he was searching for *you.*"

She stared at him in frank bewilderment. "I'm sorry; I've offended you. That was the last thing I intended to do. I . . . I'm grateful to you and to poor Captain Crawford. We all are. We . . . that is, they meant to kill us, you know. To burn us alive . . . after telling us that you were coming and that we were to be freed."

"Yes," Phillip managed, ashamed of his churlishness. "We shot three men who were running away with flares in their hands."

"They were obeying the Newab's orders," Andrea Cockayne told him. "They said it was to avenge Betarwar—perhaps you know what they meant? We had no idea. We . . . to us, it was the final act of cruelty. They let us hope—we had been waiting here for more than three hours for your boats to come. The guards had left us, except for those three. We prayed and we heard your voices, *English* voices and the . . . the splash of oars . . . so we started to sing. And then . . ." Suddenly, her control broke and she was sobbing, remembered terror in the tear-filled blue eyes.

Deeply moved, Phillip took her in his arms, shocked anew to feel through the ragged sari how thin and frail she was. Behind the brave pretence of composure, there was a frightened, half-starved child, he thought contritely. A child who had been tortured almost beyond endurance, beaten and humiliated and finally deceived by a promise of freedom which her tormentors had never intended to keep . . . And he, God forgive him, had seen fit to reproach her because, during her long ordeal, she had failed to remember the name of a man who had once loved her. He laid his cheek on her scarred one, tasting the salty bitterness of her tears, and held her close, letting her weep. Then, when the first paroxysm had passed, he stripped off his jacket, charred by the flames, and gently wrapped it about her shoulders.

"I'll take you to the boat, Andrea," he said. "Come, child, you're free now and safe, please God."

She went with him without a word. Arbor came to him when he had left her, in Highgate's care, aboard the boat. The baggage-master was white to the lips and cursing savagely. "God in heaven, I hope I never have to see the like of this night's work again!" he exploded.

"How many?" Phillip asked.

"Thirty-two, Commander, of whom eleven are children. And six dead . . . but that number could be doubled before we get back to the column. I've put the living in the first two boats, and the dead in mine. I take it we can bring the dead back with us, so that they may have Christian burial?"

"Yes," Phillip agreed, his throat tight. "That, at least, we can do for them. And . . . add George Crawford's body to your cargo."

"He's dead, poor devil?"

"Yes, you'll find him where we left him, at the top of the steps. How about our men? Any of them injured?" Arbor shook his head. "Burns, of course, but nothing serious, as far as I know. They're not complaining, any more than you are." He jerked his thumb at Phillip's blistered hands and ruefully extended his own for comparison. "We're the fortunate ones— but some of those children . . . dear God, they'd break your heart! It's a miracle any of them got out alive."

He went off, with Crawford's orderly, in search of the Captain's body and Phillip called in the sentries. The boats put off, the native boatmen still at their oars, and Petty Officer Devereux asked gruffly, when Phillip joined him beside the rocket-launcher, "Is our target still the same, sir? I reckon it wouldn't do no 'arm ter morale if we was to leave them swine with somethin' ter remember us by."

By heaven, it would not Phillip thought, with bitter satisfaction . . . it would do no harm at all. Then he remembered— the firing of the Newab's palace was to be the signal for Colonel Cockayne to launch an attack on the city, and he gave Devereux a reluctant headshake.

The pathetic survivors of the garrison had to be escorted safely to Cawnpore. Cockayne, once committed to an attack, might not pull out and, with sixty miles of hostile country to cover, the column could afford no losses. Retribution would have to be postponed.

"No, Chief," he said firmly. "We shall only return fire if we are attacked."

"But, sir!" The grey-haired petty officer regarded him in

stunned astonishment. Outraged feelings overcame the habit of discipline and he gave indignant vent to them. "With respect, sir, after what that bastard of a Newab done to them poor souls? Wimmin, sir, an' little children—you seen them with your own eyes! Are we jus' goin' ter walk out an' leave 'im ter carry on?"

"We must, Devereux," Phillip told him. "Our first responsibility is to get the women and children back to Cawnpore and there are few enough of us to do it. My order stands."

From behind him, Ensign Highgate volunteered unexpectedly, "Commander Hazard, one of the ladies told me that the Newab isn't in his palace. He left, sir, with his troops, when they did . . . they saw him when they were brought up from the cellars. He's taken flight, sir—anticipating an attack. So really"—he glanced at Devereux—"there wouldn't be much point in setting his empty palace on fire, would there? Or in attacking the town. I mean, sir, the townspeople aren't responsible for the Newab's treachery, are they? They probably don't know anything about it and we . . . truly, sir, I think we have enough blood on our hands."

Highgate's attitude had, it appeared, undergone something of a change, Phillip reflected wryly. He looked at the boy in his torn and smoke-stained scarlet jacket, noting the lines of weariness and strain criss-crossing the grime on his plump young face and drew him aside, out of earshot of the rocket-crew.

"Well spoken, Benjy!" he applauded. "And you're right—we do have enough blood on our hands, more than enough. Besides, one act of reprisal simply leads to another. You . . ." He broke off, hearing the thin wail of a child in pain, which came from beneath the straw-thatched awning. It stopped a moment or two later, and he added, forcing a smile, "You did a fine job of work this evening. Without your timely aid, we should have lost more lives than we did. Well done!"

Benjamin Highgate reddened and then, a trifle uncertainly, echoed his smile. "Sir," he said in a low voice, "I almost failed to obey your order—your second order, I mean, sir—to come ashore and aid you in saving those poor souls from the fire."

"Why, for God's sake?"

Highgate's colour deepened and spread, suffusing his smoke-grimed cheeks. "Because I'd made up my mind to take the boat out—as you'd instructed me originally, sir—and loose off your rockets at the Newab's palace. Your men hadn't heard the second order and I was going to pretend I hadn't either."

Phillip eyed him in astonishment. "The devil you were! Presumably you had a reason, Mr Highgate?"

"Well, yes, sir." Highgate avoided his gaze. "I was sure it was what the Colonel wanted. You see, sir, he as good as told me that the Newab would betray us. He said you'd return empty-handed because none of his garrison were left alive, and that taking the boats to the city was only delaying the—the inevitable. When I saw the fire break out, I thought it was a trick and that you had been fooled by the hymn singing. My own idea was to pay the Newab back in his own coin, sir, and bring the column in as quickly as I could. I realise now it would have been wrong and I—I'm thankful I didn't do it."

The Colonel was more to blame than poor young Highgate had been, Phillip thought. "What made you change your mind, Mr Highgate?" he asked curiously.

Highgate continued to avoid his eye. "The prisoner, sir," he confessed.

"What prisoner, for heaven's sake?"

"The old man—the *vakeel,* sir. You left him in my charge."

Of course, Phillip recalled, he had told Highgate to guard the old man and treat him gently. "Well?" he prompted. "Where is the *vakeel?*"

Ensign Highgate evaded the question. "He suddenly started speaking in English, sir—and he *knew,* he knew exactly what was going to happen! He was yelling his head off, saying that our women and children were in the *godown* and that the Newab intended to serve them as we had served his women in Betarwar. But he was urging me to try and save them, sir, not to let them die."

"Save them? But—"

"Yes, sir. I couldn't understand it either, but there was no time to think. I could hear the screams by then so I . . ." The boy hesitated, looking up anxiously into Phillip's face. "I ordered the boat in and I—that is, I picked the old man up and threw him overboard, sir. I didn't care if he drowned, I—"

"And did he?" Phillip demanded.

Highgate shook his head. He said shamefacedly, "One of your sailors fished him out, sir. He's in Mr Arbor's boat now. But—that's not quite all, sir. When he was in the water, he kept yelling that the hostage the Colonel's holding is *his* son, sir, not the Newab's. I think that was why he had to keep his mouth shut until the last minute and why he was so anxious for us to save our women and children."

That could well be, Phillip thought. Clearly the Newab had not wanted to risk the life of his own son and, by sending the *vakeel's* son in his place, he had made certain of the old man's silence.

"That's a very revealing story, Mr Highgate," he said. "Thank you for telling me."

The boy shuffled uncomfortably. "I wasn't going to, sir. But then I thought about it and when you said 'Well done' and called me by my Christian name, sir, I knew I'd have to tell you the truth. Although it . . . well, it doesn't reflect to my credit exactly, does it?"

Phillip flashed him a wry grin. "On the contrary, Benjy, in my view it does. And I still say 'Well done' because you came ashore in the nick of time and you kept your head. I could ask no more than that of any officer, I assure you."

Benjamin Highgate stared at him for a moment in ludicrous surprise and then with a stammered "Thank you, sir," made for the stern, his shoulders shaking.

They were nearing the point at which the column had halted and Phillip was about to hail the shore when, without warning, a fusilade of shots, coming from the city they had left behind them, brought his head round. The shots were followed by the distant roar of cannon fire and he bit back a shocked exclamation as he, too, made for the stern. The native oarsmen, hearing the ominous sound, stopped rowing and two of them dived out of Grayson's boat, which was just astern, to strike out frantically for the bank.

"What's going on, Commander?" Grayson shouted, as both boats lost way. "Can you see anything?"

Phillip, his Dolland to his eye, could see little more than cannon flashes but his heart sank, as the firing grew in volume and Oates, at the sweep, said angrily, "Those are our guns, sir! Both of 'em. They're . . ." the rest of his words were lost as an explosion rent the air and the shadowed rooftops of the native city errupted into flame. Within minutes, as they watched, the tightly packed houses on the west bank were hidden beneath a dense pall of smoke and John Arbor, bringing his boat alongside, called out in dismayed tones, "The column—for God's sweet sake, they didn't wait for us! They're attacking the city! That was the magazine they just blew up."

"Put into the bank, Oates," Phillip ordered. He gestured to the still glowing bivouac fires which marked the campsite and the native boatmen, muttering protests, sullenly yielded to the threat of his pistol and bent once again to their oars. The boat grounded and a sentry challenged hoarsely. "Wait, Benjy," Phillip cautioned. "Don't attempt to let anyone disembark until I tell you. And watch those boatmen—we may need them."

He swung himself on to the overhanging bank and Arbor, not waiting to bring his boat into shallow water, jumped in and splashed across to join him. The campsite was deserted, except for the baggage waggons and the native camp followers, and Arbor swore horribly as he took in the fact that only a sergeant and a guard of fifteen or twenty men had been left in charge of his precious train.

"The man must be mad, Hazard!" he growled resentfully. "What in hell induced him to take the column in without waiting for our return? And . . . in the name of heaven, look at that! He pointed ahead of them to where a body dangled from an improvised gallows, at the edge of a clump of trees. They were too far away to see the dead man's face but Phillip felt bile rising in his throat as he looked at the slowly gyrating body—the *vakeel's* son, without a doubt, had paid a terrible price for his brief hour of masquerade.

"Perhaps," he said, keeping a tight rein on his feelings. "The surgeon is still here. If he is, we can thank God for small mercies." He turned to the startled guard commander. "Is he, Sergeant?" The man nodded. "Then fetch him, man," Phillip bade him urgently. "Our passengers have need of his services. Tell him," he added, as the sergeant started to move away, "that they are women and children and that some of them have been badly burnt."

"Right, sir." Infected by his urgency, the sergeant put down his rifle and ran. Roused from sleep, the young assistant-surgeon, to his eternal credit, wasted no time. Within ten minutes, he and his two assistants were at work beneath the straw-thatched awnings and his *doolie*-bearers were waiting at the water's edge with their curtained litters to carry the sick and injured ashore.

"Mr Highgate!" Phillip called and, when the boy answered, he gestured to the rocket-tube. "You have my permission to fire a couple of rockets—but into the air, if you please, as a recall signal to Colonel Cockayne. Repeat the signal in five minutes."

"Do you suppose that will bring him back, Commander Hazard?" Grayson asked, doubtfully.

Phillip sighed. "It might. At least it will indicate our presence here. But if there's no response . . ." He hesitated, frowning. "I'll ride after him. Dammit, we've got to get the column back! We—"

"You'd be too late," Arbor asserted with conviction. "Colonel Cockayne won't return until he's burnt Ghorabad to the ground. That's what he came to do, isn't it? Nothing you could say or do would stop him now, Commander." He shrugged, as the first of the two rockets Phillip had ordered hissed skywards in a shower of brilliant sparks. "But it shouldn't take him long— he's evidently not meeting with much opposition. The ladies were right. The Newab has fled the city with his troops. The trouble will come when *he* returns, I very much fear."

"Unless," Phillip began, "we—" he broke off, hearing a strangled cry from the darkness behind him. None of them had realised that Colonel Cockayne's daughter was within earshot until she spoke, her voice a thin, unhappy whisper of sound as she asked, "Are you saying that my father is alive? That he's there"—her gesture took in the blazing city of Ghorabad—"and that he's responsible for . . . for that?"

All three officers regarded her with dismay and Phillip, recognising her anguish, took her small, trembling hand in his.

"Your father is alive and he is in command of this column, Miss Cockayne. I'm sorry. I should have told you. It's come as a shock to you, I'm afraid."

"Yes," she agreed faintly. "It is . . . rather a shock. I thought all the officers of the garrison had been killed—executed by the Newab—and my father with them, you see. But you couldn't have known, Commander Hazard, and . . . there has been very little time for . . . for explanations. I—" She turned away, her face deathly pale in the moonlight and Phillip, cursing his own tactlessness, released her hand.

"I'm firing the second signal, sir!" Highgate called out.

"And there'll be no response to that either," Phillip said bitterly. "For God's sake, I'll have to ride after Cockayne. He's got to be stopped."

Captain Grayson laid a hand on his arm. "John Arbor's assessment of the situation is correct, Hazard: the harm is done. It's too late to try and stop it now and the Colonel won't linger, once he's done what he set out to do. In half an hour, there'll be precious little of the town left standing and even Cockayne will have to accept that justice has been done."

"Justice?" Phillip challenged.

"For want of a better word," Grayson conceded. "The column will be back here by first light. If it's not, then it will be up to us to get the women and children back to Cawnpore, and we shall have to leave Cockayne to fight a rearguard action, if the Newab pursues us. I think," he added cynically, "he owes that to his daughter, do you not? In the meantime, there are the dead to bury and our own column to prepare for the road."

Phillip felt the anger drain out of him. "You're right," he acknowledged. "Let's make a start, then."

By dawn, the last of the bodies they had brought back had

been lowered into its shallow grave, each with a roughly fashioned wooden cross to mark it and each with a few words of the Burial Service read over it. Phillip had performed this melancholy service at sea in the Crimea, but he found himself choking over the simple words as he watched the burial party shovel sand on to George Crawford's white, shuttered face and then on to the charred body of a child—one of three who had breathed their last during the night.

The rest, the surgeon had told him—with the exception of two of the women—would stand a reasonable chance of reaching Cawnpore alive, provided their return was not long delayed.

"They've all suffered some burning," the young doctor explained gravely. "In most cases, thank God, it's fairly superficial: hands and feet. They weren't wearing shoes, you see. But all of them have been badly treated and are half-starved, and they have little resistance. They will have to be carried in *doolies,* even the comparatively healthy. And I'm afraid four or five of your rescue party will be unable to handle their rifles. Mr Highgate's hands are in a particularly bad way . . ." He went into details, his voice brittle with weariness, ending regretfully, "I have done my best for the two seriously injured ladies but, alas, I can hold out very little hope for them in these circumstances."

He had thanked the exhausted young man, Phillip recalled, and had submitted to having his own right arm dressed and bandaged, although conscious of no pain. No pain, save that of the heart.

"*Man that is born of a woman hath but a short time to live . . . he is cut down, like a flower . . . in the midst of life we are in death . . .*" The words were coming more easily to his tongue now; they were familiar, he no longer had to think of them, but they were deeply moving nonetheless . . . and not only to himself. Benjamin Highgate, he saw, both hands swathed in wadding, was weeping unashamedly as two men of his regiment laid the emaciated body of a fair-haired woman beside that of a tiny, wizened child, born, he could only suppose, during the mother's captivity. As his sister Lavinia's baby had also been born and died, un-mourned by its dying mother. *"We commit their bodies to the ground. Earth to earth, ashes to ashes, dust to dust . . ."* in alien soil, killed by an alien foe—innocents, caught up in a battle that was not of their making. Phillip caught his breath. The prayer book he was using had been Lavinia's, found in the shambles of the Bibigarh in Cawnpore and given to him by Midshipman Edward Daniels . . . the page was blurred as he looked down at it but he read on, from memory: *"In sure and certain hope of the resurrection to eternal life through our Lord Jesus Christ . . ."*

He turned away and saw John Arbor running to meet him. "The column," he said breathlessly. "It's coming back, Hazard— your guns and the infantry, but I can't see the Colonel or any of his cavalry."

It was Lightfoot who explained the reason for Colonel Cockayne's absence. "There was no opposition, sir—the Newab and whatever troops he had were long gone when we entered the city. But the Colonel ordered us to set it on fire and we crossed over to the east bank by a bridge in the centre. He went on, sir, in pursuit of the Newab, taking the Sikhs with him. He said he hoped to be back within 24 hours and sent us out to await his return."

"I fear we shall not be able to wait that long," Phillip told him bleakly, "since the lives of the unfortunate survivors of the garrison may well depend on the speed with which we can get them to Cawnpore. See that your men break their fast,

Mr Lightfoot, without delay. I anticipate that the column will move out within the hour."

Grayson, Arbor, and the recently returned Alan Williams, when he sought their opinion, gave their unanimous agreement to his proposal to set out immediately for Cawnpore.

"As senior ranking officer, Commander Hazard," Grayson suggested formally, "I take it that you will assume temporary command of the column?"

"And the responsibility for its premature departure, Captain Grayson," Phillip answered, with a wry smile. "Supposing that is ever questioned."

Grayson shook his head. "No," he asserted. "The decision is a joint one; we all share the responsibility, Hazard, my friend." He glanced at the others for confirmation and both gravely inclined their heads.

"In the column commander's defence, sir," Alan Williams offered diffidently, "I have to say that he was *not* aware of your successful rescue of those ladies being held hostage by the Newab. Had he been, I feel sure he would have returned with us to the rendezvous."

For a moment, no one spoke; then John Arbor shrugged disgustedly. "As it is, gentlemen—and since I take it we are speaking freely—I can only pray that, having raised a hornet's nest about us, the column commander will himself meet any threat this may pose."

"What on earth do you mean, John?" Williams questioned. "I don't think I follow you."

Arbor laid a hand lightly on his arm. "I'm an old soldier, Alan, grown grey in the Company's service, which inclines me to pessimism, perhaps. But we've nearly sixty miles to cover and, with no cavalry to act as our eyes and ears, I cannot feel entirely at ease. Provided Colonel Cockayne's pursuit of the

Newab is successful, we've probably very little to fear. But if it's not, if he fails to make contact, then the fact that he's razed Ghorabad to the ground may bring the Newab after *us*. And we have the lives of twenty poor, brave ladies to protect, and those of their children. After what they have endured, it would be little short of a tragedy if we were unable to deliver them safely to Cawnpore, would it not?"

Young Alan Williams hesitated, torn between loyalty to his commander and his own feelings; finally he said, with evident reluctance, "You're absolutely right, of course, John, and I agree wholeheartedly with the decision to start on our way without waiting for Colonel Cockayne. But I wish we could get a message to him, to tell him that the survivors of his garrison are here—including his daughter. Because truly he has no idea and—"

"I'm going to give the old *vakeel* his freedom," Phillip put in, reaching a swift decision. "He can take the body of his son and I will ask him to despatch a messenger. A British soldier would have no chance of finding the Colonel but a native might manage to get through to him. That's the best I can do, I'm afraid."

"Thank you, sir," Williams acknowledged. "I'm grateful. It will bring him back at once, I feel certain."

CHAPTER EIGHT

Phillip was less hopeful and, when the Colonel's daughter sought him out just before the column moved off, he was compelled to answer her question concerning her father's whereabouts with a regretful headshake.

"I don't know, Miss Cockayne. I was told by a member of his staff that he has gone, with the Sikh cavalry, in pursuit of the Newab. I've sent a messenger after him, but, for the sake of the ladies who shared your captivity, we cannot delay our return to Cawnpore in order to wait for him to rejoin us."

She did not dispute his statement, accepting its harsh necessity and he added, smiling at her reassuringly, "I don't anticipate that we shall be able to cover more than ten or twelve miles a day, if the injured are to travel in anything approaching comfort, so the Colonel should have no trouble in catching up with us. You'll be reunited with him very soon, Miss Cockayne."

"Thank you," Andrea Cockayne acknowledged. In daylight, she looked even more frail than Phillip had imagined and his heart went out to her in helpless pity. Both her feet and hands were bandaged and her fair hair was cropped short, like a boy's so that, in the ragged native robe she wore, she made an oddly incongruous figure, robbed of femininity and charm, yet possessed of a natural dignity that at once impressed and moved him.

"They've found a *dhoolie* for you?" he asked anxiously.

She gave him a quick amused smile. "Oh, yes, Commander Hazard—I shall travel in comfort, don't worry. I've promised to take care of Mrs Lennard's baby, so that she may have a chance to rest; poor soul, she is worn out."

"That will not be very comfortable for you," Phillip demurred. "I'm sure if I asked the surgeon he would arrange something for the baby."

"Do not concern yourself, please," the girl begged. "Your surgeon has been wonderful to us. He's never spared himself all night."

"Yes, but—" Phillip began.

Smiling, she cut him short. "Commander Hazard, to be carried, instead of walking barefoot, and to eat and drink in a civilised manner . . . you can have no idea what that means to us. To be treated with kindness and respect, instead of being subjected to constant humiliation, to be once again addressed by our names, why . . ." Her smile faded and he saw that her lower lip was trembling. But the blue eyes met his, bright with courage, as she confided, "I keep having to pinch myself to make certain I am not dreaming! You cannot know from what torment and despair you have saved us or how grateful we are—you cannot possibly know."

Phillip looked down at her small, pinched face, his throat aching and at a loss for words. He resisted the impulse to take her in his arms as, following her escape from the burning *godown*, he had taken her, sensing that her pain was too intense for tears to bring relief. Poor, tortured child, he thought bitterly, what must she have suffered during the four endless months of her captivity—she and the others who had been confined with her? He found himself silently cursing Colonel Cockayne. Damn the man . . . why hadn't he waited until the return of the boats, instead of indulging his own savage desire for revenge? And why, devil take him, after reducing Ghorabad to a smouldering ruin, had he gone off with the cavalry on what might well prove to be a wild goose chase, when the safety of the column—and of the pathetic survivors of his garrison—was thereby jeopardised?

As if she had read his thoughts, Andrea Cockayne said quietly, "You have made the right decision, I am sure, Commander Hazard—not to wait for my father, I mean."

"Have I, Miss Cockayne?"

"Yes, you have. Some of the poor children and several mothers are gravely ill . . . and it's not only from their burns. Dr Milton told me that if they are to have even a small chance of recovery, they must be taken away from here, right away, to where they can be cared for and can forget. This place . . ." She shivered. "It holds so many terrible memories, such terror, even for the children. None of us can sleep, as long as we remain here, the—the nightmare is still with us, you see. And now that my father has destroyed the city, I . . . but he did not know, did he? He did not know that any of us were left alive."

"No," Phillip said thickly. "He did not know that, Miss Cockayne." He offered her his arm. "I'll escort you to your *dhoolie.*"

"Thank you," the girl acknowledged and laid her hand on his.

The column moved off, the small procession of *dhoolies* in the centre and infantry detachments, in skirmishing order, in place of the cavalry at front and rear. Apart from a few peasants working in the fields—who fled at the column's approach —they encountered no one. The men were tired but cheerful and Phillip gave permission to march at ease and sing on the march, partly to keep up morale but mainly in the hope of giving the sick and frightened women a feeling of security. A two-hour halt at midday further raised spirits and when the march was resumed, the young soldiers sang lustily, led by the 88th's two fifers and Oates's fiddle, regimental marching songs alternating with hymns and the occasional lewd chorus, which shocked NCOs hastily silenced.

Dusk found them almost twelve miles on their way and, when camp was made and bivouac fires lighted, all but the most seriously ill of the rescued hostages left their *dhoolies* and ate their meal with the men, in what became almost a picnic atmosphere, sailors and soldiers vying with each other to pet the thin, grave-faced children and clowning for their benefit.

Phillip, after conferring anxiously with Grayson and Arbor —his advance and rearguard commanders—joined in the picnic atmosphere and presented a smiling face to those gathered about the cooking fires. But when it was over and the camp wrapped in sleep, he answered Surgeon Milton's summons to bury one of the two badly burnt women and spent the night wakefully with Grayson's outlying piquet. Returning at dawn from his vigil, the surgeon again summoned him and he found Andrea Cockayne kneeling, in tearful prayer, beside the small, still body of a flaxen-haired child.

"He was only five," she whispered, in answer to his shocked question. "And his name was Christopher—Christopher Hardacre. His father was the Assistant-Commissioner and they murdered him when the Residency was over-run and taken by the sepoys. I—I was there. I saw what they did . . . how they killed him. And . . . you buried his mother last night. Now there are none of them left. The other two children died whilst we were prisoners."

Phillip did his best to comfort her. Meeting Dr Milton's

gaze over her bent head, as she wept in his arms, he saw the young man's lips frame a single word and his heart sank. Cholera was the one enemy no army could defeat and five-year-old Christopher Hardacre had—if the surgeon's diagnosis was correct—died of that dread disease. And the other women, the children, perhaps even the girl whose tear-stained face was pressed against his shoulder, might be infected by it. He had seen the terrible ravages of cholera in the Crimea and it had struck down more than a score of the *Shannon*'s seamen on the journey by river steamer from Calcutta to Allahabad, he recalled, killing half of them and severely incapacitating the rest . . . men in the peak of physical condition.

He was suddenly afraid, as he visualised the possible consequences should the infection spread among his small force now, with nearly fifty miles of hostile country still to be crossed and only one comparatively inexperienced young medical officer to cope with the crisis. The prospect did not bear thinking about but . . . he continued to hold the frail, grief-stricken girl in his arms, murmuring futile words of comfort and stroking her lank fair hair with fingers whose trembling he was unable to control. Looking back, a long time afterwards, he decided that this must have been the moment when he had fallen in love with her. Then, he did not recognise his feelings for what they were, believing them to be engendered by pity but certainly from then on, Colonel Cockayne's daughter was seldom absent from his thoughts or from his prayers, and he knew no peace when the demands of duty kept him from her. And always, for her sake, he was afraid . . .

The march was resumed in the same order as before, delayed only for long enough to enable the body of the poor little cholera victim to be laid to rest beside that of his mother.

The men continued to march to the tunes played by the fifers or tapped out by the drums, joining in the more popular choruses; when they halted, just after sunrise, to break their fast, all of them made an effort to recapture the picnic gaiety of the previous night but the word had leaked out, the shadow was there and with it the fear, to which only the less sensitive were immune.

But the day passed without incident. A few footsore men fell out with nothing more serious than blisters and hopes rose when the surgeon reported that his most severely injured woman patient was still miraculously holding her own when the column halted at sunset. The following morning, the shadow had lifted and morale was again high, the men swinging along like veterans and making such good progress that Phillip decided to call an early halt to rest the baggage and gun-cattle and afford an opportunity for Colonel Cockayne and his cavalry to catch up with them. Despite the inevitable delay caused by the slow-moving *dhoolies,* by noon they had covered almost half the distance which separated them from Cawnpore and no fresh cases of illness or injury had been reported.

In optimistic mood, Phillip rode ahead with Henry Grayson to select a camp site after the mid-day halt, finding the ideal spot beside a mango *tope,* with a small stream running through it and flat, cultivated fields on either side which gave an unobstructed view of the surrounding country. The column reached the site an hour later and there was a concerted rush to the stream, the men eager to wash the accumulated sweat and dust from their faces and to enjoy the luxury of a bathe in the cool, clear water. At Phillip's suggestion, Devereux and two of the seamen rigged a canvas screen in order to provide the women and children with a private bathing place and the cries of delight with which this somewhat primitive arrangement was greeted amply rewarded the effort it had entailed.

There was a walled village a mile or so to the east and Grayson despatched Benjamin Highgate with a small party to reconnoitre it. The ensign returned, beaming triumphantly, with the headman and some of the villagers, who brought chickens, milk and a few scrawny goats which, with every appearance of willingness, they offered to the British party.

"They've brought them as gifts, sir," Highgate explained, when Phillip insisted that payment must be made. "All they ask is that we don't enter the village or molest them. They're Hindus, sir, and they seem very well disposed to us—indeed, quite friendly, although they wouldn't let us inside the walls. And I thought the milk would be capital for the children, sir."

"It will," Phillip agreed. "Nevertheless everything we take is to be paid for, Benjy."

A bargain was struck, the *ryots* departed with smiles and *salaams,* and what amounted to a feast was prepared and eaten as the sun went down in a blaze of crimson glory behind the distant hills. The women, although able to eat very little after their months of starvation, were warm in their praise of the excellence of the repast and, in particular, of the tea which the naval cooks brewed up for them and served with milk and sugar.

"To be clean and well fed, Commander Hazard," Andrea Cockayne confided, when Phillip took leave of her after the meal. "That is happiness and I thank you from the bottom of my heart. I cannot remember ever feeling happier! All I need for my cup to run over is to see and speak to my father again."

"I feel sure he will be back with us very soon, Miss Cockayne," Phillip said, smiling to lend conviction to his words as he looked down into her shining, newly washed face from which, at last, the scar left by the whiplash was beginning to fade. He took her small, roughened hand in his and kissed it gently, hoping that she believed him. But he was by no means certain and he was conscious of a growing feeling of uneasiness as he made his nightly inspection of the piquets . . . Colonel Cockayne, if he had kept to his stated time limit, was now more than 24 hours overdue.

But Arbor, to whom he voiced his uneasiness, retorted cynically, "For God's sake, he's got a squadron of first-rate cavalry at his back and the bit between his teeth—Cockayne's not worrying about us! And there's no word of him in this neighbourhood. I asked a few pertinent questions of those villagers this evening and they appear to have heard nothing, either of him or the Newab. They were very friendly, as no doubt you observed."

"Not too friendly?" Phillip asked, his earlier, half-formed doubts returning.

John Arbor shrugged. "I don't think so. It's a Hindu village and—"

"But they had heard about Betarwar, surely?"

"Yes, they must have heard—it's about ten miles from here and news of that kind travels fast. It probably scared them out of their wits and that's what prompted the gifts."

"And their anxiety to keep us away from their village?" Phillip pursued, recalling Highgate's explanation.

"Yes, I imagine so." Arbor repeated his shrug. "None of them mentioned Betarwar but, as I say, they're Hindus. In normal times they would have no truck with the Newab or any of his people."

"But these are *not* normal times, my dear fellow," Phillip reminded him. "Moslem and Hindu are united in rebellion against us . . . and I haven't forgotten their last attempt to take us by surprise when we were bivouacking." He sighed. "Perhaps I'm taking the responsibilities of command too seriously, John, but I shan't sleep until I've had a look at that village. Will you come with me?"

Arbor hesitated and finally nodded. "Yes, of course, if you think it's necessary. How many of us—just you and me?"

"And a couple of horse-holders," Phillip decided. "I'm not proposing to go into the place—simply to make sure those villagers are as well disposed towards us as they seemed."

He was, he knew, probably being over-cautious; Arbor's expression told him that but . . . damn it, with the safety of women and children at stake, it was better to be sure than sorry. Accompanied by Benjamin Highgate and an ensign of the 82nd named Miller, they rode the two miles which separated them from the village, halting under cover of a clump of trees to dismount and leave their horses in the care of the two young ensigns. With Arbor, Phillip made a stealthy approach on foot and, as they neared its loop-holed mud walls, they saw that the village was in darkness.

"Not a sign of life, Commander," Arbor said, when they had been watching for several minutes without seeing anything remotely calculated to arouse their suspicions. "They're all sleeping the sleep of the just. Shall we"—there was a hint of reproach in his deep, pleasant voice—"shall we go back and do the same? As I told you, these people are Hindus and—"

"Wait!" Phillip cautioned. "Listen—I can hear something. Over to the left." They both listened tensely. Clearly across the intervening distance came the thud of galloping hooves and, moments later, a body of about thirty horsemen could be seen, the moonlight glinting on their lance-tips as they thundered towards the sleeping village. Lights sprang up at their approach and, after a brief conference, the heavy iron-bound door between the twin watch-towers creaked open to admit them.

Arbor gripped Phillip's arm and pointed. "I apologise for my scepticism, Commander Hazard. D'you see that big, bearded fellow on the grey Arab? Look, the torchlight's shining on his face now!"

Phillip followed the direction of his pointing finger. Light from a blazing torch held aloft by one of the villagers revealed a dark, arrogant face beneath a green *pugree* and Arbor said, as the gate swung shut once more, "That's the Newab . . . come in person, it would seem, to enlist the aid of my peaceful Hindu *ryots!* My God, if only we had your rocket-tube here!" He sighed heavily. "What now? Do we move the column out or wait for them to attack us?"

Phillip had been turning over the various possibilities in his mind, his brain racing as he considered what courses of action were open to him. With the safety and well-being of the women and children his foremost concern, they were few, and he echoed Arbor's sigh. The campsite—so well chosen for the rest and relaxation he had planned—could, he thought, be made defensible, but that would take time and the women would be in constant danger should an attack be launched against it. And, even if they were to move out at once, hampered by the *dhoolies* and the baggage train, they could not hope to move far or fast enough to outdistance the Newab's cavalry. A safe refuge would have to be found for the women and the sick and wounded and then perhaps . . . His eyes narrowed, as he started across at the walled village. Clearly, the Newab would not stay there; he must have ridden ahead of his main body, to which he would return once the purpose of his clandestine visit had been achieved . . . whatever that purpose might be.

Phillip made up his mind. "John," he bade Arbor urgently, "go back, if you please, and send Benjy Highgate to rouse the column. They're to prepare to move out, but not until I send word to Grayson, you understand? Tell Benjy to rejoin me here with the rocket-launcher and thirty riflemen as fast as he can make it. Miller's to wait with our horses."

"Right, sir." John Arbor was on his feet. "You're staying here?"

"Yes, until I can work out what's going on. Come back yourself, as soon as you've given Benjy his instructions."

Arbor slipped silently away. He returned, ten minutes later. "The devil take Colonel Cockayne!" He exclaimed angrily, as he slid into a crouching position at Phillip's side. "If we had his Sikh cavalry now, we could take the Newab without any trouble. But as it is, even if Benjy breaks his neck to get here, it'll be at least an hour before he does." He swore under his breath. "Have they made any move down there?"

Phillip shook his head. He was tense and worried, wondering whether he had read the Newab's intentions aright. If he had not, they were losing precious time, and failure to use what little time they had at their disposal could cost lives— the lives of the Newab's erstwhile prisoners, *Andrea's life.* He found himself thinking suddenly and quite illogically of Mademoiselle Sophie, remembering incidents he had believed long forgotten, re-living memories that were fraught with pain. The heartbreak of their farewell in distant Odessa, his escape to the clifftop with Mademoiselle Sophie's Cossack footman, and Ambrose Quinn's attempts to abandon him there. The floggings Quinn had ordered at the *Huntress's* gratings, which his Russian captors had compelled him to witness. And . . . Mademoiselle Sophie's courageous intervention, which had brought about his release; the church bells of Odessa ringing out, as he had stepped into the *Wrangler's* gig, their joyous peals announcing the birth of an heir to the House of Narishkin —the birth of a son to Mademoiselle Sophie, the Princess Narashkin.

Phillip drew in his breath sharply. Dear God, he was like a drowning man, he told himself, seeing a vision of his past life floating before him as the waters closed over his head and it was all a long time ago. It was three years since he had taken his last and final leave of Mademoiselle Sophie and now . . . He closed his eyes, seeking to conjure up the image of her face. It came but the outline was blurred, the image indistinct. *"The heart does not forget,"* she had told him and he had not forgotten, he would never forget. But now . . . John Arbor's fingers closed warningly about his arm and the memories vanished, as swiftly as if they had never been. He was back in the present, sick with the consciousness of danger, his fears—as they had been for the past three days and nights— for Colonel Cockayne's daughter and those who had shared her tortured captivity.

"They're coming out," Arbor whispered.

The wooden gate opened on its creaking hinges and a team of oxen appeared, drawing a heavy brass gun behind them. It was followed by a second, with a long-barrelled nine-pounder lurching in the wake of the straining beasts and then the Newab and his horsemen emerged, to form up protectively about the two guns as the gate closed behind them.

"Dammit, we've lost him!" Arbor said bitterly. "And he's got what he came for." He gestured to the guns. "Which puts him in the deuce of a strong position, doesn't it?"

Phillip watched as the plodding gun-cattle were whipped and goaded into a shambling trot. They were heading due north, his mind registered, away from the camp. He waited to make sure but Arbor dashed his brief hopes. "They'll have come from the river—probably made camp a few miles behind us, which means they must have eluded the Colonel. *He's* no doubt half way to Lucknow by this time, on a false scent, perdition take him! And those confounded villagers will have given the Newab all the information he needs about our strength and position." He hesitated, eyeing Phillip speculatively from beneath frowning brows, and then offered, a harsh note in his voice, "At a rough guess, Commander Hazard, I'd say that the Newab will start after us at first light and aim to catch us on the road. What exactly do you intend to do?"

"That gives us . . ." Phillip glanced up at the moonlit sky. He was quite calm now, his mind firmly made up, his plan of action—for better or worse—decided upon. They had eaten at sunset and—he took out his watch—he and Arbor had been here, watching the village, for almost two hours . . . He made a swift mental calculation. "That gives us seven hours at the very least, John—nine or ten, if the Newab doesn't hurry himself. His main body must be ten miles or so behind us or we'd have seen them before we made camp. He must have moved pretty fast to get as close to us as he has and—"

"Most of his force will be mounted and his light guns horsed," Arbor pointed out. "He *can* move fast if he wants to."

"He'll have to rest his horses and his gun-cattle at some stage," Phillip reminded him. "My guess is that he'll aim to attack us at the noon halt and that would give us considerably longer."

Arbor looked dismayed. "Are you proposing to make a run for it, then? Because in my view we shouldn't have a dog's chance. Without the women and children perhaps but with them, even if we dig in, we—"

Phillip cut him short. "No," he returned crisply. "I'm not

proposing to run, it would be taking too great a risk. I'm going to occupy the village, John, as soon as Benjy joins us with his party."

"Occupy the village?" Arbor echoed. "In heaven's name, Hazard, why?"

"Because it's the best defensive position we're likely to find for miles and because the women will be safe there, which is my main concern. Also, my dear John"—Phillip turned, smiling, to meet the older man's anxious gaze—"if your assessment of your peaceful Hindu *ryots* is correct, because they won't offer much opposition. We'll evacuate the men but we won't lay a finger on their women and children. We can move in before first light, leave a guard and one of my guns to defend the place and, with a modicum of luck my friend, *we* might even contrive to catch the Newab on the road! I noticed a spot about three miles back which would make an admirable site for an ambush."

Arbor stared at him in astonishment for a moment and then an answering smile spread slowly across his face. "My God, Commander Hazard!" he exclaimed. "For a sailor, you make a damned fine soldier! I have to admit I had my doubts concerning your ability to command a mixed land force but— you're right, of course. That village *is* the best possible place to defend. I . . . permit me to take it for you, when Benjy Highgate brings up his riflemen?"

"With the greatest of pleasure, Mr Arbor." Phillip rose, flexing his cramped muscles. "I fancy it's a job for a soldier. Let's get our horses, shall we?"

By sunrise the following morning, the British column was in position, awaiting the appearance of the rebel force and all, to Phillip's heartfelt relief, had gone according to plan. The villagers had surrendered without firing a shot and the headmen, volubly protesting his continued loyalty to the Company's *raj*—once satisfied that his womenfolk would be unmolested—had suffered himself to be evacuated with the rest of the male inhabitants. Within three hours, the transfer of the British women and children and the wounded had been successfully completed. Leaving a strong guard and one naval gun, under Alan Williams's command, to hold it, Phillip had led the remainder of the column back along the road to the site he had chosen for the ambush.

It was not an ideal spot—the ground was too flat—but trees and underbrush on one side and a dried-up stream-bed on the other afforded adequate cover for his small force of infantry, and he sited Lightfoot's gun just behind the screening trees to the left, where it could be brought to bear on the road. The rocket-tube, with its light carriage, he advanced as far as he dared to the right and himself took command of it, intending to open with it as soon as the rebels were sighted, in the hope of dispersing their cavalry and preventing a charge. With Grayson commanding the troops on the left and Arbor those in the *nullah,* there was little he could do now save wait, with ever increasing impatience, for the Newab to make his appearance. It was nearly two hours before he did so. Highgate and Miller, who had volunteered to ride forward and reconnoitre, came galloping back on sweating horses, to report the approach of a large body of horse and foot.

"They're coming from the north, sir," Highgate said, gesturing excitedly behind him. "You'll see them for yourself when they clear the trees, because they're following the direction of the road. I should say . . ." He glanced at Miller for confirmation and he sounded more than a little awed as he added, "I should say there are over a thousand of them, mostly cavalry, sir. And we counted four guns, didn't we, Charlie?"

Young Miller nodded. "The two from last night, sir,

bullock-drawn, and the other two are horsed guns. They're moving quite fast, with the cavalry well in advance and the infantry really only a baggage-guard, sir, trailing along about a mile to the rear."

What would he not give for Colonel Cockayne's Sikh cavalry now, Phillip thought wryly, to cut off the baggage-train and the rebels' reserves of ammunition, but . . . He forced a smile. "Well done, both of you. How about scouts or skirmishers? Have they thrown out any?"

Both young men shook their heads. "None, sir," Highgate, stated positively. "They're riding in a compact body, with the horsed guns in their centre, almost . . . well, arrogantly, sir, as if they'd nothing to fear. And I don't suppose they have, really, with such a large force. Can we . . ." He looked round at the small detachment of scarlet-jacketed British riflemen in the *nullah* below them, and then at Petty Officer Devereux, placidly chewing tobacco and the only man of the rocket-crew on his feet. The others on Phillip's orders, were sprawled on the ground beside their weapon, snatching what rest they could, and Highgate took heart from their seeming unconcern. "We *can* lick them, can't we, sir? Even if we are rather . . . well, outnumbered."

Perhaps they could, Phillip thought . . . please God, they could! He had not anticipated that the Newab would be able to gather a thousand-strong force about him quite so rapidly, but at least they had a chance, with the element of surprise to aid them. It would have been a very different story if the hordes of rebel horsemen had fallen on the column when it was on the open road, hampered by the presence of the women and children and with nowhere to dig in. If they could inflict a defeat on the Newab and sufficient casualties to send him back to Ghorabad with his tail between his legs, then the safety of the women was assured and that, really, was all that mattered.

"Don't you worry, Benjy," he told the ensign, with well-simulated confidence. "We'll give them a hiding they won't forget in a hurry. Get those horses under cover, if you please, and take post here with me. Mr Miller, you'd better make your report to Captain Grayson and act as his aide."

It was half an hour before the Newab's horsemen came into view. They were still in a compact body, riding twenty or thirty abreast and spilling over on both sides of the road. As Miller had said, they were moving fast. Phillip studied them through his glass, observing with satisfaction that the horses were lathered and that discipline was, by British standards, somewhat lax. But now a party of about a dozen had been sent forward, in advance of the main body, presumably for the purpose of reconnoitring the road and the camp site, and he despatched Highgate to warn Grayson and Arbor to allow them to pass unmolested.

They did so, fifteen minutes later, cantering past the British troops' concealment without a second glance, laughing and chattering among themselves and clearly not expecting to meet with any opposition. Phillip listened tensely when they were lost to sight, fearing that their reconnaissance might include the village but Highgate, who had wormed his way to the far side of the *nullah* to watch them, reported that they were continuing to follow the road.

"Right," Phillip said, addressing Devereux. "Action front, Chief! Close up the rocket-crew . . . it won't be long now. When I give the order, I want rapid fire into the enemy centre and rear. We'll leave the riflemen to deal with their front. Our aim is to panic the horses and break up their formation—but not a move until I tell you." He waved a warning to Arbor, in the *nullah* below him and they waited, the rocket-crew lying full length on the ground, the infantrymen hidden in the *nullah*, gripping their rifles, able to hear but, as yet, not to see the advancing enemy.

Phillip closed his Dollond and flung himself flat, his heart thudding. Everything depended on the next few minutes. If one young soldier lost his nerve and opened fire prematurely, the bulk of the Newab's cavalry, and his baggage and guns, would escape the trap he had laid for them but . . . Not a man moved, although the strain of waiting became almost unbearable. The *zamindari* horsemen came noisily, even carelessly, spread out so far across the road that those on the flanks were having to pick their way over tree-roots and clumps of brushwood and Phillip, watching them between the screening leaves of an overhanging peepul tree, found it hard to believe that they had not seen the scarlet jackets of Grayson's detachment on the far side of the road and some sixty yards behind him. He let the first hundred or so pass his point of vantage; then, when he judged that Lightfoot's nine-pounder was bearing on them, sprang to his feet, yelling to Devereux to open fire.

The rockets caused even more pandemonium than he had dared to hope they might. Terrified horses bolted or, unable to escape from the tightly packed ranks, plunged and reared, flinging their riders to the ground. When Devereux directed his fire to the rear, the elephants drawing the baggage and ammunition waggons were thrown into wild confusion, some charging forward, trumpeting, into the cavalry's disordered ranks, others trampling on the men who endeavoured to control them. Lightfoot's gun sent round after round of grape into the advance guard and, on both sides of the road, the Enfields and Miniés opened a rapid and sustained fire at virtually point-blank range.

The surprise was complete; the rebel guns, trapped in the centre of the melee, could not unlimber and, as men and horses went down on all sides of them, the gunners abandoned their weapons and attempted to flee. A few of the cavalrymen, braver than the rest, bunched together and tried to charge into the trees, but Grayson's men met them with levelled bayonets and drove them back, to meet the enfilading fire of Arbor's as they sought safety in flight.

Finally, leaving scores of dead and wounded behind them, the rebels retreated, emerging from the smoke in scattered groups, intent only on escape. Devereux and his crew continued to direct a shower of rockets into their midst; Lightfoot and his gunners manhandled their weapon on to the road and opened on their rear and Phillip, with Benjy Highgate running breathlessly after him, joined Arbor's party in a bayonet charge across the fields to their right. But the rebels, although they had been hard hit, were still capable of fighting and a party of some hundred or so reformed, to conduct a courageous rearguard action. Led by a bearded native officer in the yellow chapkan of the Oudh Irregular Cavalry, they repeatedly charged the advancing British infantry and, growing bolder when they began to realise how few their assailants were, compelled them to form square to avoid being driven back.

Phillip, grabbing a Minié from a wounded soldier, took careful aim and knocked the bearded leader from his horse but the fellow picked himself up and came at him in a lunging rush, sabre raised above his head and his dark face contorted with hatred. A sergeant of the 88th shot him, a fraction of a second before the steel blade descended and Phillip grinned his thanks. The rearguard, disheartened by the loss of their leader, fell back after a while, but they had inflicted a number of casualties and bought time for their fellow rebels and Phillip saw, to his dismay, that a party of them had brought up one of the heavy brass cannon they had taken from the village the previous night and were making strenuous efforts to bring it into action.

"Withdraw your wounded, John," he bade Arbor. "And take cover. There's nothing more you can do."

"Very well," Arbor acknowledged. He passed a blood-stained hand across his sweating, smoke-blackened face, and swore, loudly and angrily. "The swine will get away, you know—God, if only we had our cavalry! The Newab is commanding that gun in person . . . look!"

Phillip nodded, tight-lipped, and repeated his order. Satisfied that it would be obeyed, he ran back along the shambles of the road in search of Lightfoot. Finding him, he said, shouting to make himself heard, "Bring your gun forward, Mr Lightfoot, and hurry!"

"Aye, aye, sir." Young Lightfoot was black from head to foot, a torn and filthy bandage wound round his left leg and he was limping badly, but he cheered as lustily as the rest when, aided by half a dozen riflemen of Grayson's detachment, the seamen dragged their nine-pounder into position on the far side of the trees. A roundshot came bounding to meet them, followed by a second, as the Newab's party brought their brass cannon to bear on the road. The men scattered to avoid the deadly missiles, but a party of Arbor's wounded were not so fortunate and the second shot ploughed through them, leaving three or four broken bodies in its wake, as the native bearers deserted their *dhoolies* and ran shrieking for cover. Devereux was still sending a steady shower of rockets into the rebels' fleeing baggage train, but he was unsighted and unable to bear on the brass cannon and Phillip yelled to Lightfoot's crew, gesturing to the belching monster, "There's your target, my boys—action front, rapid fire! The Newab's there and he's all yours, if you can hit him!"

He heard the nine-pounder open as he stumbled wearily across the road to aid Arbor's wounded and then both guns abruptly ceased fire and he heard the men cheering wildly. Benjy Highgate gripped his arm and he straightened up to see, to his astonishment, that the brass cannon was being abandoned, the gunners leaping for their horses in blind, unreasoning panic.

"What the devil—" he began, but Highgate cut him short.

"The Colonel, sir!" the boy told him, his voice shrill with excitement. He raised a scarlet-clad arm and pointed. "Look, sir—it's Colonel Cockayne with the Sikh cavalry! By heaven, what a capital sight they make!"

They did indeed, Phillip thought, his heart lifting as he watched them ride into the attack, the sun striking a myriad rainbow-hued reflections from their drawn sabres. The blue-turbanned Sikh cavalrymen increased their pace from a canter to a gallop, the whole squadron in line behind Colonel Cockayne, giving points with their flashing sabres as their charge gathered momentum and they bore relentlessly down in the Newab's panic-stricken gunners.

There was no escape for the Newab; the Colonel rode, straight as a die, for his enemy and the rebel leader, too proud to seek refuge in flight, held his ground. He and a handful of others were dismounted but, for a moment, each of the two antagonists were alone, Cockayne twenty yards ahead of the Sikhs, the Newab standing by himself in front of the great, silent brass cannon on which he had pinned his faith. He waited bravely for death, making no attempt to defend himself, and the Colonel's sabre, descending in a gleaming arc, all but severed his head from his shoulders.

It fell to the lot of one of his unhorsed bodyguard to avenge him. The man hurled himself beneath the Colonel's plunging charger, hacking at its belly and legs with his *tulwar* and the animal crashed to the ground, flinging its rider over its head. The Sikh line struck and, their impetus making it impossible for them to do otherwise, one or two of them rode over their recumbent commander. They went on in pursuit of their beaten enemy, as they had been ordered and Phillip seized the bridle of a loose horse, which one of Arbor's men was holding, and flung himself into the saddle.

"Find a *dhoolie* if you can, lad," he bade the soldier. "And send it after me. I'm going to bring the Colonel in."

He had only one thought, as he kneed his reluctant mount across the field of trampled winter corn to where the Colonel lay, and that was to restore her father to Andrea—if he was alive. He was lying, spreadeagled and motionless, a few yards from the brass cannon and the Newab's body and he appeared to be dead but, when Phillip reached him and, dismounting, went to kneel at his side, his eyes opened and were lit by a flicker of recognition.

"Your daughter is safe, Colonel," Phillip told him, uncertain whether or not he understood. "Your daughter Andrea, sir. Last night she said that all she needed for her cup of happiness to run over was to see and speak to you again."

He looked round for the *dhoolie* he had asked for but could see no sign of it. Benjy Highgate and some soldiers had, however, started after him and he measured the distance between them, suddenly conscious of danger. Not all the rebels who had fallen about the Newab's cannon were dead; several of them, although wounded, were moving about and . . . He drew in his breath sharply as he found himself looking into the muzzle of a long-barrelled flintlock pistol, hearing the click as it was cocked. Dark eyes gleamed in a white-bearded face, meeting his balefully and then softening in what, at any other time, he would have taken as friendly acknowledgement. A thin old hand came out to grasp his shoulder, as if seeking to thrust him aside.

"Not you, Hazard Sahib," the old *vakeel* whispered, in English. "I have one bullet and my life is draining away. I would take my son's murderer with me. His hands are red with innocent blood. He deserves to die, he—"

Phillip leapt to his feet. He made a grab for the old man's wrist but his fingers closed on empty air. The pistol exploded and his world seemed to explode with it, setting him adrift in a sea of pain, unable to see or to breathe. From somewhere near at hand he heard a scream; then there was silence and merciful oblivion.

Colonel Cockayne got up, his own smoking pistol in his hand, and walked unsteadily to meet Highgate and his soldiers. He saw the *dhoolie* following behind them and said, his voice shaking, "Don't worry about me, Highgate . . . tell them to pick up Commander Hazard. He . . . has just saved my life and I fear he's severely wounded. You'll . . . deal with him gently, won't you? He has a pistol ball . . . in the chest."

Benjy Highgate sobbed as he urged the *dhoolie*-bearers forward.

EPILOGUE

Early in February, the Commander-in-Chief's main force returned to Cawnpore, preceded by Hope Grant's Cavalry Brigade, and on the evening of the 12th, the Naval Brigade under Captain Peel made camp at Unao, on the Lucknow side of the Ganges.

Futtehghur had been taken and occupied and various forces of brigade strength had done all that was necessary to subdue the Doab. Following a conference with the Governor-General, Lord Canning, at Allahabad, Sir Colin Campbell began to make preparations for a second and final assault on Lucknow.

Phillip was in hospital but convalescent when a note arrived from William Peel to say that he would ride over to Cawnpore next day, in order to visit him.

"I rejoice in your recovery, my dear Phillip," the Shannon's Captain wrote warmly. "And I have a number of communications from Their Lordships and from Commodore Watson—newly appointed as Senior Officer in Calcutta—which concern you and which you will, I feel sure, regard as good news.

"First and foremost, my sincere congratulations on your promotion to post-rank, official confirmation of which reached me here only yesterday, together with that of Jim Vaughan . . . and a hint, which gratified me greatly, that I am to be awarded a KCB!

"I trust your journey back to Cawnpore was not too unpleasant and that tomorrow I shall find you—if not yet quite fit enough to resume normal duty—at least making progress towards that end. There is, do not forget, the matter of making the official presentation of the Brigade's Victoria Crosses, the arrival of which via China has been so long delayed."

Phillip smiled, as he read the letter through a second time, taking in the fact that it was addressed to "Captain P. H. Hazard, VC, RN" in William—soon to be Sir William—Peel's neat, firm hand. It was good to have attained the much coveted post-rank at last, although his promotion would probably mean a period on half-pay, possibly in England, before he could hope to be appointed to a new command. But it released him from the promise his father had exacted from him, all those years ago, when he had been the *Trojan's* First Lieutenant . . . his smile widened. He was free to marry, if the young lady of his choice would consent to become his wife . . . and Andrea Cockayne was still in Allahabad, with the rest of the survivors of the ill-fated Ghorabad garrison, awaiting transport to Calcutta and passage home, when they had recovered sufficiently from their ordeal to undertake the long journey.

He leaned back in his comfortable rattan chair, eyes half-closed, remembering. The slow return to Cawnpore in a *dhoolie,* with his chest heavily bandaged, had been a nightmare, which he preferred to forget. But there had been moments during his agony which remained in his mind and to which he had clung, when his tortured body was fighting for survival . . . moments shared with Andrea. The sound of her voice, distinctive among all the other voices, the awareness that she had wept over him, prayed for him and walked, her hand clasping his, for hour after weary hour beside his airless, swaying *dhoolie,* bringing him water when the column halted and gently wiping the sweat from his unshaven face . . . dear heaven! Those memories he cherished, since they had inspired his fight for life, when it would have been easier and less painful to die.

But he had had to let her go without revealing any hint of his feelings for her, because he had spent the first two weeks of his return to Cawnpore in a state of semi-consciousness, and only learnt—days after her departure—that, on her father's insistence, she had left for Allahabad with the others. Colonel Cockayne had accompanied her and rumour had it that he intended to retire and travel back to England with his daughter . . . Phillip sighed. He had written, of course, but had received no reply and . . .

"Phillip—Phillip, my dear fellow, my apologies if I've wakened you . . ." He opened his eyes, recognising Peel's voice with pleased surprise. "Sir Colin sent for me," the Naval Brigade Commander explained, when greetings and congratulations had been exchanged. "So I'm here a day earlier than I anticipated. Things are moving, Phillip. Reinforcements are flowing in, General Outram is more than holding his own in the Alam Bagh and the signs are that the rebels are tiring of the struggle and quarrelling among themselves. We'll be ready to move against Lucknow in two or three weeks time, I think—and with a total force of close on twenty thousand men of all arms. Our Brigade will be stronger than it's ever been." Peel grinned, with schoolboyish delight. "We captured the Carriage Works at Futtehghur intact and during our stay there, I had carriages made for our eight-inch guns—the *Shannon*'s own guns, Phillip, are coming from Allahabad!" He went into enthusiastic detail and Phillip listened, his heart quickening its beat.

"I'd give a great deal to be in at the death, sir," he said.

"Will you have any work for a newly appointed Post-Captain on half-pay, do you suppose?"

Peel laughed. "Since the Brigade already has one, in the person of Oliver Jones, I anticipate complaints from Their Lordships if I permit a second to join us. And Commodore Watson sends me repeated demands for the entire Brigade to pull out and return to Sir Michael Seymour's command in China! So far, with Sir Colin Campbell's influential help, I have contrived to avoid making any definite reply to the Commodore, in confident expectation that Their Lordships will over-rule him. We *are* needed, if Lucknow is to be recaptured without heavy losses of life, Phillip. Remove our heavy batteries and our four hundred and thirty trained and seasoned officers and men, and Sir Colin will feel the loss greatly. But—" His smile faded. "As to yourself, dear fellow, whilst if you are fit, I'd gladly risk the Admiralty's displeasure by entering you as a volunteer, like the gallant Jones . . . I regret to tell you that Commodore Watson has made a specific request for your services."

"For *my* services, sir?" Phillip stared at him in dismay. "In what capacity, if I may ask?"

William Peel laid a friendly hand on his shoulder.

"To take command of the Company's steam-screw gunboat *Falcon*," Peel told him. "On loan to the Indian Navy. Her Captain has recently died and she's under orders for China." He sighed. "Obviously the Commodore isn't aware that you have been wounded. You haven't had a medical board yet, have you?"

Phillip shook his head. "No, not yet. I'd hoped—that is the surgeons had proposed one in ten days' time. I was to be given a week's sick leave, you see, and—"

Peel's gay, infectious smile returned. "Then I suggest, my dear Phillip, that you take a fortnight's sick leave and spend it away from this station. Have you not friends in Allahabad, to whom you wish to bid farewell before they depart for Calcutta and passage to England? Your mid, Johnny Lightfoot, seemed to think you had."

Phillip reddened and then echoed his smile. "To tell you the truth, sir," he confessed, "the girl I hope to marry is in Allahabad. I'd intended to seek her father's consent to my proposal before they left, if I possibly could. Only—"

"Seek it, my dear fellow," Peel advised. "And the best of luck to you!" He held out his hand. "I'm expecting Their Lordships' to reply by overland telegraph and I don't anticipate being deprived of one of my best officers, in order to fill a temporary vacancy in the Company's Navy. I think it more than likely, however, that you'll be ordered home. Perhaps . . ." He was smiling broadly. "Perhaps towards the end of March, Phillip. And I shall expect an invitation to the wedding, you know."

Two days later, Phillip was on his way to Allahabad.

HISTORICAL NOTES

On events covered in *The Sepoy Mutiny,*
Massacre at Cawnpore, The Cannons of Lucknow,
and *Guns to the Far East.*

T*he mutiny* of the sepoy Army of Bengal on Sunday, 10th May, 1857, began with the rising of the 3rd Light Cavalry in Meerut. Despite the fact that he had two thousand British troops under his command, the obese and senile Major-General William Hewitt handled the crisis so ineptly that, after an orgy of arson and slaughter, the Light Cavalry and their sepoy comrades of the 11th and 20th Native Infantry were permitted to reach Delhi, with scarcely a shot fired against them.

Here, supported by the native regiments of the garrison, they proclaimed the last of the Moguls, eighty-year-old Shah Bahadur, as Emperor of India, and seized the city, murdering British civil and military officers and massacring hundreds of Europeans and Indian Christians, who had been unable to make their escape. Hampered by both lack of British troops and inadequate transport for those available to him, the British Commander-in-Chief nevertheless contrived to establish a small force on the Ridge by 8th June. This force, which consisted of fewer than three thousand men of all arms—although it had won two pitched battles against the mutineers on the way to Delhi—was so greatly outnumbered and deficient in heavy artillery that it could only wait for reinforcements, unable, until these arrived, to attempt to recapture the city or even effectively to besiege it.

In Oudh—recently annexed by the East India Company and already, on this account, seething with discontent—the situation rapidly became critical as, in station after station, the native regiments broke out in revolt. A source of grave anxiety was Cawnpore, 53 miles northeast of Lucknow and on the opposite bank of the Ganges River. With some 375 women and children to protect, the commanding General, Sir Hugh Massey Wheeler, pinned his faith on the friendship of a native prince, the Nana Sahib, Maharajah of Bithur. He had only two hundred British soldiers in his garrison—among these seventy invalids and convalescent men of Her Majesty's 32nd Regiment—about the same number of officers and civilian males, forty native Christian drummers, and a handful of loyal native officers and sepoys.

Betrayed by the Nana, the garrison held out for three weeks with epic heroism, in a mud-walled entrenchment at the height of the Indian summer, under constant attack by nine thousand rebels and surrounded by batteries of heavy calibre guns. Compelled finally to surrender when two hundred-fifty defenders had been killed and with their food and ammunition exhausted, the survivors were treacherously massacred on the river bank, where they had gone, on the promise of safe passage to Allahabad, on 27th June. By the time the Nana called a halt to the awful slaughter, all but 125 women and children and some sixty men had been killed. The men were shot; the women and children, many of them wounded, were held as hostages in a small, single-storey house known as the Bibigarh, together with female captives from other stations.

When the small, poorly equipped relief force, under Brigadier General Henry Havelock, fought its way up country from Allahabad and recaptured Cawnpore, it was learned that all the hostages had been brutally murdered on 15th July, when the British column was still engaging the Nana's troops outside the city. Feeling ran high among Havelock's soldiers, when details of the massacre became known, but the stern and deeply religious little General would permit no indiscriminate reprisals against the civilian population of Cawnpore. Punishment would be meted out to the guilty, but the most urgent task facing the column was the relief of Lucknow, which was now under siege by an estimated twenty-five to thirty thousand rebels.

Due to the foresight of the Chief Commissioner of Oudh, Sir Henry Lawrence, his Residency had been provisioned and preparations made for its defence but he, too, had insufficient British troops—a single regiment, the 32nd—and over twelve hundred women, children, and non-combatant males, who had all to be sheltered, protected, and fed. At the end of June, Lawrence suffered a disastrous reverse when he led a small force of his defenders to Chinhat, in an attempt to drive off the rebels and was himself mortally wounded when a round-shot entered through the window of his upper room at the Residency on 2nd July. Command was handed over to Colonel Inglis, of the 32nd, who sent urgent messages to Havelock, requesting aid.

General Havelock made his first attempt to relieve the garrison on July 29th, when he crossed the Ganges with fifteen hundred men—twelve hundred of them British and the rest Sikhs of the Ferozepore Regiment—and ten light field guns. He took no tents and twenty of his gunners were invalids of the Veteran Battalion; to his scant force of twenty Volunteer

Cavalry were added some forty infantrymen, with experience of riding, whose cavalry training had of necessity been completed in less than a week. His four European regiments—Her Majesty's 64th, 84th, and 78th Highlanders and the Company's 1st Madras Fusiliers—had already suffered heavy casualties in the four actions they had fought between Allahabad and Cawnpore, and the terrible ravages of cholera, dysentry, and sunstroke daily reduced their number.

To hold Cawnpore and cover their crossing into Oudh, Havelock ordered the construction of an entrenchment, considerably stronger than General Wheeler's had been, sited on a plateau overlooking the river, and well armed with guns. The Commanding Officer of the Madras Fusiliers, James Neill—whose promotion to Brigadier General was the reward for his ruthless suppression of the mutiny in Benares and Allahabad—was left to defend the newly constructed entrenchment with three hundred men. No sooner had Havelock departed than Neill set about executing any native who was even remotely suspected of complicity in the mutiny, reserving a terrible vengeance for those believed to have had a hand in the massacre at the Suttee Chowra Ghat or in the Bibigarh. His reign of terror earned him the unenviable title of "Butcher of Cawnpore."

Havelock's attempt to bring relief to the "heroic garrison of Lucknow" was, from the outset, doomed to failure. He had too few troops, inadequate transport, and sick carriage, and, in the ancient Kingdom of Oudh, every man's hand was against him—the mutineers' ranks swollen by the armed *zamindars* and peasants who flocked to join them in the insurrection. His small force was victorious in every action, fought against overwhelming odds; it attacked with deathless courage, taking fortified and entrenched positions at the point of the bayonet and inflicting twice and three times the number of casualties it suffered. But the rebel losses could be made good— Havelock's could not and, although his column bravely battled its way to within thirty miles of Lucknow, the little General was compelled to retire to his base at Mungalwar, six miles into Oudh from the river crossing, no less than three times.

Havelock's constantly reiterated plea for reinforcements was, at last, answered. On his return to Cawnpore on 17th August, he received news—via the *Calcutta Gazette* of 5th August—that command of the Dinapore Division had been given to Major General Sir James Outram, under whom he had served in the recent Persian campaign. Outram's new command was to include that of Cawnpore, and he was reported to be moving with all possible speed up country with the two regiments for which Havelock had so often begged, the 5th Fusiliers and the 90th Light Infantry. Sir Colin Campbell, of Balaclava fame, had succeeded the somewhat ineffectual Patrick Grant as Commander-in-Chief, and Havelock's chagrin, caused by his apparent supersession, was tempered by the new hope that the appointment of Colin Campbell engendered. It vanished completely when Outram, with a chivalrous generosity that was typical of him, announced that Havelock was to continue to command the now augmented relief column until Lucknow was entered. He, himself, he stated, would accompany the column in his civilian capacity as Chief Commissioner of Oudh and serve under his junior as a volunteer.

Outram reached Cawnpore on 15th September, bringing 1,268 men with him and a battery of heavy, elephant-drawn guns. These reinforcements brought the total number of troops to a little over three thousand men—twenty-four hundred of them British—with three batteries of artillery. By the evening of 20th September, leaving three hundred men to hold Cawnpore, the whole force had crossed the Ganges, with General Havelock in official command, and his two brigades under General Neill and Colonel Hamilton, of the 78th. The Sye was crossed on 23rd September in fine weather. After a hard-fought battle with some ten thousand rebels two miles from the city, the Alam Bagh Palace was captured.

The British Column bivouacked in and around the Alam Bagh that night. The next day was spent resting by the troops and in careful reconnaissance by Havelock and Outram and their senior staff officers. The two Generals were not in agreement as to the best way in which to gain the Residency, but, owing to the waterlogged state of the ground—which rendered moving the heavy guns well-nigh impossible—Havelock finally consented to abandon his own plan in favour of that put forward by Outram.

This entailed crossing by the Char Bagh bridge and— instead of advancing through a maze of heavily defended streets direct to the Residency—taking a circuitous route along the canal bank to the then undefended Sikander Bagh Palace, from the shelter of which the final advance would be made under cover of two other walled Palaces, leaving only five hundred yards of the Khas Bazaar between the column and its objective, the Bailey Guard gate of the Residency.

The men, too, despite their weariness, were eager to reach their objective, the memory of the Cawnpore massacre still vivid in their minds. They had been inspired also by the news which had reached them in camp at the Alam Bagh, that Delhi had been recaptured, and they greeted their little General's decision to "push on and get it over" with heartening cheers.

Accordingly, all the sick and wounded and half of Eyre's heavy guns were brought within the walls of the captured

Alam Bagh, and, leaving three hundred men under Major MacIntyre of the 78th to defend it, the final advance on Lucknow began on 25th September.

The casualties were appalling. Out of the two thousand men who made the assault, 535 fell dead or wounded, among them James Neill, shot through the head at point-blank range by a rebel sniper. Havelock and Outram reached the Residency unscathed—although Outram had earlier suffered a wound in the arm—to find themselves the centre of a crowd of cheering, exultant defenders, who sallied forth, rifles at the ready, to assist them over a low mud wall in front of the Bailey Guard gate, just as darkness fell. After five long and anxious months, the Residency at Lucknow had been relieved.

Major General Sir James Outram, as Chief Commissioner for Oudh in succession to Sir Henry Lawrence and senior military officer, formally took command of both the relief force and the garrison on the morning of 26th September. It was evident even then that the original plan—which had been to evacuate the Residency garrison to Cawnpore—would have to be abandoned. There were four hundred-seventy women and children, and to the garrison's sick and wounded had now been added those of the relief force, making a total of some fifteen hundred, for whom there was insufficient carriage available. The original defenders had been reduced to seven hundred fifty gaunt and famished men, of whom half were Sikhs and loyal sepoys but, their ranks swelled by the addition of the relief force, Outram decided that he could hold Lucknow until the troops Sir Colin Campbell was gathering arrived to reinforce him.

On 16th July, 1857, having embarked the Earl of Elgin and his staff, the frigate *Shannon,* Captain William Peel, VC, accompanied by the *Pearl,* Captain Edward Sotheby, sailed from Hong Kong to Calcutta. At 5 p.m. on 8th August, the steam-screw *Shannon* dropped anchor off the Esplanade, Calcutta, and the Governor-General, Lord Canning, gratefully accepted Lord Elgin's offer of the two frigates to the Indian Government to aid in the suppression of the Sepoy Mutiny.

On the afternoon of the 18th August, the first party of the *Shannon*'s Naval Brigade was embarked aboard a river steamer and flat to travel up the Ganges River to Allahabad. Under the command of Captain Peel, this party consisted of 408 officers and men, including Royal Marines, with ten of the frigate's sixty-eight-pounder guns, a twenty-four-pounder howitzer, eight rocket-tubes and field-pieces, with four hundred rounds of shot and shell for each gun. A second detachment, under the First Lieutenant, James Vaughan, numbering one hundred twenty, left Calcutta a month later. Both detachments reached Allahabad at about the same time—early in October—and, coming under the orders of General Sir James Outram and later, the Commander-in-Chief, Sir Colin Campbell, at first undertook garrison duties in the fort at Allahabad. By the end of the month, however, the whole Brigade—with the exception of two hundred forty, including sick and convalescent men—advanced to Cawnpore to join the Lucknow Relief Force, under Sir Colin Campbell, taking part in the successful evacuation of the Residency garrison on 22nd–23rd November. In the fierce fighting which preceded the evacuation and in the subsequent battle for Cawnpore, the Naval Brigade won high praise—in particular during the attack on the strongly held Shah Nujeef Mosque.

In his despatch, Sir Colin Campbell wrote: *"Captain Peel led up his heavy guns with extraordinary gallantry, within a few yards of the building, to batter the massive stone wall . . . It was an action almost unexampled in war. Captain Peel behaved much as if he had been laying the* Shannon *alongside an enemy frigate . . ."* A total of two hundred seamen and Marines fought in the Relief of Lucknow, with six 24-pounder guns, two 8-inch howitzers and two rocket-tubes, the Marines and seamen rifle companies forming a strong infantry escort to the guns.

The *Pearl* Brigade went up country to Dinapore in September and, although none took part in the relief of Lucknow, they, too, played a gallant part in the suppression of the Mutiny.

BOOKS CONSULTED

Government of India State Papers: Edited G.W. Forrest, Calcutta Military Department Press, 1902. 2 vols.

The Sepoy War in India: J. W. Kaye, FRS., 3 vols., W.H. Allen, 1870.

History of the Indian Mutiny: Col. G.B. Malleson, CSL., 3 vols., Longmans, 1896.

History of the Indian Mutiny: T. Rice Holmes, Macmillan, 1898.

The Tale of the Great Mutiny: W. H. Fitchett, Smith, Elder, 1904.

The History of the Indian Mutiny: Charles Ball, 6 vols, London Printing & Publishing Co., circa 1860.

Addiscombe: Its Heroes and Men of Note: Col. H.M. Vibart, Constable, 1894.

Way to Glory: J.C. Pollock, John Murray, 1957 (Life of Havelock).

1857: S.N. Sen, Government of India Press (reprinted 1958).

The Sound of Fury: Richard Collier, Collins, 1963.

The History of India: James Grant, Cassell, circa 1888.

The Bengal Horse Artillery: Maj. Gen. B.P. Hughes, Arms & Armour Press, 1971.

Lucknow and the Oude Mutiny: Lt. Gen. Mcleod Innes, VC,
   R. E. A. D. Innes & Co. 1896.

Journal of the Siege of Lucknow: Maria Germon, edited
   Michael Edwardes, Constable (orig. pub. 1870).

The Orchid House: Michael Edwardes, Cassell, 1960.

Accounts of the Siege and Massacre at Cawnpore: Lt. Mowbray
   Thomson, 53rd. N. I., and G. W. Shepherd (Survivors).

The Illustrated London News, 1856–8.

Naval Brigades in the Indian Mutiny: Edited
   Cdr W. B. Rowbotham, RN, Naval Records Society.

Shannon's Brigade in India: Lt. Edmund H. Verney, RN,
   Saunders, Otley & Co., 1862.

The Defence of Cawnpore: Lt. Col. J. Adye, CB, Longmans,
   Brown, 1858.

GLOSSARY OF INDIAN TERMS

Ayah: nurse or maid servant

Baba: child

Bearer: personal, usually head, servant

Bhisti: water bearer

Boorka: all-enveloping cotton garment worn by purdah women when mixing with the outside world

Brahmin: high-caste Hindu

Chapkan: knee-length tunic

Charpoy: string bed

Chitti: a chit, a written order

Chuprassi: a uniformed door-keeper

Daffadar: sergeant, cavalry

Dhoti: a loincloth worn by men in India

Dhoolie: stretcher or covered litter for conveyance of wounded

Din: faith

Ekka: small, single-horse-drawn cart, often curtained for conveyance of purdah women

Eurasian: half-caste, usually children born of British fathers and Indian mothers

Fakir: itinerant holy man

Feringhi: foreigner (term of disrespect)

Ghat: river bank, landing place, quay

Godown: storeroom, warehouse

Golandaz: gunner, native

Havildar/Havildar-Major: sergeant/sergeant major, infantry

Jemadar: native officer, all arms

Ji/Ji-han: yes

Lal-kote: British soldier

Log: people (baba-log: children)

Mahout: the keeper and driver of an elephant

Mem: wife, woman

Moulvi: teacher of religion, Moslem

Nahin: no

Nana: lit. grandfather, popular title bestowed on the Mahratta chief

Oudh: kingdom of, recently annexed by Hon. East India Company

Paltan: regiment

Pandy: name for mutineers, taken from the first to revolt, Sepoy Mangal Pandy, 34th Native Infantry

Peishwa: official title of ruler of the Mahratta

Pugree: turban

Raj: rule

Rajwana: troops and retainers of native chiefs

Rissala: cavalry

Rissaldar: native officer, cavalry

Ryot: peasant landowner, cultivator

Sepoy: infantry soldier

Sowar: cavalry trooper

Subadar: native officer, infantry (equivalent of Captain)

Sweeper: low-caste servant

Talukdar: minor chief

Tulwar: sword or sabre

Vakeel: agent

Zamindar: landowner

Zenana: harem

More Action, More Adventure, More Angst . . .

McBooks Press invites you to embark on more sea adventures and take part in gripping naval action with Douglas Reeman, Dudley Pope, and a host of other nautical writers. Sail to Trafalgar, Grenada, Copenhagen—to famous battles and unknown skirmishes alike.

All the titles below are available at bookstores. For a free catalog, or to order direct, call toll-free 1-888-BOOKS-11 (1-888-266-5711). Or visit the McBooks website, www.mcbooks.com, for special offers and to read excerpts from McBooks titles.

ALEXANDER KENT
The Bolitho Novels

___ 1 Midshipman Bolitho
  0-935526-41-2 • 240 pp., $13.95

___ 2 Stand Into Danger
  0-935526-42-0 • 288 pp., $13.95

___ 3 In Gallant Company
  0-935526-43-9 • 320 pp., $14.95

___ 4 Sloop of War
  0-935526-48-X • 352 pp., $14.95

___ 5 To Glory We Steer
  0-935526-49-8 • 352 pp., $14.95

___ 6 Command a King's Ship
  0-935526-50-1 • 352 pp., $14.95

___ 7 Passage to Mutiny
  0-935526-58-7 • 352 pp., $15.95

___ 8 With All Despatch
  0-935526-61-7 • 320 pp., $14.95

___ 9 Form Line of Battle!
  0-935526-59-5 • 352 pp., $14.95

___ 10 Enemy in Sight!
  0-935526-60-9 • 368 pp., $14.95

___ 11 The Flag Captain
  0-935526-66-8 • 384 pp., $15.95

___ 12 Signal – Close Action!
  0-935526-67-6 • 368 pp., $15.95

___ 13 The Inshore Squadron
  0-935526-68-4 • 288 pp., $13.95

___ 14 A Tradition of Victory
  0-935526-70-6 • 304 pp., $14.95

___ 15 Success to the Brave
  0-935526-71-4 • 288 pp., $13.95

___ 16 Colours Aloft!
  0-935526-72-2 • 304 pp., $14.95

___ 17 Honour This Day
  0-935526-73-0 • 320 pp., $15.95

___ 18 The Only Victor
  0-935526-74-9 • 384 pp., $15.95

___ 19 Beyond the Reef
  0-935526-82-X • 352 pp., $14.95

___ 20 The Darkening Sea
  0-935526-83-8 • 352 pp., $15.95

___ 21 For My Country's Freedom
  0-935526-84-6 • 304 pp., $15.95

___ 22 Cross of St George
  0-935526-92-7 • 320 pp., $16.95

___ 23 Sword of Honour
  0-935526-93-5 • 320 pp., $15.95

___ 24 Second to None
  0-935526-94-3 • 352 pp., $16.95

___ 25 Relentless Pursuit
  1-59013-026-X • 368 pp., $16.95

___ 26 Man of War
  1-59013-091-X • 320 pp., $16.95

___ 26 Man of War
  1-59013-066-9 • 320 pp., $24.95 HC

DOUGLAS REEMAN
Modern Naval Fiction Library

___ Twelve Seconds to Live
  1-59013-044-8 • 368 pp., $15.95

___ Battlecruiser
  1-59013-043-X • 320 pp., $15.95

___ The White Guns
  1-59013-083-9 • 368 pp., $15.95

___ A Prayer for the Ship
  1-59013-097-9 • 288 pp., $15.95

___ For Valour
  1-59013-049-9 • 336 pp., $15.95

Royal Marines Saga

___ 1 Badge of Glory
    1-59013-013-8 • 384 pp., $16.95
___ 2 The First to Land
    1-59013-014-6 • 304 pp., $15.95
___ 3 The Horizon
    1-59013-027-8 • 368 pp., $15.95
___ 4 Dust on the Sea
    1-59013-028-6 • 384 pp., $15.95
___ 5 Knife Edge
    1-59013-099-5 • 304 pp., $15.95

DUDLEY POPE
The Lord Ramage Novels

___ 1 Ramage
    0-935526-76-5 • 320 pp., $14.95
___ 2 Ramage & the Drumbeat
    0-935526-77-3 • 288 pp., $14.95
___ 3 Ramage & the Freebooters
    0-935526-78-1 • 384 pp., $15.95
___ 4 Governor Ramage R. N.
    0-935526-79-X • 384 pp., $15.95
___ 5 Ramage's Prize
    0-935526-80-3 • 320 pp., $15.95
___ 6 Ramage & the Guillotine
    0-935526-81-1• 320 pp., $14.95
___ 7 Ramage's Diamond
    0-935526-89-7 • 336 pp., $15.95
___ 8 Ramage's Mutiny
    0-935526-90-0 • 280 pp., $14.95
___ 9 Ramage & the Rebels
    0-935526-91-9 • 320 pp., $15.95
___ 10 The Ramage Touch
    1-59013-007-3 • 272 pp., $15.95
___ 11 Ramage's Signal
    1-59013-008-1 • 288 pp., $15.95
___ 12 Ramage & the Renegades
    1-59013-009-X • 320 pp., $15.95
___ 13 Ramage's Devil
    1-59013-010-3 • 320 pp., $15.95
___ 14 Ramage's Trial
    1-59013-011-1 • 320 pp., $15.95
___ 15 Ramage's Challenge
    1-59013-012-X • 352 pp., $15.95
___ 16 Ramage at Trafalgar
    1-59013-022-7 • 256 pp., $14.95
___ 17 Ramage & the Saracens
    1-59013-023-5 • 304 pp., $15.95
___ 18 Ramage & the Dido
    1-59013-024-3 • 272 pp., $15.95

ALEXANDER FULLERTON
The Nicholas Everard WWII Saga

___ 1 Storm Force to Narvik
    1-59013-092-8 • 256 pp., $13.95
___ 2 Last Lift from Crete
    1-59013-093-6 • 272 pp., $13.95
___ 3 All the Drowning Seas
    1-59013-094-4 • 320 pp., $14.95

PHILIP McCUTCHAN
The Halfhyde Adventures

___1 Halfhyde at the Bight of Benin
    1-59013-078-2 • 224 pp., $13.95
___2 Halfhyde's Island
    1-59013-079-0 • 224 pp., $13.95
___3 Halfhyde and the Guns
   of Arrest
    1-59013-067-7 • 256 pp., $13.95
___4 Halfhyde to the Narrows
    1-59013-068-5 • 240 pp., $13.95
___5 Halfhyde for the Queen
    1-59013-069-3• 256 pp., $14.95
___6 Halfhyde Ordered South
    1-59013-071-5 • 256 pp., $14.95
___7 Halfhyde on Zanatu
    1-59013-072-3 • 192 pp., $13.95

DEWEY LAMBDIN
Alan Lewrie Naval Adventures

___ 2 The French Admiral
    1-59013-021-9 • 448 pp., $17.95
___ 8 Jester's Fortune
    1-59013-034-0 • 432 pp., $17.95

JAN NEEDLE
Sea Officer William Bentley Novels

___ 1 A Fine Boy for Killing
    0-935526-86-2 • 320 pp., $15.95
___ 2 The Wicked Trade
    0-935526-95-1 • 384 pp., $16.95
___ 3 The Spithead Nymph
    1-59013-077-4 • 288 pp., $14.95

JAMES L. NELSON
___The Only Life That Mattered
    1-59013-060-X • 416 pp., $16.95

V.A. STUART
Alexander Sheridan Adventures

___ 1 Victors and Lords
    0-935526-98-6 • 272 pp., $13.95

___ 2 The Sepoy Mutiny
    0-935526-99-4 • 240 pp., $13.95

___ 3 Massacre at Cawnpore
    1-59013-019-7 • 240 pp., $13.95

___ 4 The Cannons of Lucknow
    1-59013-029-4 • 272 pp., $14.95

___ 5 The Heroic Garrison
    1-59013-030-8 • 256 pp., $13.95

The Phillip Hazard Novels

___ 1 The Valiant Sailors
    1-59013-039-1 • 272 pp., $14.95

___ 2 The Brave Captains
    1-59013-040-5 • 272 pp., $14.95

___ 3 Hazard's Command
    1-59013-081-2 • 256 pp., $13.95

___ 4 Hazard of Huntress
    1-59013-082-0 • 256 pp., $13.95

___ 5 Hazard in Circassia
    1-59013-062-6 • 256 pp., $13.95

___ 6 Victory at Sebastopol
    1-59013-061-8 • 224 pp., $13.95

___ 7 Guns to the Far East
    1-59013-063-4 • 240 pp., $13.95

___ 8 Escape from Hell
    1-59013-064-2 • 256 pp., $13.95

C. NORTHCOTE PARKINSON
The Richard Delancey Novels

___ 1 The Guernseyman
    1-59013-001-4 • 208 pp., $13.95

___ 2 Devil to Pay
    1-59013-002-2 • 288 pp., $14.95

___ 3 The Fireship
    1-59013-015-4 • 208 pp., $13.95

___ 4 Touch and Go
    1-59013-025-1 • 224 pp., $13.95

___ 5 So Near So Far
    1-59013-037-5 • 224 pp., $13.95

___ 6 Dead Reckoning
    1-59013-038-3 • 224 pp., $15.95

___ The Life and Times of Horatio
   Hornblower
    1-59013-065-0 • 416 pp., $16.95

DAVID DONACHIE
The Privateersman Mysteries

___ 1 The Devil's Own Luck
    1-59013-004-9 • 302 pp., $17.95
    1-59013-003-0 • 320 pp., $23.95 HC

___ 2 The Dying Trade
    1-59013-006-5 • 384 pp., $16.95
    1-59013-005-7 • 400 pp., $24.95 HC

___ 3 A Hanging Matter
    1-59013-016-2 • 416 pp., $16.95

___ 4 An Element of Chance
    1-59013-017-0 • 448 pp., $17.95

___ 5 The Scent of Betrayal
    1-59013-031-6 • 448 pp., $17.95

___ 6 A Game of Bones
    1-59013-032-4 • 352 pp., $15.95

The Nelson & Emma Trilogy

___ 1 On a Making Tide
    1-59013-041-3 • 416 pp., $17.95

___ 2 Tested by Fate
    1-59013-042-1 • 416 pp., $17.95

___ 3 Breaking the Line
    1-59013-090-1 • 368 pp., $16.95

NICHOLAS NICASTRO
The John Paul Jones Novels

___ 1 The Eighteenth Captain
    0-935526-54-4 • 312 pp., $16.95

___ 2 Between Two Fires
    1-59013-033-2 • 384 pp., $16.95

Classics of Nautical Fiction

CAPTAIN FREDERICK MARRYAT

___ Frank Mildmay OR
   The Naval Officer
    0-935526-39-0 • 352 pp., $14.95

___ The King's Own
    0-935526-56-0 • 384 pp., $15.95

___ Mr Midshipman Easy
    0-935526-40-4 • 352 pp., $14.95

___ Newton Forster OR
   The Merchant Service
    0-935526-44-7 • 352 pp., $13.95

___ Snarleyyow OR The Dog Fiend
    0-935526-64-1 • 384 pp., $16.95

___ The Phantom Ship
    0-935526-85-4 • 320 pp., $14.95

___ The Privateersman
    0-935526-69-2 • 288 pp., $15.95

RAFAEL SABATINI
___ Captain Blood
0-935526-45-5 • 288 pp., $15.95

MICHAEL SCOTT
___ Tom Cringle's Log
0-935526-51-X • 512 pp., $14.95

WILLIAM CLARK RUSSELL
___ The Yarn of Old Harbour Town
0-935526-65-X • 256 pp., $14.95
___ The Wreck of the Grosvenor
0-935526-52-8 • 320 pp., $13.95

A.D. HOWDEN SMITH
___ Porto Bello Gold
0-935526-57-9 • 288 pp., $13.95

Military Fiction Classics

R.F. DELDERFIELD
___ Seven Men of Gascony
0-935526-97-8 • 368 pp., $16.95
___ Too Few for Drums
0-935526-96-X • 256 pp., $17.95

The Alexander Sheridan Adventures

BY V. A. STUART

FROM THE Crimean War to the Sepoy Mutiny, the Alexander Sheridan Adventures deftly combine history and supposition in tales of scarlet soldiering that cunningly interweave fact and fiction.

Alexander Sheridan, unjustly forced out of the army, leaves Britain and his former life behind and joins the East India Company, still in pursuit of those ideals of honor and heroism that buoyed the British Empire for three hundred years. Murder, war, and carnage await him. But with British stoicism and an unshakable iron will, he will stand tall against the atrocities of war, judging all by their merit rather than by the color of their skin or the details of their religion.

"Stuart's saga of Captain Sheridan during the Mutiny stands in the shadow of no previous work of fiction, and for historical accuracy, writing verve and skill, and pace of narrative, stands alone."

—*El Paso Times*

1 **Victors and Lords**
ISBN 0-935526-98-6
272 pp., $13.95

2 **The Sepoy Mutiny**
ISBN 0-935526-99-4
240 pp., $13.95

3 **Massacre at Cawnpore**
ISBN 1-59013-019-7
240 pp., $13.95

4 **The Cannons of Lucknow**
ISBN 1-59013-029-4
272 pp., $14.95

5 **The Heroic Garrison**
ISBN 1-59013-030-8
256 pp., $13.95